Murthen Island

Murthen Island

Book Two: Tales of Golmeira

Marianne Ratcliffe

Published by Marianne
Ratcliffe
Macclesfield, UK

Printed in the United Kingdom

First Printing, 2015

ISBN 9780993400100

Published by Marianne Ratcliffe
www.marianneratcliffe.com

Dedication

This book is dedicated to Richard and Sylvia Ratcliffe, for their continuous support and encouragement

Chapter One

Kylen snapped her telescope shut in satisfaction and retreated into the shadow cast by a sun-baked boulder.

'At last,' she said in a low voice. 'The shipment of weapons. Just like that drunken Golmeiran captain told us. Time we sent a message to Grand Marl Thorlberd.'

'We've been sending such messages for the last year, my Lady. I'm not sure anyone is listening.' Her huge Sendoran companion was almost as large as the rock behind which they were hidden.

'Then we need to do more. I'll make him wish he had never even thought of invading Sendor.'

'I just... I have a bad feeling about today.'

Kylen sighed wearily.

'Again, Hylaz?'

'We've stretched our luck as it is. We can't keep going up against such numbers and surviving.'

'Survival is overrated. I'd rather die by a Golmeiran sword than live as their slave. My father would agree, if he were alive.'

'Lord Mendoraz died defending the people of Golgannan against the entire Golmeiran army and their monstrous migaradons. He wouldn't venture his life over a few wagons of supplies. I'm not sure it's worth the risk.'

'We are down to our last few crossbow bolts and your sword has been patched more times than a beggar's blanket. If those wagons are carrying weapons, it will certainly be worth it.'

The big man squinted through a telescope that appeared as small as a twig in his giant hands. 'Must be a hundred of them, and we are only twenty.'

Kylen slapped his broad back.

'It wouldn't be fun if it was too easy, now would it?'

'I wouldn't mind easy, just for once,' muttered her companion. 'Instead of odds of five to one.'

'Remember every one of our people is worth ten soft-bellied Golmeirans. I make that two to one in our favour.'

'Well, when you put it like that...'

Kylen stood up and made a signal with her right hand. She received small movements of acknowledgement from positions triangulated above the narrow defile. Her team was ready.

Below them, soldiers wearing black uniforms with a green gecko emblazoned on their chests rounded a bend and marched slowly up the narrow track towards them. Kylen allowed the leading line of soldiers to pass by, waiting until the first of the wagons creaked into position directly beneath her. She tapped Hylaz on the shoulder. He cupped his hands around his mouth and gave out the pre-arranged signal, mimicking the bellow of a male fellgryff. Kylen lifted her elmwood Golmeiran crossbow, sighted at the driver of the wagon and fired. The driver sagged forward in his seat. Hylaz spat at the ground.

'Say what you like about Golmeirans, they make a good crossbow.'

Thank you, Zastra. Her bow had been a parting gift from the only Golmeiran that Kylen didn't despise. Her shot was echoed by a volley of sharp twangs as the rest of her team fired their own bolts. Cries of alarm came up from the track below and the figures in black scattered. Kylen had chosen the site of the ambush well. The track had been carved through the mountainside and the Golmeiran soldiers found themselves hemmed in by sheer rock. There was nowhere to hide as Kylen and her fellow Sendorans released their second and third bolts. Once her crossbow was empty, Kylen threw it aside. Using Golmeiran tactics had given them the advantage but now it was time to wage battle the Sendoran way. *Show the enemy your face.* Hylaz brought forward Breeze, her fellgryff. She met the creature's intelligent eyes and he dipped his head, bucking as she leapt on his back. He was always temperamental, but today the scent of the Golmeirans added to his excitement and she had to grip hard with her legs to cling on. When Breeze settled under her, she eased him towards the edge of the ledge and brandished a sword above her head, her outline framed against the clear blue sky. A Golmeiran bolt whipped past her ear, so close she felt its breath on her cheek. Grinning in wild abandon, she spurred Breeze forward. Sure footed, he sprang from rock to rock, down into the defile and landed on the track in front of the invaders. For a moment she was alone amongst the enemy, before her fellow rebels leapt down onto the track to join her as she had known they would. They were still outnumbered by far, but that was unimportant.

'For Sendor!' she cried. If this was to be her last day, she would not die alone.

Chapter Two

Zastra clenched her toes to grip the rough trunk of the jula tree as it swayed alarmingly beneath her bare feet. The slender tree grew straight out from the steep mountainside, bowing under her weight as she inched towards its crown to reach the jula berries that would be her reward for risking her neck. She listened attentively for any tell-tale creaks that would give her warning of a flaw in the wood. The tree was old. If the trunk snapped she would be sent flying down the steep incline onto the unforgiving rocks below.

'It's too dangerous,' Dalbric cried as she leaned out to tug at a bunch of the orange fruit. Below her, his untidy mop of straw-coloured hair shook in disapproval.

She laughed, increasingly confident as she rode each dip and roll of the tree. 'You should try it. There's a great view from up here. I can even see our fields.'

The Border Mountains stretched away in all directions, swathed in dense forest, summits of barren rock poking up above the treeline like bare heads above a rich green cloak. To the far north the snow-capped tips of the Northern Wastes were, as usual, obscured by clouds. Much closer, on the neighbouring ridge, she could just make out the tiny patch of cleared land that marked out their homestead.

'Stop showing off and hurry up.'

'It's not my fault you're scared of heights.'

She flung a bunch of thick-rinded jula berries at him. He side-stepped smartly and caught the bunch one-handed.

'Hey! Careful. You'll bruise them.'

Ignoring his pleas, she rained more fruit down on him. A strange moaning noise made them both pause. Dalbric looked anxiously to the north.

'A wind-gust. You'd better come down.'

Zastra glanced across the slope. A wave of vigorous movement swept across the treetops and accelerated towards her. Yet there were more jula berries to be had, the best too, right at the tips of the branches. She stretched out and tore off the last few remaining bunches of fruit, grabbing hold of a sturdy limb just as the wind-gust slammed into the tree, forcing it to bend so much that its crown pressed against the mountainside. Judging the moment carefully, Zastra sprang to the ground a mere instant before the tree trunk whipped back, released as the wind-gust passed. She placed the fruit into Dalbric's hand with a triumphant flourish.

'One day your luck will run out and you'll be catapulted halfway to the moons,' he said. 'I wouldn't mind, only Ma will blame me and I'll be on double chores for a week.'

'A week, eh? As long as that? Then I'd best be more careful.'

'We'd better head back. If we're late, it'll only give Ma time to think up more jobs.'

The sun was low in the sky and the pale outline of Horval, the larger of the twin moons, was already ascending.

'Fine.' Zastra wriggled into her backpack. She began to slide down the steep slope. 'Last one back cooks supper.'

'Hey!' Dalbric snatched up his own bag and scrambled after her. 'Not fair.'

'Come on, slowcoach.' Zastra reached the treeline at the bottom of the slope and sprinted into the forest.

'Save your breath for grovelling,' Dalbric called back. He put on a spurt and overtook her, thundering between the trees to her left, breaking through the shafts of evening sunlight that slanted through the thick canopy overhead. Zastra increased her pace, ducking under familiar branches and hurdling fallen trunks. Side by side they raced until they burst into their home clearing, Dalbric ahead by a whisker. Their house sat above them, a log cabin at the top of a grassy incline. Seeing she was about to lose, Zastra dived for Dalbric's legs, sweeping his ankles together so he sprawled to the ground, a mass of long limbs all tangled up in the straps of his dislodged backpack. Pressing her advantage, Zastra leapt on top of him and grabbed his arms so that he couldn't move.

'No fair!' Dalbric grunted, his nose squished against the grass.

'You're getting slower,' Zastra panted. 'I reckon it's the weight of all that hair. Still, I expect Hanra will like it. It does hide those big ears of yours.'

A door slammed. They both leapt up, like soldiers jumping to attention. A small woman with the same straw-coloured hair as Dalbric strode down the slope towards them, her lips pressed together in disapproval.

'What are you playing at? Don't you know there's work to be done? I suppose you expect me to do it all myself?'

'It's my fault, Etta.' Zastra hung her head sheepishly.

'It usually is. I was beginning to think you'd got lost, the pair of you.'

'Ma, we know every last tree and path in the forest within two days' walk,' protested Dalbric.

'Then you've no excuse for being this late, have you?' Etta pulled Dalbric's bag from his grasp and examined the contents. 'These had better not be damaged—'

Before she could finish her scolding, Etta broke into a hacking cough. Her body bent forward under the force of it. Dalbric reached towards her in concern, but Etta batted his hand away, straightening up and pumping her chest with her fist as if she could beat the cough out of her slight frame.

'Layna!' A boy, barely six years old, galloped down from the house, covered head to foot in mud.

'Oh, Fin,' Zastra sighed. 'I only washed your clothes yesterday. What in the stars have you been doing?'

'Making mud castles,' the boy explained proudly. He tugged her sleeve. 'Layna, come look.'

Layna. Even though she had been called that for many seasons, Zastra still found it odd that her little brother didn't know she had once had a different name. It was more than five years since they had escaped from Golmer Castle after their treacherous uncle and his mindweavers had killed their parents. Five hard years, toiling to farm the stony ground of the Border Mountains, hoping their goatswool fetched a good price and every year risking her life for the jula berry harvest. No one would look at Zastra, clad in Dalbric's ill-fitting cast offs, and think she had royal blood. Fin had been too young to remember anything of his life before the mountains. Too young to remember his twin sister, Kastara, left as a baby in the care of Bodel, the mother of one of Zastra's childhood friends, deep within Golmeira. It was safer that he did not know these things. Even in the mountains, you never knew when a mindweaver might come by and dig out the secrets held inside your head. She allowed Fin to drag her up the slope.

'Don't be long,' wheezed Etta, still recovering from her coughing fit. 'Did you catch anything for supper?'

Zastra shook her head. 'There wasn't time for fishing.'

'But time enough for fighting, I see. We'll have to make do with halsa paste again then, won't we? You can think about your priorities as you clean the wool tonight, young lady.'

Zastra sighed but did not protest. After a brief detour to admire five misshapen lumps of mud that Findar insisted were castles, she took him back to their tiny kitchen and began grinding up a few handfuls of misshapen halsa nuts, adding water and salt to make a pale green paste. She set it to heat on the stove until the mixture bubbled and then served it up. Dalbric pulled a face.

'If I eat any more of this, I'll turn into a halsa nut myself. Then you'll be sorry.'

Findar pushed his plate away in alarm. 'Don't want to turn into a nut. Can I please have cabbage instead?'

Zastra prodded her fork in Dalbric's direction.

'Now look what you've done.'

'Patience, little man.' Dalbric nudged Findar's plate back towards him. 'The ground has only been thawed a little while. Even though we planted our first seeds straight away, it'll be next Moonscross before anything starts to grow.'

'Beans?' Findar asked hopefully.

'They'll come after the cabbages. It's the yellow-root I can't wait for. If I close my eyes, I can almost taste it. Salt roasted and covered in cheese. Yummy.'

Fin clapped his hands in agreement.

'Want yellow-root. Now!' he exclaimed.

'Dalbric, sometimes you can be a real idiot,' Etta scolded.

'Only sometimes?' Zastra queried. 'Come on, Fin. Eat up. You won't turn into a halsa nut, I promise. And tomorrow, I'll take out my bow and find us something nicer.'

Fin wavered, but when he saw there was no other food to be had, he ate up his green paste with no further protest and even licked out the bowl.

After supper, Etta set up her spindle. Clumps of wool were draped all the way along a length of rope that was slung across their cabin. Dalbric took one down, checked it was dry and picked up the combs with a smug grin. Zastra sighed and headed through the kitchen to the cold storeroom that lay at the back of the house. A second batch of goats' wool had been soaking in barrels for the past two days and was now ready for rinsing. Zastra rolled up her sleeves and stuck her hands into the foul smelling liquid, a special concoction of Etta's. All the muck and dead insects from a year's worth of mountain living floated in a scum at the top. Zastra scooped off the rancid layer, pulled out a ball of wool, wrung it out and rinsed it thoroughly in a second barrel of clean, cold water. Her hands were soon chafed and stinging, but she continued until all the wool was clean. They desperately needed the money. It was a long way from Golmer Castle and the luxuries of her childhood, but it was worth it to keep her brother safely out of their uncle's reach.

Chapter Three

A high ranking general in the Golmeiran army brushed a speck of fluff from the shoulder of his immaculate uniform and knocked firmly on the panelled blackwood door. He waited for an acknowledgement before entering.

'Ah, Ixendred. Come.' Grand Marl Thorlberd's deep tones reverberated against the bare stone walls of his office. Ixendred presented a neat bow, exactly to protocol. Thorlberd was standing beside a desk of highly polished elmwood. Before him was the trembling figure of Higina, Master at Arms and Ixendred's commanding officer. Word had it that she had just returned from Sendor. Her uniform was faded and dirty. She was carrying a little extra weight these days, Ixendred noted, and dark circles of sweat spread out beneath her armpits.

'Continue, Higina.' The woman stirred like a leaf buffeted by a wind-gust at the Grand Marl's command.

'I-I am sorry to report that Sendoran rebels have captured the supply of weapons meant for our garrison at Finistron,' she stuttered.

'How many rebels were there?' Thorlberd glowered darkly.

'A-at least three hundred, m-my Lord.'

'You lie!' Thorlberd crashed his fist down on the desk. A large crack opened up within the grain. 'Don't you know that I can see into the depths of your mind, even though you try to block me? Your thoughts scream your guilt.'

Higina flinched backward as Thorlberd narrowed his eyes.

'I see twenty rebels, against a hundred of what you laughably believed to be your best troops.'

'I... we killed five of them—'

Thorlberd cut through Higina's protest. 'But not the daughter of Mendoraz, who I see was among them. Killing the heir to Sendor might have rescued something from this abysmal failure. It is three years since we first invaded that miserable country. A year since you assured me it was subjugated. I will suffer this failure no longer.'

He beckoned Ixendred, who stepped forward promptly and snapped to attention.

'Have you any ideas on how this rebellion might be crushed, Ixendred?'

Ixendred cleared his throat with confidence. His contacts had told him the news from Sendor and, being a most practical man, he had anticipated that Thorlberd might be looking for someone to replace Higina.

'Yes, my Lord. First, we must cut off support for the rebels; deal firmly with any peasants that feed and shelter them. Anyone suspected of helping them must be punished. Also, we must commit more troops. We hold the towns and cities, but the countryside remains vulnerable.'

'What would you recommend, were you to be my new Master at Arms?'

The two men paid no heed to the strangled squeak of protest from the increasingly perspiring Higina.

'I propose we reassert control across Sendor, my Lord. And this time, it must be absolute. The Sendorans are seasoned warriors, willing to die for their cause. If we are to succeed, we need the help of experienced soldiers, equally ferocious and determined.'

'Where do you propose we find such soldiers?'

'The Kyrgs, my Lord. You used them before, and what a masterstroke it was. Why not call on them again?'

Thorlberd scratched his beard. 'The exchequer is still deep in debt from the bribes I had to pay the Kyrgs to help overthrow my brother. This Sendoran business is a constant drain. I've already increased taxes twice and squeezed the marls for all they have. There is no more money.'

'Why not use a mind lock, my Lord? I understand such things are possible for a skilled mindweaver. If you can control Jelgar, the Kyrg chieftain, the absolute obedience of the Kyrg army would do the rest. No need for money at all.'

'I had considered this, when I seized control from my brother, but in order to ensure the lock remains in place, a mindweaver must stay close to Jelgar at all times. There was no one to whom I could entrust such a task without my brother finding out.'

Ixendred nodded in understanding.

'But now, my Lord, secrecy is not required.'

Thorlberd acceded the point.

'What mindweaver in their right mind would volunteer to live with those animals in the Northern Wastes?' spluttered Higina. Thorlberd straightened his back.

'A mindweaver who is anxious to make up for her recent failures, lest she meet the fate of my last two Masters at Arms.'

Realisation and horror chased each other across Higina's broad features. Her predecessor had been executed for failing to capture one of Sendor's major cities quickly enough. The one before that had so earned Thorlberd's displeasure that it was said that he had driven her mad before releasing her to wander Golmeira in perpetual mental torment.

'Start packing your furs, Higina. I hear that winter in the Northern Wastes is cold enough to freeze your fingers off. Deliver me the Kyrginites and I will let you live. I may even allow you to return once Sendor is under control.'

'But...but...' protested Higina, desperately searching for a flaw in the plan. 'What if Jelgar's guthans refuse to obey him? They would kill me, quick as blinking.'

'As long as Jelgar is alive, they will obey his orders. It is the Kyrg way. Only if someone kills him does the leadership pass on. You must not let that happen. I will supply you with a small troop, to protect Jelgar.'

'Protect Jelgar? What about me?'

Thorlberd furrowed his brow in annoyance.

'I will give you another mindweaver, someone also eager to regain my good opinion. The two of you will have to keep each other alive.'

'Kyrgs will not be enough. What about our fleet? It is desperately undermanned.' Higina was clearly not going to give up without a fight. 'We need to protect our shipping from pirates and Skurgs. I'll bet General Ixendred hasn't an answer to that problem.'

Ixendred coughed politely.

'I believe I do have a solution. Our folk in the Border Mountains are tough and contribute little in taxes. Decree that everyone living there between the ages of sixteen and twenty-five must serve in the Golmeiran army. It would not be popular, but would solve our manpower problem.'

'Popularity is irrelevant.' Thorlberd waved a large hand dismissively. 'See to it. Let that be the Kyrgs first task. They are good at sniffing out their prey and they know how to deal with anyone who refuses to co-operate. You are hereby appointed my new Master at Arms.'

Ixendred bowed.

'You can count on me, my Lord.'

Chapter Four

'Come on, Fin,' urged Dalbric. 'At this rate we'll have to start back before we even get to Fivepeaks.'

Fin was trying to choose whether to take his wooden soldier or his pressed leaf collection. In his opinion, both were essential supplies for the trek down to Fivepeaks, but Etta had insisted that he could only take one. Dalbric picked up a large skein of yarn and made for the door. 'If you can't make up your mind, you'll just have to stay here.'

'I could stay behind with him,' Zastra offered. Etta shook her head firmly.

'We've been through this before. Folk'll be suspicious if you don't come down to the village.'

'Nice try,' Dalbric remarked. 'I don't understand how you can be happy to nearly break your neck climbing a jula tree and yet be scared of a few villagers.'

Zastra glared at him.

'I'm not scared. I just don't trust them. Especially the likes of Hanra, always asking questions.'

'If you tried a bit harder to make friends, maybe they'd let it alone. I would have thought someone brought up in a castle would be more polite.'

Zastra frowned, and lowered her voice.

'Careful, Fin might hear.'

Luckily, her brother was still pre-occupied in choosing what to take on the trip and was oblivious to their conversation. Dalbric mouthed a silent apology. At last Findar thrust aside the leaf collection and stuffed the soldier in his waistband and they set off. As they met the treeline, the little boy picked up a stick twice his height, which he proceeded to use as a staff. Within a few minutes he grew tired of carrying it and planted it upright in the centre of a patch of mud.

'Will it grow into a tree?' he asked hopefully.

''Course not,' Dalbric said, laughing. 'Has your sister been teaching you such nonsense?'

Fin looked upset.

'Would it have hurt to pretend?' Zastra whispered.

'Lies won't help him survive in the mountains.'

Zastra plucked the stick from the ground and threw it for Dalbric to catch. She stepped off the path and snapped a slim branch from a sapling, stripping off the side shoots and she balanced it on her palm to feel its weight.

'I remember my first spring in the mountains, you told me yellow roots grew at the top of silver ferns. I nearly killed myself on the thorns trying to climb up.'

'Ain't my fault you believed me,' grinned Dalbric. 'The clue was in the word "root".'

Zastra swung her stick sharply. Dalbric used his own to parry her blow. They began to circle each other. Zastra had taught Dalbric how to spar to fill the time when they were shut indoors during the long winters. He thrust towards her chest, but she side-stepped smartly, and rapped him across the hand.

'Ow!' he yelped, dropping his stick and sucking on his knuckles. 'Do you have to hit so hard?'

'Never attack unless you have your defence prepared. You wouldn't last a minute against a trained fighter.'

'Stop playing at soldiers, will you?' snapped Etta. 'Layna, if that wool gets spoiled—' She was brought up short by another coughing fit that lasted so long her face turned an angry shade of red. Zastra threw aside her stick and fumbled to release the flask of water from her waistband. She offered it to Etta.

'Ma, you should talk to Lindarn about that cough. It's been getting worse even though winter is behind us.'

'I'm not going to bother the healer over a little cold. I'll be right in a few days.'

'Fin!' Zastra cried, horrified by the sight of her brother on the brink of investigating his way into a fast flowing stream.

'Look – a fishy.' Findar leaned out and dipped his pale fist into the water. Zastra only just managed to grab the back of his shirt before he toppled in.

'Fish for lunch?' he suggested hopefully. Zastra looked along the stream. Further down the mountainside it dropped into a shallow pool. She wedged her precious bag of wool next to a large rock and clambered along towards it. Settling onto her stomach she sank her left arm beneath the water so that it lay on the bed of the stream. The water was ice cold and ate into her flesh, needles of pain slowly replaced by numbness. She resisted the urge to flex her fingers. Out of the corner of her eye, she saw a flash of silver as a fat river trout shot down the stream and into the pool.

'Is there a fish? Where is it? Where?' Fin had followed behind and leaned over Zastra's shoulder to peer into the water.

'Hush, you'll scare it.'

With a flick of its tail, the grey-scaled fish glided towards a patch of sunlight and paused above Zastra's submerged arm. In a single fluid movement, she flicked it out onto the bank, reached for her knife and chopped off its head.

'Ugh!' cried Fin. 'Poor fishy.' He ran back to Etta and buried his head in her skirts as Zastra grabbed her pack and followed, holding up the large trout in triumph. Etta, who seemed to have recovered from her fit, led Fin away down the mountain with his head still buried in her skirts.

'No need to show off,' remarked Dalbric. 'I taught you well, is all.'

Zastra pulled him back, until Etta and Fin were out of earshot.

'I'm concerned about Etta. That's more than just a cold, whatever she says.'

'You heard her. She refuses to see Lindarn.'

'What if I bring him to Frecha's? She can hardly refuse to see him then.'

Dalbric looked astonished at such a bold suggestion.

'She'll be real mad at you.'

'Well, we're both used to that. As soon as Etta and Frecha get gossiping, I'll sneak out and find him.'

They reached the outskirts of Fivepeaks village just before noon. At the first farm they passed, a tall, muscular man was ploughing furrows with great intensity.

'Kikan!' Findar waved vigorously at the man. However, Kikan

paid them no heed, but continued on, forcing his hand-held plough into the earth as if it were an enemy to be defeated.

'Why didn't he say hello?' Fin asked, downcast.

'He's busy,' explained Etta. 'Kikan knows the importance of getting the oats planted early. And it doesn't look as if Raurak is helping him. That's what he gets for marrying a soft valley man. More trouble than they're worth.'

Zastra wondered if that remark was aimed at her. After all, like Kikan's husband, she had not been born in the mountains. In the eyes of Etta and the other villagers, she was one of the soft valley folk and always would be, no matter how hard she worked to prove herself.

They passed a few more scattered farmhouses before the narrow path widened into a track that marked the entrance to Fivepeaks itself. Houses were packed more densely together there, one of the largest having an upper floor with elaborately carved shutters flung open to let in the spring air. A youth with short hair leaned out of an upstairs window and waved at them. Three moles lay in a line down his left cheek.

'Ho, Layna!' he called a sing-song voice.

Zastra increased her pace, refusing to look up.

'You look so fine, please be mine, oh Lay—naaa.'

Dalbric nudged her.

'Looks like Gonjik still likes you. Can't think why. I see now why you were scared to come – afraid he'll try and kiss you again?'

'If it was you he wanted to kiss, you'd be running back up the mountain as quick as blinking.'

'True,' Dalbric acknowledged. Gonjik's head disappeared. Moments later he skipped out of the door into Zastra's path, forcing her to stop.

'Trade a kiss to let you past?'

Zastra shoved him aside. 'I'd rather kiss a goat's backside. It's prettier and less smelly.'

'Layna, don't be rude,' admonished Etta.

Gonjik was followed out of his house by his mother, Mexun, a pinched-faced woman who served as the village carpenter. Etta stiffened, but greeted her politely.

'Off to see Frecha, I suppose,' the carpenter remarked. 'Geort hasn't made it back yet. I expect he's found a younger woman to spend all that firedust money on.'

'Geort would do no such thing,' Etta protested. 'I won't listen to such ugly gossip. And before you ask, we don't need any furniture, thank you very much.'

'I was only saying hello,' Mexun began, but Etta moved them briskly along before the carpenter could continue. When it was clear she would be getting no gossip and no business, Mexun turned away, dragging Gonjik back into the house with her, much to Zastra's relief.

When they reached the weaver's house, the door was yanked open before they could knock by a plump girl of about Zastra's age.

'Dalbric,' she exclaimed brightly, breaking into a dimpled smile. 'How nice to see you. Oh, and here's Etta and dear little Fin.'

'Hi, Hanra,' mumbled Dalbric, in the general direction of the floor. He surreptitiously licked his palms and pressed them down on his hair in an unsuccessful attempt to flatten it down.

'Hello,' Zastra said pointedly. Hanra flicked her eyes briefly towards her and then skipped back into the house, leaving them to follow. Dalbric stood fixed in the doorway, gazing in adoration at Hanra's receding figure. Zastra planted two hands on his back and shoved him forwards. The dark hallway widened into a pleasant room with a large window. An older version of Hanra in miniature sat by a loom, eyes shining in pleasure. She did not get up, but opened her arms and wiggled her fingers in welcome.

'Etta, Dalbric, how lovely. Oh, and here's Layna and my darling little Fin. How he has grown! Come here, duckie, and sit on my knee. How is everyone?'

'We are all quite well,' Etta said quickly, before anyone else had chance to speak. 'We brought the first batch of wool.'

Frecha reached out to twist the yarn between her thumb and forefinger.

'This is lovely. Very soft. Should fetch a good price. I'm glad. Mexun has been pestering me for money, even though I keep telling her Geort won't be back from the Helgarths until midsummer.'

'Why so late?'

'Shortage of firedust, so they've extended the mining season. I suppose he'll get more money, but I could really do with some now.'

'Us too,' remarked Dalbric. 'Our axe has so many chips and cracks, it's a wonder it's still in one piece.'

'You surely need new trousers too, duckie.'

Dalbric had been victim of a grown spurt over the winter and the lower part of his calves protruded below the hem of his trousers.

'I don't agree, Ma,' Hanra interjected. 'Dalbric has such strong calves. He should have them on display more often.'

Dalbric blushed furiously.

Zastra held up the trout.

'We brought lunch.'

'Oh, how kind!' Frecha exclaimed. 'Hanra – get the stove going, will you, duckie?'

'Um, shall I chop some wood?' offered Dalbric, his face still in high colour. He picked up an axe that was resting against the wall.

'Be careful you don't do anything to damage those lovely calves,' Zastra remarked.

'I don't feel too well,' said Hanra, affecting a cough, 'Layna won't mind cooking, will you?'

Zastra minded very much. Not only because Hanra didn't look at all ill, but she could hardly go and fetch Lindarn if she was stuck in the kitchen.

'I was hoping to go for a walk,' she protested. 'Round the village.'

'But you've just walked all that way down the mountain,' Hanra returned smugly. 'Why would you want to go out again?'

'No business of yours.' Zastra felt herself getting angry.

'Always so secretive, ain't you? You've never even told us where you are from. Anyone can see you ain't no mountain girl.'

'I told you, she's my cousin's girl,' Etta interjected.

If you knew who I really was, you'd be a lot nicer, I'd bet, Zastra thought, glaring at Hanra. *I can almost picture the look on your face.* However, she bit back a retort and began to descale the fish.

'Oh, how kind of you Layna,' said Frecha. 'My back has stiffened up today, and Hanra seems to have another of her fevers, poor dear.'

Hanra offered up a pathetic hiccup, as if to confirm her incapacity, whilst still finding the energy to give Zastra a look of sly triumph when no one else was looking. Zastra found a frying pan, and began to cook the fish. Meanwhile, Etta began to help Frecha set the yarn upon the loom.

'Kikan seemed hard at work when we passed,' she remarked. 'He didn't even say hello.'

Frecha stopped dead, the spool of yarn still in her hand.

'Haven't you heard, duckie? Raurak is missing. Old Haq's donkey too.'

Etta stared at her.

'Missing? What do you mean?'

'They had some bags of oats spare after the winter so Raurak took them down to Kirkholme to sell, along with some of their bamboo cloth. He and the donkey were due back last week, but there's been no sign of them.'

Kirkholme, the nearest trading post, lay several days journey away. Whenever the villagers had goods to trade, they paid Haq a small fee to hire his donkey and cart.

'I bet Raurak has run off with another man,' Hanra said with a giggle. 'He's always had roving eyes, that one. And Kikan is *so* much older than him.' Frecha looked at her disapprovingly.

'Even if that were true, Raurak would never take the donkey and not bring it back. He knows how important it is to all of us. Kikan says if he's not back by tomorrow, he'll go down to Kirkholme himself.'

'He'll kill Raurak if he finds him. I'd never run away from *my* husband.' Hanra sidled up to Dalbric and put her arm through his. Dalbric's face went bright red. Zastra reached between them and banged the hot pan down on the table.

'Lunch is ready.'

'Don't want to eat the poor fishy,' protested Fin.

'What do you mean?' Zastra asked. 'You were the one that asked for fish for lunch. That's why I caught it in the first place.' Fin pouted and crossed his arms.

'He was happy and you killed him.'

'Ain't no such thing as a happy fish,' scoffed Dalbric, but Fin still refused to touch his plate. Frecha found some bread and syrup for him to have instead.

When they had eaten, Frecha stood up and began clear away the dishes, wincing with the pain. Hanra made no offer of help, so Zastra leapt up and took the plates from Frecha's hands.

'You rest, Frecha.' She shot a pointed glance at Hanra, but it was wasted. The weaver's daughter rested her head on Dalbric's shoulder and sighed as if she didn't even have the energy to sit up properly. Resisting the temptation to throw something at her, Zastra scrubbed the plates and pots so hard that they shone. When she was done, she was at last free to go in search of Lindarn.

'I'm just popping out to see Gonjik. To apologise for being so rude.'

However, her lie was unnecessary as no one paid her the remotest attention. Etta and Frecha were working the loom, Hanra and Dalbric were deep in some secret discussion, and Findar...was nowhere to be seen.

'Where's Fin?'

Etta, roused by Zastra's worried cry, shot to her feet.

'I thought he was with Hanra.'

'What?' Hanra turned towards them. 'No – not since we finished lunch. Ain't he in the bedroom?'

Zastra dashed into the bedroom. It was empty. She searched every other room in the house, but there was no sign of her brother.

Chapter Five

Zastra shot out into the street. A fog had descended and the outer edges of the village were shrouded in a pale grey curtain. Findar was nowhere to be seen. Where could he be? Had he disappeared, just like Raurak? A figure loomed out of the mist. Gonjik, smirking as usual.

'Looking for something?'

'My brother. Have you seen him?'

Gonjik hopped from one foot to the other. 'Maybe, maybe not. I might remember, if you were nice to me. Just one little kiss.'

Zastra gathered a fistful of Gonjik's shirt in her hand and pushed him backwards until he was pressed up against the trunk of a tree.

'Tell me where he is. Right now.'

Gonjik just grinned and spread his hands wide

'Why resist this attraction, Layna? You can't keep your hands off me.'

Zastra dropped him in disgust and stormed off down the street, looking behind every fence and knocking on every door. No one had seen her brother. The fog thickened until she could see barely three paces in front of her.

Gonjik skipped after her. 'I'll help you look.'

'Just leave me alone,' she growled. She began to run, yelling her brother's name, panic beginning to flutter in her chest. Then, out of the grey mist, a thin cry echoed her own. She followed the sound and found herself at the healer's house. Fin was pounding on the door with both his little fists. Zastra gathered him up in her arms.

'Fin, thank the stars. Where have you been?'

'Fetching healer for Etta. Make her better.'

'Oh, Fin, you are a love.' She hugged him close and planted a big kiss on his cheek. Her brother giggled and tried to wriggle out of her grip but Zastra held firm. She wasn't going to let him escape again, not with the mountain fog thickening by the moment.

'If you're wanting Lindarn, he ain't here.' Gonjik emerged from the murkiness. 'He's gone to Steepcrest to help his son's wife have her baby. Won't be back for days.'

'Fin? Layna?' Zastra recognised Etta's voice. She set Fin down, but kept a firm hold of his hand.

'Come, Fin. We mustn't tell anyone that we were looking for Lindarn. It's our secret.'

'Secret,' echoed Fin with utmost seriousness. Etta and Dalbric emerged from the mist.

'You found him. Thank the stars!' Etta cried in relief and planted a kiss on the top of Fin's head. Dalbric peered behind them.

'Where's Lindarn?' he asked expectantly. Zastra shot him a look of exasperation.

'Lindarn's a secret.' Fin's exaggerated whisper was so loud that everyone in the village must have heard. Etta pinched her left earlobe between her thumb and forefinger, a sure sign she was seriously displeased. She waited a moment before speaking, and when she did, she was dangerously calm.

'I see. Sneaking around behind my back, the lot of you. We're going home. This instant. And when we get there, Layna can start cleaning the next batch of wool and Dalbric, you can dig a new waste pit. You should have plenty of energy after mooning at Hanra all day. It seems I'm not keeping you busy enough if you have time to hatch plots behind my back.'

Zastra and Dalbric exchanged glances as Etta strode off up the mountain, coughing.

'I don't care how many chores we get, I'm going to find Lindarn,' Zastra insisted. Dalbric nodded in silent agreement, and they headed home.

Chapter Six

Kylen squinted through the branches of a tree at the familiar village. Something was wrong. Breeze sensed it too and nudged her nervously in the back with his nose. She scanned every house carefully. There was no sign of Golmeiran soldiers, but her intuition told her not to move. *Something is different from the last time we were here.*

'What are we waiting for?' Hylaz broke her concentration. 'I'm starving. The thought of Loran's pancakes gets my taste buds itching. And we need to get the rest of these Golmeiran weapons hidden away.'

His stomach emitted a loud rumble. Kylen frowned in annoyance.

'I don't know what's worse. Your grumbling, or that of your belly. We'd best hope there aren't any Golmeirans nearby. I was hoping to remain unnoticed.'

'I don't understand. If there were a hundred soldiers in this village, you'd have already sent us in to fight them.'

'Because then we'd have known what we were facing.' Kylen

continued her scan of the village. Her eyes came to rest on a large house of clay bricks that sat opposite the watchtower.

'See Loran's house? There's something odd about the door.'

Hylaz took out a telescope and peered through it. 'Looks as if it's been boarded up.'

Kylen snatched the telescope from him so that she could see for herself.

'That's odd. Why would Loran close up his house?'

'Only one way to find out,' offered Hylaz hopefully. His stomach rumbled again and Kylen relented. As she led her small group and their fellgryffs into the village, it became even more apparent that something was amiss. Sendorans were usually keen to welcome their own, and they had many friends in this village. But today no one came out to greet them. A woman emerged from her house carrying a large bucket, but the moment she saw them, she ducked back inside and slammed the door behind her. Others lowered their eyes as Kylen passed, with no word of welcome. When they reached Loran's house, Kylen peered between the rough boards that had been nailed across the doorframe. There was no sign of movement, even when she banged her fist against the wood.

'There go my pancakes,' Hylaz remarked sorrowfully.

'Shut up about your stupid pancakes.'

Kylen strode to the house next door to Loran's and thumped on the door. No one answered. Resting her ear to the wood, she gestured for quiet. She closed her eyes, cutting off all other senses. She attuned herself to the swish of the wind playing through the highest branches of the trees. A raven squawked somewhere in the treetops and further down the village a door creaked. She acknowledged these sounds and searched for something more.

There it was; soft, nasal, pulsating in time with her own breathing. She stepped back and pounded so hard that the door threatened to come free of its hinges.

'I know you're in there!'

A small crack appeared between the door and the jamb.

'Noonan, isn't it?' Kylen peered into the darkness. 'There's no need to hide from me. We are all friends here. I just want to know what has happened.'

The door inched open and a woman stuck her head outside, scanning the village nervously.

'Golmeirans. They knew we'd been supplying you with food, Lady Kylen. I don't know how, but they knew. Someone had to take the blame.'

'So you gave up Loran?' Kylen swelled with rage. She grabbed Noonan by her arm and dragged her bodily into the street. 'Who gave him up?'

Hylaz prised Kylen away from the woman.

'These people are not our enemies, my Lady.'

Kylen shrugged him off and jabbed her finger towards Noonan.

'They gave up Loran. That makes them traitors to Sendor.'

Noonan returned her gaze levelly.

'Loran gave himself up. They were going to burn all our food, so Loran stood forward to take the blame. Then they burned the food anyway.'

'What, all of it?' Kylen exclaimed in dismay. 'They left you nothing?'

'We managed to keep some supplies hidden, but we must hope for a good harvest.'

'And Loran?'

'They took him away. He was a good man.' There was bitter

accusation in her voice, and it seemed that it was not only directed at the Golmeirans. Kylen strode towards the edge of the village, chewing her lower lip. She gathered her small band of fighters and issued a few, brief orders. Her comrades mounted their fellgryffs and scattered, reappearing just as the sun was setting, bearing the fruits of a day's hunting. Kylen ordered the meat to be placed in front of Loran's door.

'We are not your enemy,' she called out into the dusk. But she was answered only by the slamming of doors and closing of shutters. One by one the lights in the village were extinguished until they were left in darkness.

Chapter Seven

It was several days before Etta let Zastra or Dalbric out of her sight. She kept them working from before dawn until well after sunset, barely speaking to them except to deliver orders, or think of new chores. However, when the final batch of wool was all cleaned and spun, she had no choice but to allow the two of them to take it down to Frecha.

'I won't come with you,' she said. 'I need to start making the cheese. Make sure you come straight back. No dallying.'

As they were preparing their backpacks, Findar ran up to Zastra.

'Can I come? Want to show Frecha my knee.' He pointed proudly at a small scab at the top of his shin. A she-goat had taken offence when he had tried to cuddle her newborn kid and kicked him.

Zastra chewed her lip. She didn't want Fin to come, but couldn't explain why, not with Etta listening. Dalbric interjected bluntly.

'You'll slow us down, little man. We are late already and you're getting too big to carry.'

Findar's face fell and his eyes moistened with tears, but his protest remained unspoken. As soon as they were out of sight of the house, Zastra gave her pack of wool to Dalbric. He added it to his already heavy load.

'I feel like Haq's donkey,' he protested.

'Oh, stop moaning. Just think how it will help firm up those lovely ankles of yours.'

'Very funny. Just make sure you find Lindarn. It's not like Ma to turn down a chance to visit Frecha. She looks ready to drop. Did you hear her last night? She was wheezing and coughing so much I didn't get a wink of sleep.'

The grey bags under his eyes told the truth of his remark. With a quick goodbye, Zastra left the path, skirting round the crown of the mountain before heading downwards in a southerly direction. She had only been to Steepcrest once before and hoped she was going the right way. It was hard work at first. Prickly silver ferns grew densely at this point and there were no paths. She prised her way between entwined limbs and several times was forced to crawl under low lying branches in order to make progress. She had been going for some time when yet another set of low hanging branches forced her to crouch down on her belly and wriggle beneath them. In this uncomfortable position, she felt something she had not felt for many years; the sharp pain and pressing weight of a mindweaver trying to enter her thoughts. Taken unawares, she had no mental barrier in place and she was fixed, utterly helpless as a dark shadow fell across her. *I thought I'd taught you better, Zastra.* To her relief, the pain vanished and she was free to move again.

'Dobery?'

An old man, his ugly face blemished by a large brown birthmark, held out his hand to pull her up. Zastra jumped up and squeezed her old teacher in a fierce hug.

'Your mental defences are weak,' he clucked. 'Remember what I taught you? You must practice every day without fail, or else you will be vulnerable to any passing mindweaver.'

'Well, you should come more often and make me. Besides, we've barely seen anyone except the villagers. Soldiers and mindweavers don't come this far up from the valleys.'

'You have been fortunate. But I'm afraid your luck may be about to run out.'

The lines across his face were deeper than she remembered. He had always been an old man, but now he looked drained and frail.

'What do you mean?'

'There is a shift in Golmeira. A turn for the worse. There are tales... well, I have not time to tell them now. Suffice it to say, there are soldiers everywhere and the Kyrgs are back. There was a whole troop of them at Kirkholme when I passed through, wearing your uncle's uniform.'

'Kyrgs? Zastra shuddered. She'd had brushes with Kyrginites on her escape from Golmer Castle and had seen for herself how brutal and merciless the race of warriors with red faces and flat nostrils could be. 'What are they doing out here?'

'The last time Thorlberd called on them it was to defeat your father. He must have something big in mind, to risk such an unpopular move. Sendor perhaps. He thought it conquered years ago, but he should have known better. You must be on your guard, my dear.'

He darted a probe into her mind. This time, she was prepared, offering him only the mind of Layna, a mountain girl. Dobery nodded in satisfaction.

'Why don't our people stand up to my uncle?' Zastra asked.

'Everyone is scared. He controls all the mindweavers and to even think the wrong thing is a crime. He also has many supporters. Invading Sendor was a popular move and the marls that sided with him when he overthrew your father have been rewarded for their loyalty. Unfortunately that means the most greedy and selfish are now in positions of power.'

'I feel so useless,' Zastra said bitterly. 'Hiding in the mountains, while that traitor rules Golmeira. The thought of what he did to my parents makes me want to pull up trees with my bare hands. Is there nothing to be done?'

Dobery looked thoughtful.

'You ask that, my dear and I almost dare not answer. I have long debated whether I should even come.'

'That's not an answer.'

'Our people are almost without hope. Unless we act now, I fear Thorlberd's grip on power will become absolute. We must show them that someone can dare to stand against him.'

'By someone, you mean me?'

'Only you could bring together those who are faithful to your father's memory. He and your mother both inspired considerable loyalty, especially amongst the soldiers. They would support you, if only you have the courage to reveal yourself. You are the rightful heir to the throne of Golmeira after all.'

Zastra yanked a twig from a nearby tree and snapped it in half.

'What would you have me do? Walk down to Kirkholme, proclaim myself the daughter of Leodra and politely request to have back my rightful position as Grand Marl?'

'That would be foolish. Although my plan may hardly be less so. The question is, are you ready?'

'I've been ready since the day Thorlberd murdered my parents. What is this plan?'

'There are some who refuse to kowtow to Thorlberd. They are barely more than a thorn in his side at present, but at least they stand up to him. Their leader is called Lord Justyn. I have made contact with one of his followers and she waits for us a few leagues south, where a small waterfall falls into a narrow lake. Do you know it?'

Zastra nodded.

'She has horses ready and a boat that can take us down to Castanton. I have told her you are alive and may be willing to join them, but you must come now.'

'You can't be serious? What about Fin? I can't just leave him, especially if Kyrgs are around.'

'If we don't act soon, then nowhere in the whole of Golmeira, or Sendor for that matter, will be safe. The future for Findar, Kastara and any other children growing up in Thorlberd's Golmeira will be bleak indeed. We can leave word for Etta, but we must be on our way before nightfall.'

A chance for revenge. One she had been waiting for ever since her uncle's betrayal. But what about Findar? He would be safer with Etta and Dalbric than if she took him to meet this Lord Justyn, but the idea of leaving him behind made her feel sick. The old mindweaver suddenly twirled round, eyes narrowing.

'What is it?' Zastra asked.

'Kyrgs. Many of them and close. You must make up your mind and quickly.'

Even as Dobery spoke, a harsh cry rang through the forest, followed by a scream. It came from further down the slope.

'Steepcrest!' exclaimed Zastra.

'We have no time—' Dobery began to protest, but Zastra was already scrambling down the mountainside. The shouts became louder and she slowed to a crawl, inching forward until she was behind a leafy bush. She parted the branches and all of Steepcrest village was laid out below her. A few moments later, Dobery eased himself into position next to her, his joints cracking in protest.

Flaxen-haired men with red faces were rousing the villagers from their houses. Zastra recognised the Kyrgs instantly. They divided the villagers into two groups. The middle aged and the elderly were placed together, along with the children, while the tallest teenagers and all of the younger adults were rounded up and their hands bound. Zastra recognised Lindarn's stocky figure. He was arguing with a large Kyrg with a tattooed face. The Kyrg grabbed the healer and flung him to the ground.

'Can't you do something?' Zastra whispered to her companion. 'Something mindweavy?'

Dobery shook his head. 'I'm afraid there are too many, even if we had time. Which we don't.'

'Please, Dobery.'

Dobery's face went blank, and she knew he was concentrating all his powers on the Kyrgs. Not for the first time, she cursed the fact that she had no mindweaving abilities. All that talent had fallen to her uncle and cousin. She could do nothing to help. Dobery roused himself.

'There may be something I can do. Watch the guthan.'

'What's a guthan?'

Dobery was already lost in concentration. The Kyrg with the face tattoo staggered backwards, shaking his head. He then barked out a series of orders and gestured away from the village.

Astounded, Zastra watched as all the Kyrgs charged out into the forest, leaving the villagers behind. She jumped up and raced into the village.

'Layna!' cried Lindarn as she emerged from the forest. 'What are you doing here? You must leave, or they'll take you too.'

'I came to ask you to see Etta. She's not well. What in the stars is going on?'

'They are taking all the youngsters. They said they'll kill all of us if we tried to stop them. Yet they have gone, for no reason that I could see.'

'You must all flee,' Dobery limped down the slope towards them. 'I've bought you a few moments, no more. They'll soon be back.'

Lindarn's eyes narrowed. Mountain folk were generally suspicious of strangers.

'Who are you?'

'Never mind who I am, my good man. Suffice to say, I bring news that you are surrounded and the Kyrgs have orders to capture every young man and woman in these mountains and force them to serve in Thorlberd's army.'

'Everyone?' cried Zastra. 'Fivepeaks too?'

Dobery's hesitation was enough.

'I must warn Dalbric and the others.'

Dobery barred her path.

'You have a responsibility to our people, Zastra. This is bigger than a single village. I cannot get Justyn's woman to wait, not with Kyrgs everywhere.'

She pushed him aside.

'Dalbric and Etta saved my life when they took us in. I will not leave them or Fin to the mercy of Kyrgs.'

As she ran, she felt him reach into her mind. Her defensive stonewall snapped into place, and she sensed a sharp flash of frustration. She paid it no heed. Fivepeaks was further from the main valley road than Steepcrest, so there was a chance the Kyrgs hadn't reached it yet. She only hoped she could make it in time.

Chapter Eight

There was no time for stealth. Birds flapped up from the treetops with angry squawks as Zastra thundered past. Her breath rasped against the back of her throat and her mouth was as dry as sand but she dare not stop for a drink. The difference between being in time and being too late might only be a moment. The sun beat down through gaps in the leafy canopy and she was soaked with sweat by the time she reached the outskirts of Fivepeaks. She came out, chest heaving, just above the set of parallel wheel tracks that had been formed by the passage of Haq's cart whenever it headed down the valley towards Kirkholme. Below her, a large band of Kyrgs was coming into sight round a bend, heading towards Fivepeaks. Zastra forced herself into a final sprint, her legs giving way beneath her as she stumbled into the village and clattered into the muscular frame of Kikan.

'Layna,' he cried. 'What's the matter? Lost your little brother again?'

'Fetch everyone,' she gasped. 'Hurry!' The urgency in her voice was enough. Kikan rounded up the village while Zastra used the last of her strength to bang on the door of Frecha's house. Dalbric and Hanra emerged, squinting in the light.

'What's wrong? Is it Ma?' asked Dalbric. The villagers gathered around them as Zastra sucked desperately for air.

'Kyrgs... coming... for the young folk. Dalbric and Hanra. And the others. They're just behind me. We've got to hide.'

'What are you talking about?' cried Hanra. 'Layna, it's not funny.'

Zastra was dismayed to see that no one had moved. They all just stood staring at her.

'Dalbric, please, make them listen.'

'Right.' Dalbric roused himself at last. 'Layna wouldn't say this if it weren't true. Everyone split up.'

'Head up the mountain. They come from the valley.' Zastra gestured toward the gap in the trees through which the Kyrgs might appear at any moment. The young people began to scatter, disappearing into the forest. Dalbric, Hanra and Zastra went together. Dalbric helped Hanra up into the branches of a blackwood tree, its dense needle-like foliage providing excellent cover. Zastra felt a strong shove help her up into a neighbouring tree and then Dalbric hauled himself up behind. They were only just in time. An instant later, the Kyrgs entered the village and began to search the houses. They became increasingly enraged as they found only old people and children. One of the Kyrgs dragged Frecha out of her house and appeared to be shouting at her. When she shook her head, he shoved her to the ground. Dalbric growled and started to climb down the tree. Zastra restrained him. She heard a stifled whimper from the neighbouring tree. *Hanra.* A jaunty whistle came from the northern edge of the village. Through the tree branches, Zastra saw Gonjik sauntering towards his house, unaware of the danger. He would walk straight into the Kyrgs. Cursing under her breath, Zastra lowered herself down from her branch.

'What are you doing?' Dalbric whispered fiercely. 'It's too dangerous.'

Zastra disregarded his warning. She bent low and crept forward, hoping to intercept Gonjik, but as she reached the edge of the track, a triumphant cry went up and two Kyrgs ran past her to grab the youth. Zastra shrank down behind the trunk of a silverfern. As they dragged their prize back to the centre of the village, one of the Kyrgs paused near Zastra's hiding place and began snuffling the air like a hunting dog. Zastra tensed and held her breath. The Kyrg took a step towards the silver fern.

'You monsters!' Mexun appeared from nowhere and began to attack the Kyrgs with a large chisel. Zastra took advantage of the diversion to retreat, erasing her tracks with a leafy branch as she went. Dalbric reached down to haul her to safety. Mexun was thrown aside and Gonjik tied up and dragged away. A heavily silence descended on the village. Zastra's legs began to cramp after her long run and she was desperately thirsty, but she dared not move.

'Can we get down yet?' Hanra whispered plaintively. 'My bottom is numb from sitting on this horrid branch.'

'Wait,' whispered Dalbric and Zastra in unison. They sat silently, even as the sun began to set. Zastra sighed inwardly. *Nightfall.* Dobery would be leaving now, along with Lord Justyn's contact. With them went any chance Zastra had to take up the fight against her uncle. She did not regret choosing to warn Dalbric and the others, but she was sad that she had left Dobery so abruptly. She had felt his anger as he had tried to stop her. *You have a responsibility to our people.* The words had been Dobery's, but in Zastra's mind it was as if her father were talking to her, urging her to avenge him. Once again, she had failed him. She doubted Dobery would ever come back. Dalbric grabbed her wrist, rousing her from her thoughts. A pair of Kyrgs were circling around the village, using the forest as cover. The same Kyrgs who had captured Gonjik. One of them crouched down every so often and sniffed the ground. They halted directly beneath Hanra's tree.

'We are wasting time,' one of the Kyrgs grumbled.

'This is our last chance to fill the quota,' replied the other, snuffling noisily through his flattened nose. 'I was sure I could smell another Golmeiran. A female.'

The scar on Zastra's back began to itch, a reminder of the time she had nearly been killed by a migaradon. *Why did it always itch when she was scared?* She fought the urge to scratch her back against the tree trunk and remained as motionless as if she were hunting for vizzal. Beside her, Dalbric was equally still.

'Have you got a scent or not?' the first Kyrg asked impatiently.

'The trail leads here, but then stops. Makes no sense.'

'The guthan said we had to be back at the rendezvous by nightfall. We'll be in trouble if we're late.'

With one last sniff, the Kyrgs gave up and jogged away down the valley road. Zastra and the others waited until they were sure the Kyrgs had gone before heading back into the village.

'Are you all right, Frecha?' Dalbric looked the weaver over with concern.

'Oh, don't worry about me, duckie. You're all safe, that's the main thing. Except poor Gonjik. I told them the blue fever had done for all the young folk last spring. They might have believed me if the poor lad hadn't turned up at the wrong time.'

'Do you think they'll be back?' Hanra shivered.

'Who knows?' Kikan said grimly. 'You younguns should make yourself scarce tonight. Camp out in the forest. They might come back at night, hoping to catch everyone sleeping.'

Hanra did not like the idea of camping out in the forest and Dalbric invited her to come up to the cabin and stay with them. Etta, looking pinched and tired, nonetheless welcomed Hanra as an honoured guest. Hanra thanked her profusely and did not stop talking all evening, hanging on to Dalbric's arm and repeating the events of the day over and over again. Zastra knew it was just Hanra's way of trying to cope with what had happened, but she wished the weaver's daughter would shut up. Every time Gonjik was mentioned, Zastra felt guilty. If only she had run faster from Steepcrest, she might have been in time to save him. He was annoying, but she didn't like to think of him in the hands of Kyrgs. She also wanted to tell Dalbric about Dobery, but there was no chance of that, not with Hanra clinging to him like a baby goat nestling against its mother.

Eventually, Zastra took herself off to bed, leaving the others talking. She was so exhausted that she fell asleep almost immediately. She woke to find Dalbric clutching her shoulder, a candle trembling in his hand. Shaking her head to clear it, she sensed it was past dawn, as pale light filtered in through the cracks in the doors and shutters.

'It's Etta. She needs help.' Dalbric's voice was fractured with panic. Zastra sprang up, instantly alert and stumbled to Etta's bed to find her half sitting, half lying. Her face was purple and she strained for breath as if she was being throttled by an invisible hand. She was trying to speak, but could not get the words out.

'She can't breathe. I don't know what to do.' Dalbric grasped

Etta's hand between his. Zastra propped a pillow behind Etta's head to try and make her more comfortable, but other than that, she could think of no other way to help. Etta's whole body jerked with the effort of trying to draw breath.

'Ma, don't leave us,' Dalbric sobbed. Fin woke up, took one look at Etta and started to howl. Hanra's head popped up from her blanket, her eyes heavy with sleep.

'Wassmatter?'

'Ma can't breathe.'

'Try steam,' Hanra muttered, before her head dropped back onto her pillow and she fell back to sleep.

'Steam?' It didn't make any sense, but they had no other ideas so Zastra stoked the stove and put a pan of water on to boil.

'Wake Hanra up again. Get her to tell you what she means,' she told Dalbric.

'She won't like that.'

'Tough.'

Hanra took some rousing. She had no recollection of what she had said about steam, nor why she had said it.

'I'm sorry,' she yawned. 'I must have been dreaming.'

'You mean there's nothing we can do?' Dalbric tugged at his hair in horror. From Etta's throat came a horrid whistling sound, like the wind trying to force its way through a narrow crack in the wall. Her eyeballs began to swell. Dalbric grabbed hold of her hands again and sucked in air, as if he would breathe for both of them. At that moment, a rap at the door made them all jump. Zastra shot across the room and flung it open. The stocky form of Lindarn stood dark against the morning mist. She had never been happier to see anyone in her life. Wordlessly, she dragged him inside. The healer took one look at Etta and dug into his

bag and pulled out a small brown bulb that looked like a miniature onion. He asked for a knife and chopped the bulb into tiny
pieces and threw them into Zastra's pan of boiling water. A pungent scent filled the room and Zastra almost gagged. Lindarn carried the steaming pan to Etta's bedside, careful not to spill any and
signalled for her to breathe the fumes. Within moments Etta had
stopped wheezing and was able to lie back, weak and shaken, but
capable of breathing at last. Dalbric sobbed with joy. Findar, who
had been howling the whole time, jumped up onto her bed and
flung his arms around Etta's neck.

'Careful, Fin.' Zastra eased her brother away. 'Let Etta recover.'

Lindarn took the opportunity to examine the patient. He listened to her chest and asked questions in a low voice.

'Well?' Dalbric enquired.

'Miner's lung,' was the verdict.

'But Ma doesn't work in the mines.'

'I did once,' Etta admitted, with a weak cough. 'Me and your
father met working the Helgarth mines. We both needed the
money. His family was starving and my first herd of goats had died
from foot-rot. But the mines are no place to bring up a child, so
when I was pregnant with you, we saved every tocrin to buy our
first pair of goats and moved here.'

'Da.' Dalbric looked at her thoughtfully. 'I remember now that
he used to cough a lot. Was it the same thing?'

Lindarn nodded. 'Most likely.'

'Is there a cure?'

'I'm afraid not.' Lindarn began to pack up his bag. 'But the yaya-
root infusion will help Etta to breathe better, if used regularly. It
was fortunate that I had some on me. It's the last of my supplies.
Lucky too you had some water on the boil.'

'Somehow, I just knew.' Hanra flushed with pleasure. 'Wait 'til I tell Ma how I saved Etta's life. Maybe I've a natural gift for healing.'

'I've prescribed Geort yaya-root before,' Lindarn remarked. 'Perhaps you saw your father breathing the steam when you were a littlun?' Hanra looked crestfallen at such a rational explanation for her apparently miraculous knowledge.

'Where can we get this yaya-root?' Dalbric asked.

'The herbalist in Kirkholme may have some. It's expensive, mind.'

'No,' Etta croaked. 'We can't afford it.'

'Stop it, Ma! Just stop it.'

Etta gaped at her son and Zastra thought it was lucky she was still weak from her ordeal. Dalbric would surely pay later for raising his voice. When Lindarn left, Dalbric accompanied him to the path. Zastra knew he would be arranging to pay for the healer's service. *If I have to hunt every night until next Moonscross to fill Lindarn's larder, I will*, she vowed. If the healer hadn't turned up when he did, Etta would certainly be dead. Fin reached up and stroked Etta's hand. 'We'll make you better, won't we, Layna?'

'We'll do everything we can, little man.'

When Dalbric returned, he looked oddly calm. He knelt down beside Etta.

'When were you going to tell us?' he asked softly. 'You must have known what this cough meant, after what happened with Da. Were you ever going to tell me?'

Bright tears leaked down his cheeks. Etta, for once, could find nothing to say. Dalbric stood up, took Zastra's crossbow from its hook and left the house, not bothering to close the door behind him. That night, he did not return home.

Chapter Nine

Ixendred had been summoned to Grand Marl Thorlberd's office. As he approached the door, he found his path blocked by a slender young man with dark hair and a thin beard carefully shaped to give definition to his pale features. He was handsome and well aware of the fact, judging by the self-assured way he swept a lock of hair away from his eyes. Ixendred bowed low.

'My Lord Rastran,' he said with utmost politeness. The young man stared at him insolently.

'Hello, Ixy. Come to see Father, have you?'

'Indeed I have, my Lord.'

Rastran flung open the door.

'Look who I've found skulking in the corridor, Father.'

Ixendred ground his teeth but knew better than to protest. Anyone in Thorlberd's service knew not to make an enemy of Rastran. He presented his report. Thorlberd frowned.

'Your conscription activities in the Border Mountains has given us fewer recruits than anticipated.'

Rastran smirked.

'Tut, tut, Ixy.'

Ixendred forced himself to take a moment before replying and kept his voice neutral.

'Word spread quickly amongst the villages and some of the young people escaped. I have put in place a secondary plan to soak up the dregs. I guarantee we will get all the recruits we need.'

Rastran heaved himself nonchalantly onto the edge of Thorlberd's table and crossed one leg over the other.

'I don't suppose you found a girl among them? About eighteen, she'd be. Chestnut hair. Vicious as a migaradon that hasn't been fed.'

'Silence boy!' Thorlberd barked. 'And stand up straight in my presence, instead of lounging about like a Far Islander.'

Rastran leapt off the table as if he'd been bitten. Ixendred's curiosity was piqued.

'There were many girls,' he remarked. 'If you tell me what is so interesting about this particular one, I might be able to find out more.'

'It is of no matter.' Thorlberd's abrupt response put an end to that particular line of conversation. Ixendred tucked away the information in a corner of his brain. Interesting. A girl, someone Thorlberd did not want to discuss. Could it be that Leodra's daughter, Zastra, had not been killed after all? There had been rumours at the time, but anyone gossiping about such things had tended to disappear. *She would be about eighteen by now.* Thorlberd broke into his thoughts.

'When will you be ready to move on Sendor?'

Ixendred noted the sudden change of subject, but knew better than to show it.

'Just give the word, Grand Marl. The supply lines are already in place. The Kyrgs are ready for some real fighting. We will make a feint from the west with a small Golmeiran force, while the Kyrgs attack in strength from the north.'

'Good. Take Rastran with you. It's time my son learned something of the art of war, rather than idling about here.'

Ixendred indicated his assent with a tiny inclination of his chin. Rastran's eyes shone.

'At last you've listened to my requests to lead our army in battle. I shall enjoy putting down some Sendoran animals.'

'Ixendred will be in charge. You are there only to watch and learn. Do not let your enthusiasm get the better of you. Remember, we have need for Sendoran prisoners. Alive, not dead.'

'Yes, Father.' Rastran responded with a meekness that Ixendred felt pretty sure was faked. 'The Murthen Island project. I hear we are making great progress.'

Ixendred pricked up his ears again. He considered himself well informed, yet he had nothing of this Murthen Island. More secrets. He felt Thorlberd's attention on him, and had a sudden concern that the Grand Marl might be reading his mind. *I am loyal, I swear!* Thorlberd gave him a level stare.

'We have various schemes in motion, designed to ensure the continued glory of Golmeira. I prefer to keep them known only to a few. I'm sure you understand, Ixendred.'

'As you command, my Lord.'

'Yes, Ixy. Since you aren't a mindweaver, you can't be trusted,' Rastran crowed. A tempting idea began to form in Ixendred's mind, but he decided that strangling the Grand Marl's heir was probably not the wisest move if he wished to remain Master at Arms.

'Quiet, boy!' thundered Thorlberd. 'You will learn discretion if

I have to beat it into you. And don't think I won't. Go and get ready. Do as Ixendred tells you, or you'll answer to me.'

There was a moment of awkward silence before Rastran sidled out. Ixendred followed, trying not to let his mind show how very much he hated the idea of babysitting the Grand Marl's eldest son. He had work to do, information to gather. If Leodra's daughter was indeed alive and living in the Border Mountains, Ixendred would be the one to find her. Thorlberd was sure to be grateful. He decided to send extra mindweavers to scan every conscript. If Zastra was among them, the mindweavers would find her out.

Chapter Ten

Frecha sent word that all their wool had been woven into cloth and was ready to take to Kirkholme. Not a day too soon. The axe had finally broken and they would soon need to begin laying down wood stores for the winter, so that the logs would have enough time to dry out before the cold weather arrived. They also needed a new firering. The one Zastra had been given, many years ago by a man called Hedrik, had been whittled away to just a few small fragments. Most important of all, Etta needed her medicine. However, there was a problem. In previous years, Dalbric and Etta had taken their wares down to Kirkholme using Haq's donkey and cart, but Raurak and the donkey had never returned. It was suspected that Raurak, like Gonjik, had been captured by Kyrgs and forced into service in the Golmeiran army. Any hopes of recovering the donkey and cart had long since faded.

'Dalbric and I will have to carry everything down to Kirkholme on foot,' Zastra said.

'It's too dangerous,' protested Etta. 'What if you are recognised? That's why we never let you go before. What if the Kyrgs are still around? I don't think either of you should go.'

Dalbric gave her a hard stare.

'I'm going, Ma, and there's nothing you can say to stop me.'

He rooted around inside the large store cupboard.

'Anyone seen my large pack?'

Zastra pulled two backpacks from behind a stack of jula oil barrels and handed one to Dalbric.

'I'm coming with you. There's no way you can carry everything yourself. We'll just have to be careful. If we spot any soldiers, we'll hide until they've gone.'

Etta reached out towards Dalbric, but he pulled away. Ever since Lindarn's visit he had been distant, particularly to his mother. Etta picked up one of the barrels of jula oil and handed it to her son. The crop had been good that spring. Dalbric had spent many evenings pressing out the oil, and they had two spare barrels to sell along with their cloth.

'Promise me you will come back safe.'

Dalbric shoved the barrel into the bottom of his pack.

'I promise, Ma,' he mumbled eventually. Fin ran into the kitchen and flung himself at Zastra's legs.

'Don't go,' he begged. 'Bad soldiers catch you.'

Zastra bent down and levered him up into her arms, pretending to groan with the effort.

'You're getting too big to lift, little man.'

Her brother buried his face in her neck. Zastra kissed the top of his head. His hair felt soft against her cheek. She steeled herself and prised him away.

'It's good you're so big, because I need you to do something very important. I need you to take care of Etta while we're gone.'

Her brother looked at her with a serious expression. Zastra rummaged around in the pocket of her trousers and pulled out the

last two pieces of her broken firering. The ends of the two fragments fit snugly together. She gave the smaller piece to Findar.

'See how they link together? If you touch this whenever you are
missing me, I'll do the same. It will be like we are connected.'

Fin eyed the small tube of metal in his palm, his forehead
creased into a frown. Zastra and Dalbric packed their bags quickly,
before Fin could make any other protest and before Etta could
think up a way to stop them.

'Fin, you be sure to do exactly as Etta tells you,' were Zastra's
parting words. Her heart almost broke at the sight of her brother's
woebegone face staring at her from the doorway. They headed
down the mountain, stopping at Frecha's only long enough to
pick up the wool. The bundles of cloth were large and when added
to the heavy oil barrels, there was no space left for food or water.

'We'll just have to get what we need from the forest,' Dalbric
remarked bluntly. They bid Frecha and Hanra farewell and set off.

It was a four day journey, much of it beating against the strong
winds of the high mountain passes. Zastra formed a healthy
respect for Haq's donkey as the straps from her heavy pack dug
into her shoulders and her thighs trembled under the weight.
They trudged on, mostly in silence, conserving all their energy
for carrying their burdens. When they could walk no more, they
made camp by the nearest stream or spring. Too tired to hunt,
they made do with small meals of tree fungus or nuts and berries
plucked as they travelled, before falling asleep by a small fire that
they sunk into a pit to screen it from prying eyes.

On the evening of the third day, disaster struck. They had to
ford a large stream, swollen by recent rainfall. The water flowed
deep and strong and it took the last of Zastra's flagging energy to
wade through water that rose as high as her waist. She made it to

the far side of the stream but, as she scrambled towards safety, she slipped on the wet rocks and fell backwards, her backpack crashing down hard against a boulder. Dalbric helped her to the top of the bank, where a check of her backpack revealed that the barrel of jula oil had sprung a leak. The oil was gone. Worse, it had drenched one of the precious bundles of wool, and it could not be salvaged. Zastra sank to the ground in wordless grief. Dalbric said nothing, but Zastra could see that he was upset. They made camp by the side of the cruel stream, but Zastra, exhausted as she was, could not sleep and lay awake for most of the night, silently berating herself for her clumsiness.

At noon the next day they reached the long descent into the valley of the Thrashing River, at the head of which lay Kirkholme. Zastra shifted her load slightly to ease her aching shoulders.

'If we hurry, we may be able to do our business today. We don't want have to stay overnight.'

They hastened down the track together and entered the outpost late in the afternoon. Zastra pulled a shapeless cap from her pocket and pulled it low over her forehead so that it shaded her eyes. It was unlikely that anyone in these parts would recognise her as Leodra's daughter, but there was no point in taking chances. Dalbric also tried to look inconspicuous, raising the hood of his woollen cape, in case any Kyrgs were about, looking for more young people to conscript.

Kirkholme was a sizeable village, almost large enough to be called a town. The main streets were paved and filled with people, but Zastra saw no sign of Golmeiran uniforms or black robed mindweavers. The noise and bustle seemed strange after the peace and quiet of the mountains. Dalbric led her via narrow backstreets to a store belonging to Miray, the cloth merchant who always bought their wool. The silver-haired woman greeted them warmly. Running an expert hand over one of the bales, she offered two tocrins a bundle.

'But this is the best quality goats' wool,' Dalbric protested.

'I'm sorry, Dalbric. I don't question the quality. That's why I've offered what I have. Coarser wool raises only one tocrin a bale these days. Taxes are so high we've had to lower our costs and raise prices just to scratch a living. You can ask anyone else, they'll tell you the same.'

'Last year it was three, and the wool wasn't as good.'

'Look, I'll give you an extra quarter tocrin a roll, seeing as it's such lovely wool. But only because it's you,' Miray offered.

'So how much is that?'

'Let's see. Seven bales, that's thirteen and a quarter tocrins total.'

'Fifteen and three-quarters,' insisted Zastra darkly.

'Um, yes, that's right.' The merchant gave Zastra a sharp glance. 'It's a good thing they are teaching you counting now, up in the mountains.'

'It is, isn't it?' returned Zastra. She wasn't about to tell Miray where she had really learned arithmetic. At the chandler's they sold their single remaining barrel of jula oil for three tocrins. Then to the blacksmith's where, after a great deal of haggling, they purchased a second-hand firering and a new axe. Once they had set aside Frecha's share of the wool money they were left with two tocrins. As they were looking for the herbalist's store, Zastra caught sight of a flash of flaxen hair at the far end of the street. She grabbed Dalbric and pulled him into an alley and behind a stack of crates.

'Ouch!' Dalbric yelped. Zastra realised she was gripping him so tightly that her fingers were white. She released him and put a finger to her lips. Moments later, four Kyrgs marched across the end of the alley. Zastra and Dalbric cowered behind the crates until they had passed.

'That was close,' Dalbric whispered. 'If you hadn't seen them...'

'Come on.' Zastra pulled him to his feet. 'The sooner we're done here, the better.'

They made it to the herbalist just as he was closing for the day. He had only one other customer, a thickset man in a green jacket who couldn't decide whether to take a large or small bottle of a purple medicine.

'Yaya-root is it?' the herbalist said in response to Dalbric's enquiry. 'Well, it's very hard to get hold of these days. There's a lot of demand.'

'Do you have any?' Dalbric looked in no mood for small talk.

'I've only three bundles left. Very precious. Three tocrins per bundle.' He opened a tin and placed a bundle of the tiny bulbs on the counter.

'Three tocrins for that?'

Zastra placed a calming hand on Dalbric's arm

'We have only two tocrins,' she explained. The herbalist snatched up the yaya-root and put it back in the tin.

'I've told you the price and, before you ask, I don't give credit. I've been swindled by you mountain folk before. Always wanting what you can't afford.'

'Please!' Dalbric begged. 'My Ma will die without it.'

The herbalist placed the precious tin on a high shelf behind his counter. Dalbric eyed it longingly.

The herbalist scowled. 'I'm good friends with the captain of the guards. So don't think of trying anything,' he warned.

The man in the green jacket stepped forward and placed the smaller of the bottles of purple liquid on the counter.

'You could try Pugara,' he suggested. 'She sometimes sells herbs. Cheaper than here.'

The herbalist glared at the interloper, scooped up the bottle of medicine and began to wrap it in brown paper.

'Pugara is a rogue and thief,' he said. 'She's not even registered and doesn't pay taxes.'

The green-jacketed man shrugged. 'My friend, I would much rather these fine folk purchased from your excellent establishment, but it seems you cannot supply their needs at a price they can afford.'

'Where can we find this Pugara?' Zastra asked.

'She does her business out of the Smithy Inn, down near the river.'

Dalbric frowned.

'Etta always warned me to stay away from that part of Kirkholme. Full of thieves and worse, she says.'

The man paid the herbalist, took his parcel and put it in his pocket.

'It isn't the prettiest part of town, for sure. But the poor need somewhere to live and if you want something cheap, that's where you'll find it. Besides, you two look like you can take care of yourselves.'

Zastra didn't like the way he was looking them up and down. There was something greedy in his appraisal, as if he was setting a value on them.

'Why are you helping us?'

The man rolled his eyes. 'Everyone's so suspicious these days. Look, take my advice, or don't. It's up to you.'

He turned to leave. Zastra and Dalbric exchanged glances and together they ran out after the man.

'Where is this Smithy Inn?' Zastra asked.

The man pointed towards a large building, painted yellow. 'Turn left at the Payment Office and then follow the path down the hill. The inn is the one with the horseshoe sign over the door. I'd take you there myself but—'

'You're too scared to go to that part of town?' Zastra finished.

'Listen, girl. You seemed desperate, so I told you what I know. Your gratitude is most welcome, or it would be, if you bothered to show any.'

The man didn't wait for a response before heading away, shaking his head.

'I don't like this,' Dalbric murmured.

'I don't see that we have a choice. If there's any chance to get Etta this medicine, we must give it a try.'

They headed towards the yellow building where, just as the man had said, they found a muddy path leading downhill through a sparse patch of trees. The well-kept shops and houses of the main part of Kirkholme changed into canvas tents and rickety sheds of rotting wood. Here and there animal skins were stretched out to dry alongside patched-up clothing on lines of fraying rope. Zastra thought she recognised scrittal skulls amongst the piles of rubbish and ashes that lay in front of the dwellings. There were few people about, and those that were stared at them in an unfriendly manner. The path became muddier as they approached the river. Puddles of brown water filled imprints made by passing boots. They tried to skirt the worst of these puddles, but even so their boots got sucked into the sticky morass. Zastra shuddered as she felt cold water seep through her laces and down between her toes.

'That must be it.' Dalbric nodded towards a low building constructed of moss-covered logs as thick as his waist. There were no windows, just a narrow door hanging unevenly on its hinges. A rusty horseshoe hung above the entrance. They waded through mud that came up to their calves and pushed open the door. Zastra's eyes took a few moments to adjust to the gloom. There wasn't much to look at. The floor was just a square of compacted mud and the moss on the logs was not limited to the outside. The whole place was dark, dank and dismal. There were only three people inside. A man sat slumped against a narrow bar in one corner. He raised his head briefly, gave them a glassy stare, and sank back down. In the far corner, a plump woman with grey hair tied in two thick plaits sat in an equally plump armchair, surrounded by piles of crates and suitcases and next to her stood a huge man, with a nose that appeared to have been broken in many places.

'Are you Pugara?' Zastra stepped towards the armchair, only to find her path blocked by the giant.

'Who sent you?' Pugara's border accent was strong, her tone sharp.

'A man. Short and stocky, wearing a green jacket.'

The woman nodded and beckoned them forward. Her huge bodyguard gave Zastra a hard stare before allowing them just enough room to squeeze past. Pugara's lips twitched upwards in what might have passed for a smile, but Zastra noted that her eyes stayed sharp and, just like the green-jacketed man, she looked them up and down closely.

'Sit down, dearies.' Despite the endearment, it was a command, not a suggestion. Zastra looked around for a chair but Pugara was occupying the only available one, so she squatted down on the corner of a small crate. Dalbric found a perch on a small barrel. He kept his backpack on his shoulders ready to move quickly if he had to. Zastra did the same.

'What is it you need?'

Zastra glanced at Dalbric, who nodded at her encouragingly.

'Yaya-root. Do you have any?'

Pugara raised a thick eyebrow.

'Miner's lung, eh? Not one of you though, I hope? You both look too young for such a disease. How old are you, dearies?'

'Is that important? Do you have any or not?'

Zastra didn't bother to hide her impatience. She wanted to get their business done and leave this place as soon as possible. She scanned the room. Aside from the door they had entered through, the only other exit was a narrow opening behind the bar in the corner.

'I like to know who I'm selling to.' Pugara sat back in her chair and folded her arms. She was clearly not going to sell them anything until they had answered her questions.

'We don't know how old we are,' Zastra lied. 'We don't count these things in the mountains.'

That turned out to be only the first of Pugara's questions. Some they answered truthfully, sometimes they lied, and the questioning went on and on. Zastra became increasingly apprehensive. It was almost as if Pugara was trying to keep them here. When the plump woman asked her what her favourite food was, Zastra decided that enough was enough. She leapt off her crate, took their two precious tocrins from her pocket and thrust them under Pugara's nose.

'I don't see why you need to know my favourite food to sell us yaya-root. Here's our money. If it's not good enough for you, we'll leave.'

'Calm down, dearie.'

Pugara eased herself out of the armchair and began to rummage around in her various crates and suitcases. At length she found a bamboo cloth sack and opened it out. Zastra recognised the small brown bulbs. They were poor specimens compared with that of the herbalist. Some of the the bulbs were tiny, others had damaged skins, but it was a big bundle and she reckoned it might be enough to see Etta through the winter. The bodyguard held out his hand for the money and Zastra had just placed the coins in his giant palm when the door to the inn burst open. Three Kyrgs charged in, their serrated scythal blades flashing in the dim light.

'It's a trap!' Zastra cried. She snatched the yaya root from Pugara's grasp and dragged a stupefied Dalbric towards the corner exit she had seen earlier. It was their only hope of escape. The man who had been slumped across the bar the whole time chose that moment to rise up to block their way, but Zastra kicked out and swept his feet out from under him, knocking him to the floor. She ducked as a scythal blade flashed by her ear.

'Don't kill them, idiots,' she heard Pugara shout. 'I only get my reward if they're alive.'

They ducked through the opening and into a store room even darker and damper than the room they had left. A rectangular outline opposite indicated another doorway, perhaps to the outside. They dodged around stacks of barrels and crates. As she ran past, Zastra kicked at the barrels, causing them to crash down into the path of their pursuers. They reached the door, but it refused to open. Dalbric tried to force it with a shoulder charge, but it held fast.

'Locked!' he groaned. Zastra's heart sank. Of course. Pugara was no fool. She had meant to trap them all along, and would have made sure there was no way to escape.

Behind them the Kyrgs struggled to scramble over the barrels that Zastra had knocked down into their path, but that wouldn't hold them much longer.

'The axe!' Zastra cried. Dalbric swung his backpack from his shoulders and pulled out their new purchase. With a few hefty swings he smashed the door to pieces. A large hand clapped onto Zastra's shoulder. She spun round and used both hands to lever the Kyrg off her and aimed a stout kick at his stomach. Her opponent doubled over with a grunt of pain and she took her chance to follow Dalbric through what was left of the door. They came out into the gloom of late evening with just enough light to see that they were on a narrow wooden walkway that was raised above the surface of the river. It skirted round the back of the inn. As they dashed round the corner, a huge shadow stepped out and grabbed Zastra by her collar, lifting her into the air. It was Pugara's bodyguard. She wriggled as hard as she could but he was too strong and she could not escape. Zastra threw the yaya-root bundle at Dalbric.

'Run!' she cried. 'I'll catch you up.'

Even as she said the words, she knew that her position was hopeless. There was no escape for her, but Dalbric still had a chance, if only he would take it. Two Kyrgs pounded round the corner of the walkway and, with a last look of remorse, Dalbric fled into the gloom. Zastra tried once again to wriggle free, but the Kyrg who she had kicked in the stomach stopped in front of her and grinned as he aimed a blow at her head. Stunned, she could only struggle feebly as her arms were yanked behind her and her wrists bound together. Another blow sent her spinning into darkness.

Chapter Eleven

Kylen hated the ruined city of Golgannan. What had once been a vibrant city with paved streets, tall fountains and stately buildings was now a wasteland of broken rocks and splintered wood, left empty and desolate at Thorlberd's command as a deliberate reminder to the Sendoran people of the futility of resistance. She shivered, but not from the cold, even though dusk was beginning to settle upon the deserted streets of the city that had once been the capital of her beloved Sendor. Its ancient buildings had been well known; the tower of the ancient warriors, the glorious fighting arena, and the vast music dome renowned for its pink granite walls decorated with eye-catching fellgryff engravings. All the work of Joraz, Sendor's greatest stoneworker, and all now destroyed. The ghost of her father walked these streets, and as much as she had loved him, she had no desire to meet it. Sendoran lore said that the spirits of defeated warriors were destined to walk the earth for a thousand years as punishment for failure. Her father's shade would be tormented by what had become of his country. Perhaps Hylaz was right. What use was capturing a few wagons of weapons when Golgannan was gone and Sendor ruled by Golmeirans? Better she had died here with him. Hylaz was watching her closely.

'You could have done nothing had you been here, my Lady. Your father did right to send you and Lord Zadorax away. You were both too young.'

Kylen did not want comfort. She needed to feel the pain that she deserved for being alive whilst so many were dead. For being helpless, unable to stop the suffering of her people.

'You presume too much on our friendship, Hylaz.' The words came out more harshly than she intended and the big man said no more.

General Alboraz, leader of the largest of the Sendoran resistance groups, had sent word that he needed to speak with her. She suspected he chose Golgannan as their meeting place deliberately. Alboraz had been charged with protecting Kylen and Zax, and the old general still resented being forced into the role of babysitter rather than taking part in the last great battle for Sendor. He had never forgiven Kylen for it. It annoyed her that Alboraz felt he had the right to summon her. She would be his liege lord, just as soon as she was of age, yet he treated her like a child.

The sharp cry of a hawk was followed by the rumble of iron clad wheels.

'About time.' Kylen stepped forward, but even as she did so, her intuition told her something was wrong. Beside her, Hylaz cupped his hands and gave their usual signal. The only response was a horse's whickering. Kylen drew her sword.

'It's not Alboraz.'

Hylaz made a few silent signals and the team spread out. A covered wagon rolled towards them, driven by two Golmeiran soldiers. Two outriders on horses were oblivious to their danger. Kylen stepped out from behind a broken column and yanked one of the outriders from his horse by the ankle and had her sword at his throat before he even knew what was going on. Hylaz unseated the other outrider and knocked her out with a sharp blow to her head. The wagon driver threw her hands up in instant surrender. Hylaz walked round to the back of the wagon and pulled aside the hemp covering. Inside, three Sendorans were chained to an iron bolt that had been sunk into the wagon's base.

'Thank the stars!' said one of them, a stocky woman with a strong jaw and well-defined biceps.

'What is the meaning of this?' demanded Kylen. 'How did you allow yourselves to be captured?'

'We were betrayed. A Golmeiran mindweaver infiltrated one of the villages we used as a base. His soldiers were waiting for us.'

'And you surrendered?' Kylen didn't hide her contempt. The woman bowed her head in shame as Hylaz instructed the driver to free the prisoners.

'Where were they taking you?'

The prisoner directed her reply at Kylen's feet.

'I heard them say Castanton. We were to be put on a ship.'

'A ship?' Kylen asked in disbelief. 'Golmeirans usually kill Sendorans. Where were they sending you?'

'Why don't you ask them?' The woman nodded towards the Golmeiran prisoners, who were huddled together in a group.

'We don't know anything,' the driver protested hastily. 'We were to pass them over to a ship's captain, that's all I know.'

'What ship?'

'The *Valiant*.'

Hylaz snorted. 'Fine name for a Golmeiran ship.'

The driver knew no more and neither did any of her compatriots. Kylen ordered them to be chained to the wagon in place of the Sendorans. A strong bellow boomed out from the edge of the city. Hylaz answered and two men emerged from the gloom mounted on prancing fellgryffs. They dismounted and one threw back his hood to reveal a man of middle years, his head and beard both closely shaved. His blue eyes were colder than a mountain spring.

'I might ask why you are making enough noise to scare up a troop of Golmeirans.'

'Nice to see you too, General Alboraz,' Kylen returned stiffly, leaving it to Hylaz to explain.

Alboraz rubbed his chin thoughtfully. 'This is not the first time I've heard of our people being taken down to the coast. We don't know what happens to them. None have ever escaped, or returned.'

'So you have no firm information,' Kylen remarked. 'How is my brother?'

Alboraz returned her look levelly. 'I left the lad safe, as per my last orders from my Lord, your father. The lad wants to fight, even though his broadsword as yet lies too heavy in his hand. The spirit of Sendor is strong within him, like his father, but unlike some, he does as he's told.'

'I will soon be of age. When I am your liege lord, I will expect—'
He cut her off brusquely.

'Until you are old enough, you will obey me. Your father granted me stewardship. We've more important things to worry about than your pride, lass. The Golmeirans have recruited a new army. My sources say they plan to destroy us as punishment for our resistance. I am taking all the remaining strength left in Sendor with me west to meet them.

'Very well. I am ready to fight.'

Alboraz shook his head.

'I have another task for you. There are rumours of Kyrgs massing by our northern border. I must know if it is true.'

'Kyrgs!' spat Kylen. 'I won't have it. In fact, I don't believe it. The Kyrgs would never dare invade us. This is a ploy to keep me away from the real fighting. I won't be denied. Not again.'

The general grabbed her upper arm. His grip was so firm that her fingers went numb.

'I do not lie. Perhaps the Kyrgs see our weakness and mean to take advantage. Or Thorlberd may have renewed the old alliance. Either way, we must know.'

Something in his manner convinced Kylen he was speaking the truth. Besides, he was right. Until she was of age, she was bound to obey him.

'Fine.' She shrugged him off. 'I shall go and find these mythical Kyrgs and teach them a lesson in Sendoran manners. You can have these.' She waved dismissively in the general direction of the woman and the other Sendorans

they had rescued. 'I have no need for such poor soldiers.'

Alboraz bowed in an exaggerated Golmeiran style. An obvious insult, but she had no choice but to let it go. She only hoped Alboraz was as good a soldier as everyone said he was. If the Golmeirans were indeed sending another army, a miracle would be needed to save them.

Chapter Twelve

Zastra looked around the dim interior of the wagon as it clattered and juddered along the uneven track. Her fellow prisoners were an odd bunch, she could see that even in the gloom. By her side, a young girl with a dark complexion sat hugging her legs, her forehead resting on her knees. Opposite, a wiry youth grinned at her with knowing impudence. Most surprising of all was the Kyrg. Like Zastra, his hands were tied behind his back. He stared straight ahead, refusing to look at anyone else. Unlike every Kyrg Zastra had ever seen, he was not wearing the black uniform of her uncle's army. A column of air on either side separated him from his nearest neighbours. Zastra was not surprised. No one wanted to touch a Kyrg. You never knew what disease you might catch. The only good thing about Zastra's situation was the absence of Dalbric. Hopefully, that meant he had escaped. Four Golmeiran soldiers sat at the back of the wagon, penning them in.

'Nice of Grand Marl Thorlberd to send us a personal escort,' said the wiry youth. 'Where are we going?'

'Shut up, flekk,' barked one of soldiers, a dark-skinned South-land woman.

'Make me,' retorted the youth. The woman stood up, raised a baton and clonked the youth on his head. He collapsed forward onto the wooden slats that formed the base of the wagon.

'Request granted. The rest of you keep quiet, unless you want the same as this loudmouth.'

They continued their journey in uneasy silence. Zastra glanced out of the back of the wagon. By the direction of the long evening shadows, she could tell that they were heading south. The soldiers sat taut and alert, swords unsheathed. One rested a loaded crossbow across her knee, her forefinger tapping the trigger. Zastra's stomach lurched. There was no possibility of escape. She silently cursed the man in the green jacket and Pugara for their treachery. Beside her, the young girl started to shiver.

'It'll be all right.' Zastra tried to sound reassuring. The girl kept her forehead pressed against her knees.

'I'm scared.'

'What's your name?'

'Yashni.'

'Mine's Layna. Try not to be afraid. They've paid out good money to have us on this wagon, so they must want us alive and well. Let's wait and see before we get too worried.'

'No talking!' The curt order from Southlander ended their conversation and the wagon continued its slow journey. The twin moons were high in the sky before the wagon eventually pulled off the dirt track and stopped on a shelf of rock that overhung a fast flowing river. The prisoners were ushered out into the night. Zastra felt cold spray against her face. Beyond the rock shelf, a waterfall thundered into boiling rapids, the white foam reflecting the light of a pair of swaying lamps. The shadow of a barge loomed dark against the swirling water. Zastra and the others were marched on board. Her bonds and that of the Kyrg were cut before they were forced down a narrow wooden ladder into the depths of the hull.

'Where are you taking us?' Zastra received only a sharp shove in response to her question. The ladder was hauled up behind them and a square hatch was locked in place. They were left in utter darkness. Zastra felt a choking sensation as the dark closed around her. Ever since the night she had been forced to flee the horrors of Golmer Castle via a dark underground tunnel, she had hated enclosed spaces. A strangled squeak at her shoulder told her that Yashni was similarly afraid. She reached out a hand and brushed against trembling flesh.

'Here, hold my hand.'

'Layna?'

'Yes, it's me.'

Zastra felt a cold hand slip inside hers. Somehow, Yashni's need for reassurance gave her the courage she needed not to scream. She bit down on the bile that was rising in her throat and reached out into the darkness, shuffling forward until she felt the damp wood of the hull. A cold sweat broke across her forehead and she eased herself down, just before her legs gave way. She pulled Yashni down to the floor with her, comforted slightly by the solid-ity of the rough wood against her back. *Breathe. One, two, three, breathe.* The barge began to move, lurching with the river swell. Bodies stumbled and slid across the hold, followed by a shower of curses and muttered apologies as limbs crashed against each other in the dark, until everyone found a space to sit down.

'Where are we going?' Yashni sobbed. No one offered an answer. Zastra put her arm around the girl and pulled her close. *One, two, three, breathe.*

The barge settled into a monotonous motion. Long passages of time were broken occasionally by a succession of bumps and grinding noises.

'A lock,' someone muttered at the first of these events. 'They're taking us down to the coast.'

The air inside the barge began to thicken with the stink of sweat and damp wood. Zastra felt a familiar terror squeezing the air from her lungs.

'I can't breathe,' sobbed Yashni, echoing Zastra's internal panic. 'They mean to choke us to death.'

'Don't worry.' Zastra forced out the words. 'They don't mean to let us die or they wouldn't have gone to all this trouble. You'll see.'

She began to stroke Yashni's hair, as her own mother had once done for her, many years ago.

'Do you have some special knowledge, mountain girl?'

She recognised the voice of the cocky boy who had been knocked senseless by the Southlander.

'Who's that?'

'Name's Jerenik. We need to break down the walls of this tub before we suffocate.'

'Fool,' a voice growled in the dark. Zastra shuddered involuntarily. She recognised the harsh, scratchy tones of the Kyrg. Jerenik also appeared to recognise the Kyrginite tones.

'Is that an animal grunting?'

'You want to drown, boy?'

'Um...' Jerenik sniffed the air. 'Yes, definitely some kind of wild animal. Seems to think we can understand its gruntings.'

This brought forth quite a few chuckles and the Kyrg said no more. The enclosed space grew hotter, the air becoming thick and pungent until the sound of bolts being slid back was followed by the appearance of a bright square of light in the deck above them. The prisoners shielded their eyes from the harsh glare, but as Zastra's eyes adjusted, she saw that the sky above them was an overcast grey. A burlap sack was thrown down and a grate placed across the square. Zastra sucked in the fresh air gratefully as Jerenik made a grab for the bag and opened it. It contained a small barrel of water and some dry-roasted halsa nuts.

'Is this all?' he protested.

'Be grateful,' a voice shouted down. 'Make the most of it. That's to last you until tomorrow.'

Jerenik pulled the cork and lifted the barrel to drink but before he could put his mouth to the opening, the barrel was plucked from his hands by the Kyrg.

'Hey!' A thin, yellow-faced man shuffled into the patch of light. 'That's for us, not for you, you dirty animal.'

'My *name* is Ithgol.' The Kyrg raised the barrel to his lips and gulped down the water.

'Ooh, it thinks it's got a name,' Jerenik remarked. 'Well, I suppose even insects have names, don't they? Fleas, lice, they all—' He broke off as Ithgol lowered the barrel and issued a deep throated rattle.

'Easy there. No need to get cross.' Jerenik backed away towards the comfort of the shadows. Ithgol raised the barrel to his lips once more, keeping one eye on Jerenik's rapidly retreating form. Zastra stepped forward and grabbed the Kyrg by his arm. His bicep was thicker than her thigh and felt as solid as the wooden timbers of the ship. Still, it was too late to back down now. At least, now there was some light and air, she felt alive again. Although by the look on Ithgol's face, that state of affairs might not last much longer.

'The water is for us all to share.'

She tried to keep her voice firm and steady. This close, the powerful bulk of the Kyrg was intimidating, but she refused to stand by and let him take all their food and water. Slowly, the Kyrg set the barrel down and replaced the cork. Then, without warning, he sprang. The speed of his attack almost caught her out and she only just managed to duck beneath the powerful swing of his arm. For a moment, he was off balance and she shouldered him as hard as she could in the midriff, hitting exactly where she intended. To her dismay, he didn't even flinch. It was like fighting a giant tree. He grabbed her around her ribs, squeezing so that she could not breathe. She wriggled desperately but his grip was as firm as metal clamps. All the air was squeezed out of her body and then he tossed her aside as casually as if he were throwing a fish back into a stream. She crashed hard into the side of the barge and collapsed to the floor, sucking desperately for air.

'Strongest first.' Ithgol took another drink from the barrel, then grabbed a large handful of nuts before striding to the rear of the hold.

The other prisoners dived towards the supplies, hitting and gouging each other in their desperation to reach them first. Fists and curses flew about. Zastra saw Yashni floored by a stray elbow. Jerenik and the yellow-faced man had laid hands on the barrel and were each trying to tear it away from the other. A sudden swell caused the barge to tilt and the prisoners were sent sprawling. The barrel bounced off the hull and rolled towards Zastra. She pinned it beneath her left foot, still trying to catch her breath. Jerenik sprang for her, but she fended him off with a well-aimed jab to his stomach, leaving him gasping.

'I'm not in the best of moods.' Her chest still felt compressed and her voice came out low and harsh. She hoped it sounded imposing, rather than weak. 'So I suggest you let me share this out fairly and save yourself some pain. Unless anyone else wants what he just got.'

Zastra was relying on no one realising that she had barely enough breath to stand, let alone fight. Luckily, her bluster seemed to work and no one challenged her. She began to divide up the nuts, making sure everyone received an equal share. There was a metal ladle clipped to the barrel. Zastra filled it with water and offered it first to Yashni, who drank gratefully.

'Who's next?'

'That dirty animal's had his mouth all over it,' Jerenik complained. 'Who knows what kind of diseases it's got?'

'Then don't have any,' Zastra said shortly. 'There'll be more for the rest of us.'

Jerenik made a show of wiping the barrel opening with his sleeve before he let her pour his water, but he still drank his share. The other prisoners took their turn, although many grimaced at having to drink from the same barrel as a Kyrg. Jerenik sidled up to her.

'You're lucky that I felt sorry for you. That Kyrg gave you such a beating, it didn't seem fair to make you fight again.'

'That would have been very thoughtful,' she responded, 'if it wasn't complete rubbish.'

After everyone had taken their portion, she served herself, then addressed the darkness at the rear of the hold.

'Next time we share, Kyrg.'

There was no reply.

Chapter Thirteen

The next time food and water were thrown down, Ithgol was in position to catch the bag. The prisoners muttered under their breath, but none of them challenged him directly. With a sigh, Zastra stepped forward, ignoring the warning of her aching ribs.

'Stupid Golmeiran.'

'You may have a point,' she conceded, 'but I'd rather be a stupid Golmeiran than a selfish Kyrg.'

He made a grab for her, but she was ready. She kept on the balls of her feet, skipping away from his crushing grip every time he tried to close in on her. He charged and she swayed to one side and landed a solid kick in the ribs even as she danced away from him. Ithgol grunted; in pain or anger she couldn't tell.

'Go on, mountain girl!' Jerenik cheered. Some of the other prisoners added their encouragement, crowding around them and clapping her on.

'You show him, girl.'

'Get the animal where it hurts!'

Unfortunately, as the ring of prisoners closed around them, the lack of space made it easy for Ithgol to corner her. Just as before, Zastra was encased in his powerful grip, squeezed like a damp sponge and tossed aside. The crowd parted, grumbling at her defeat.

'I guess she is as stupid as she looks.'

'That fight was as one-sided as a mirror.'

Zastra ruefully noted that her sudden popularity had ended as quickly as it had begun. The Kyrg had taken his share of the food and water before she could recover, but as she staggered forward, Jerenik and others stood back and let her share out the rest without protest. As the grate was replaced by the hatch and they were plunged into darkness, Zastra racked her brains to think how she could defeat the Kyrg. He was stronger than her and apparently impervious to her stoutest blows. Without a weapon of some kind, her cause was hopeless.

The barge continued downriver. Every so often, more prisoners were thrust down into the hold. Zastra noted they were all young and healthy, just like Gonjik and the youngsters of Steepcrest. She almost sobbed in frustration. She had allowed herself to be taken as fodder for her uncle's army. Dobery would be appalled. Instead of standing up to her uncle, she would be forced to fight for him.

The hold became uncomfortably crowded. Zastra and Yashni found themselves squashed in between Ithgol and Jerenik, so close that their elbows and thighs pressed against each other. They hit rougher weather and the barge began to lurch from side to side. Jerenik threw up on Zastra's feet.

'Sorry,' he mumbled. Around them, other prisoners were also sick and the air became thick and rancid. Water and food was thrown down, but everyone was too ill to eat or drink, even Ithgol. Just as it seemed as if the nightmare journey would never end, they ground to a halt against something solid. Cries came from the deck and footsteps thudded overhead. The hatch opened to reveal the blue-grey sky of late evening. The prisoners were ushered out onto the deck and into a line. A lively wind snatched at their hair and clothes. The barge was tied up against a stone jetty. In front of them lay the sea, its grey horizon merging with low clouds in an indistinct haze. Four ships were moored out in the bay with sails furled, their outlines fading into the evening gloom. A man in a black uniform marched across a gangway and onto the barge.

'Welcome to the Golmeiran fleet,' he said.

Chapter Fourteen

The man held himself with military stiffness and his voice was hoarse, as if worn out by shouting.

'I am Captain Dastrin. You are now members of the Golmeiran Fleet. Do not think to escape. Desertion will be punished by death. Insolence will be punished by death. Cowardice will be punished...'

'Let me guess,' Jerenik muttered under his breath.

'... by death.'

'How original.' Jerenik rolled his eyes.

'You will obey my orders and those of my officers without question...'

Jerenik raised his hand. Dastrin shifted his icy stare towards the youth.

'Without *question*,' he repeated.

'I didn't agree to this,' Jerenik protested. 'You can't just force us into your crew.'

'Burgal.' Only Dastrin's lips moved; the rest of his body remained rigid. A Kyrg stepped forward, short of stature, with broad shoulders. In his hand was a thick leather strap, folded back on itself to form a loop. With a violent flick of his wrist he struck Jerenik across his chest and then across his shoulders. The youth lifted his arms to protect himself, crying out in pain as more blows landed. Burgal did not stop. If anything he redoubled his efforts, even as Jerenik cowered down on the deck and rolled himself into a ball. Dastrin looked on with naked satisfaction as the beating continued. The prisoners stiffened at the brutality of it. At last Burgal stopped, leaving Jerenik whimpering on the deck. Dastrin continued his speech as if he had not been interrupted.

'Grand Marl Thorlberd has decreed that our army and fleet be expanded. Any loyal citizen of our great country must be willing to serve. Those not willing are traitors and will be treated accordingly.'

He paced slowly up the line of prisoners.

'Make no mistake, I have the right to take you. I do not tolerate questions or protests. Do not think you can escape this fate. If you heed my words, then you shall be rewarded for your service at a rate of twenty tocrins per year.'

He had reached Yashni, whose shoulders were shaking with suppressed sobs.

'We have no use for snivellers. Ours is a tough life, one you must get used to quickly.'

Yashni gulped. A cloaked figure approached the barge. Zastra recognised the black robes. She breathed deeply, silently urging herself to remain calm. She needed to put everything she had learned from Dobery into practice if the mindweaver was not to uncover all her secrets. For her own sake and Findar's, she must be strong. They must not find out who she was. The mindweaver came aboard and pulled back her hood. She was an elderly lady with a surprisingly gentle face. The sort of woman you would happily invite into your house for a cup of chala and a chat. Zastra was not deceived. She knew what was coming.

'We will ensure we have no traitors,' Dastrin remarked.

The mindweaver moved along the line, stopping in front of each prisoner in turn. A small nod indicated the prisoner had been passed as fit and loyal. When she reached Ithgol, she stepped back in distaste. Dastrin beckoned forward his Kyrg officer.

'What have we here, Burgal? Is this one of yours?'

Burgal circled Ithgol and began to snuffle the air around him. Ithgol stood rigid, but Zastra thought she saw something flash across his face. Not fear, but something like it. The Kyrg officer stopped circling, grabbed hold of Ithgol's wrist and wrenched his forearm upward to examine it. A guttural sound rattled in the back of his throat and he whipped his scythal from the scabbard on his back and pressed the serrated blade against Ithgol's neck.

'Stand down, Guthan,' Dastrin barked.

'He is *Mordaka*. He must die,' Burgal growled.

'Not until I command it.'

Dastrin gestured the mindweaver to examine Ithgol. Before she could do so, he sprang forward and grabbed her throat. The elderly woman shrank back with a squeal of horror. Burgal and two other Kyrgs wrestled Ithgol to the ground, and Burgal looked towards Dastrin, seeking permission. The captain nodded and Burgal and the others began to kick Ithgol with a great deal of relish and didn't stop until he had been beaten unconscious.

Zastra was next in line. She couldn't resist a small shiver. As Dobery taught her, she hid her mind behind a mental stone wall and overlaid it with images of her life as Layna, the mountain girl. Would it be enough to fool the mindweaver? Zastra felt the probe dig into her mind, deep and painful. It lasted only a few moments, but it seemed much longer. Images of Dalbric and Etta were stolen from her and she concentrated hard on thoughts of climbing the jula trees and cleaning wool to try and divert attention away from Findar. Fortunately, the mindweaver was flustered following Ithgol's attack and seemed eager to get the job completed. She moved down the line. Zastra had passed the test. She forced herself not to show relief.

The remaining prisoners were also deemed fit for duty. They were divided into groups, each destined for a different ship. Zastra, Yashni and Jerenik were placed together with a few others from the barge. Ithgol's inert body was dumped beside them. Their wrists were bound together in front of them and then looped onto a length of thick rope so they were all joined together. Burgal kicked Ithgol until he stirred and secured him to the end of the line. He looked terrible. One eye was swollen shut, and thick globs of blood oozed from his flattened nostrils. They were marched along the jetty and forced down some stone steps into a small yacht that rocked in the ocean swell. The rope that held them together was looped around the mast.

'Anyone stupid enough to try and escape will take the rest of you with them,' said Burgal. 'We won't jump in and save you.'

The sail was raised and the little boat shoved off. They weaved their way between rowboats that fought against the swell as they ferried stores from the shore to the ships. Other yachts skipped across their bows, tacking to catch the breeze as they took the other prisoners to their respective ships. Gulls shrieked overhead, diving down to pluck discarded detritus from the surface of the sea. Zastra shivered as the wind threw up a spray, the salt water making her clothes damp and cold.

Their destination was an impressive three-masted ship with *'Wind of Golmeira'* carved into the side of the hull in large letters. Their little sailboat was dwarfed as it laid up alongside the ornate 'G' of Golmeira.

'Up you go,' ordered Burgal. Zastra looked in vain for a ladder but all she could see were small blocks of wood protruding at intervals from the hull. One by one, their bonds were cut and the prisoners ordered to scramble up the side of the ship. Zastra was one of the last, with only Yashni and Ithgol behind her. The wooden handholds were damp and slippery and she took great care as she hauled herself upwards. Behind her, a terrified scream was followed by a splash. She looked down. Yashni's dark head emerged from the water, her arms flailing. Ithgol stared at her from the prow of the yacht, motionless, as Yashni's head disappeared beneath the choppy surface.

Zastra sprang down, gasping at the sudden cold as she hit the water. She kicked out to where Yashni had disappeared. The girl re-surfaced and Zastra grabbed her, shouting at her to be calm, but Yashni thrashed wildly and dragged them both under. Zastra kicked hard with her legs to drive them upwards. They surfaced, but an evil wind-gust squeezed the yacht closer to the side of the ship. They were trapped between the two. As the gap narrowed, someone reached down and fished Yashni out of the water. Zastra felt a sharp blow to the back of her head and she was forced back beneath the water. She kicked for the surface but her head banged against a solid object that refused to move. She was trapped. Disorientated, she opened her eyes, but the water was clouded with dirt and she could see nothing. Her lungs were fast running out of air. Through a fug of panic she reasoned that the barrier above her must be the hull of the yacht. She dived downwards and breast-stroked sideways before kicking upwards with the last of her strength. With relief, she broke the surface and gulped in a lungful of precious air. She was within touching distance of the *Wind of Golmeira*. Ithgol was above her, clinging to the small wooden blocks. He reached down a hand, but she shook her head mutely. She wanted no help from him. She pulled herself up the side of the ship and was prodded into line with the other recruits.

Before them stood Dastrin and a thick-necked woman whose greasy hair was tied in a tight ponytail. Like Dastrin, she wore a black uniform, although Zastra noticed that she had two small diamonds embroidered on her cuffs in silver thread, compared with Dastrin's three. The woman cleared her throat.

'I am Lieutenant Jagula, second in command of the *Wind of Golmeira*. Guthan Burgal, who commands our Kyrginite soldiers, you have met already. Each of you will be assigned to a Watchmaster who will show you what to do. Learn quickly. Your good health and the survival of this ship will depend on it.'

Zastra and Yashni shivered as the wind tugged at their wet clothes.

'Bring forward the one who defied us,' commanded Dastrin.

Ithgol was dragged towards a large barrel that stood behind the main mast of the ship.

'This animal attacked a mindweaver. Such disobedience will not be tolerated. Burgal, you know what to do.'

Burgal lifted the lid from the barrel. It was brim full of foul smelling water. Ithgol's face creased with horror. He struggled in vain as Burgal and two other Kyrgs grabbed his legs and tipped him upside down, forcing his head and shoulders into the barrel. Displaced water splashed onto the deck. Ithgol's body writhed like a fish flicked onto dry land but the Kyrgs refused to let him surface. They had rolled up their sleeves for the job and Zastra noticed that each had a line of circular tattoos of various colours running up the inside of their left forearms. Ithgol stopped twitching and they pull him out, choking and spluttering. Burgal glanced questioningly at Dastrin, who nodded, his lip curled in a cruel smile. Ithgol's head was returned to the water. The process was repeated, until on the fifth occasion Ithgol did not move when released. His body was dumped face down on the deck.

'He's dead,' gasped Yashni, in a horrified whisper.

Burgal stamped down on Ithgol's back with his foot with the sole of his boot. A spurt of foul water shot from Ithgol's mouth but there was still no movement from the drowned Kyrg. Burgal continued to pound on the lifeless body as Dastrin looked on impassively. With a hacking cough, Ithgol came to life, his breath rattling from his sodden lungs.

'Thank the stars,' Yashni murmured. Dastrin seemed disappointed.

'It looks as if this one wants to live,' he remarked. 'Since the Kyrgs don't want him, he can work the ship like the rest.' He looked at the shivering Yashni in disgust and then his disapproving eyes travelled on to Zastra before coming to rest on the puddles of seawater that had formed by their feet.

'Lieutenant Jagula, I will not tolerate such a mess on my deck.'

'Aye, Captain.' Jagula threw some dry rags at Zastra's feet. 'Clean that mess up.'

The curt order was reinforced by a savage swipe of Burgal's leather strap. Zastra and Yashni dropped to their knees and began to mop up the water.

'I can't take this,' sobbed Yashni. 'Poor Ithgol...'

'He'll live,' Zastra said bitterly. 'Save your sympathy for some-one who deserves it.'

'He saved my life.'

'No he didn't. He stood watching while you nearly drowned.'

'He pulled me out of the water. He'd have done the same for you too, after you fell in. Why didn't you let him?'

Zastra stared at her in disbelief. 'I didn't fall, I...'

But the girl wasn't listening. She was staring in worship at Ith-gol as he knelt down to clean up his own puddle of water.

'Put your back into it,' ordered Burgal and Zastra felt another sharp blow across her back. She forced herself not to answer back. She had already nearly drowned once today and had no desire to share Ithgol's punishment. Once they had cleaned the deck to Jagula's satisfaction, they were assigned to their Watch-masters, and given uniforms of grey vests and three-quarter length trousers. Zastra and Yashni were quartered in the forward deck with the rest of the female crew, while Jerenik and Ithgol were placed in the mid-deck with the men. As they were finding their berths, the *Wind of Golmeira* weighed anchor and set sail. Zastra went up on deck and looked wistfully at the receding land. She put her hand in her pocket and fingered her piece of firering, wondering if Fin was doing the same. Would she ever see her brother again?

Chapter Fifteen

The rumours turned out to be correct. An army of Kyrgs had assembled just beyond Sendor's northern border. Their camp was basic and temporary and they weren't bothering to hide themselves. That could only mean one thing; they would attack soon.

'I won't allow it,' Kylen declared. 'Not in my Sendor.'

'I'm not sure what we can do, my Lady.' Hylaz trained his telescope on the camp. 'There must be more than a thousand. I can see some of Thorlberd's black ravens with them. He must have renewed the alliance.'

'We have to stop them crossing the border.'

'Even if we could stop these, there's sure to be more.'

'All the more reason to make a stand now. See that outcrop, above the stream? They'll have to slow down and move to single file to get through the pass. We could hold them off there with our crossbows.'

'My Lady, perhaps you did not hear me. There are a thousand, maybe more. And we are but twelve now.'

'I can add up, Hylaz,' snapped Kylen. 'And before you start reminiscing fondly about odds of five to one, I'll remind you that Alboraz ordered me to hold the northern border.'

'The general can hardly have meant taking on an army. We should find him and tell him.'

'And then what? He has only a few hundred soldiers himself. What could he do? Besides, he needs every last man and woman to hold our western border against the Golmeirans. We are here. It is our duty to try something. I refuse to stand aside and let Kyrgs into our lands.'

Hylaz sighed.

'Well, I suppose a scythal in the belly will stop me feeling hungry.'

They had travelled so fast across the northern territories that they had not had time to hunt. Their last rations had been consumed two days earlier.

'That's the spirit.'

'At least let me think of a fall back plan. Not for me, but for the others. We've asked so much of them, and they have never let us down.'

Kylen took in the sunken eyes and tired faces of her depleted team. They would be willing to sacrifice everything for Sendor. As any Sendoran should. But maybe Hylaz had a point. Even their fellgryffs were little more than skin and bone.

'See to it. If only to stop you whining. Although I have never, ever fallen back in battle. A Sendoran keeps her face to the enemy.'

'Of course, my Lady.'

'Fall back!' cried Kylen. A mound of dead Kyrgs bore witness to the accuracy of their shooting, but they had run out of bolts and enraged Kyrgs began to swarm through the narrow pass towards them, scythal blades glinting in the sunlight.

'I've got your back.' Hylaz inserted his huge frame between her and the oncoming Kyrgs.

'No,' Kylen said quietly. 'We use the fall back plan.'

Hylaz hesitated. Kylen tugged his arm.

'You're not passing up a chance to gloat are you?'

'I would never dare, my Lady.'

'Let's go.'

Kylen waved her team backwards. They leapt from rock to rock with the sure-footed confidence of those born and bred in the mountains. Plodding Golmeiran troops would have been left far behind, but the Kyrgs scrambled across the difficult terrain almost as quickly as the Sendorans. They couldn't shake them off.

'There it is,' cried Hylaz, as they reached a narrow waterfall, plunging down from the top of a cliff that rose in front them. Kylen held back, making sure all her group were accounted for. The leading Kyrg, only twenty paces behind them, launched a spear. It clattered against the rock barely a handswith above her head. The Sendorans were already scrambling up the wet cliff face beneath the waterfall. Hylaz had made them practice the ascent the previous day so that everyone knew where the hand-holds were. Kylen was the last to jump up, her fingers reaching for a hidden crevice. As she levered herself up, a scythal clashed against the rock where her foot had been just an instant before. She clambered upwards until she found herself in a chimney in the rock. As they had rehearsed, she wedged herself into it, bracing her legs against the sides. The Kyrgs massed at the base of the cliff, searching for the handholds. Kylen eased herself up the chimney until it narrowed and merged into the sheer rock, worn smooth by the waterfall. It was impossible to climb further. Shielding her eyes from the spray, she reached out blindly. Her hand found the end of the rope they had hung from a tree at the top of the cliff. Beneath her, a dexterous Kyrg had reached the base of the chimney and began to work his way up. Kylen formed a loop with the end of the rope, put her foot into it to use it like a stirrup and whistled. The Kyrg was close enough for her to spit in his face as the rope jerked her upwards. Hylaz reached down from the top of the ridge and hauled her to safety. The Kyrg could not follow.

'What now, my Lady?' asked Hylaz quietly. She stared down at the Kyrg army laid out beneath her. She had failed.

'Get the fellgryffs. We must find Alboraz and Zax and warn them. We have to warn them all.'

Chapter Sixteen

Zastra's first weeks aboard the *Wind of Golmeira* were filled with confusion and exhaustion. The crew was split into what were called the First and Second Halves. Zastra was placed in the First Half and Yashni in the Second Half and they were assigned as each other's 'alternate Halves.' This meant they shared a single bunk, each occupying it while the other was on duty. Jerenik and Ithgol were in the same Half as Zastra, under the command of Watchmaster Koltan. He was a taciturn man, who didn't understand or accept that the new recruits needed time to learn. He viewed their mistakes, which were frequent, as deliberate acts of insubordination to be punished with a swift blow of the strap. Most times, Zastra didn't even know what it was she was being punished for, such was her confusion over the multitude of strange new tasks and rules she had to learn. There were so many ropes, each with a different name and function, which all had to be hauled, tied or cast off, according to Koltan's curt commands.

Under the unforgiving gaze of their Watchmaster they learned how to make sail as well as the arts of trimming, tacking and wearing. The *Wind of Golmeira* was lateen-rigged. Each mast carried a single triangular sail hung from a huge, slanted spar. In order to wear ship, the spars had to be pivoted and brought before their mast, so that the spar and sail could be swung round the mast to the opposite side. Zastra and the other recruits hated the treacherous spars with a passion. Their arms ached from levering the top end of the spar with lengths of ropes called vangs. Reefing the sails involved a treacherous climb aloft and a precarious shimmy along the slanted spar to its peak. Their palms became raw from chafing against the vangs and reefing cords, and their ribs and shins were covered in bruises from vicious blows when the spars jerked and flexed unexpectedly in even the smallest gusts of wind. Zastra began to wonder if the foremast spar was possessed by some kind of evil spirit, a living thing whose only pleasure was in hurting the puny people who tried to tame it.

They had to learn quickly. Zarvic, a young Southlander with two years' experience, took pity on the new recruits. He showed them the skills they needed, translating the initially incomprehensible orders from the officers into understandable tasks. Everyone was forced to forget their differences and work as a team. Since his terrible beating from Burgal, Jerenik had lost some of his cockiness and he often helped Zastra by passing on whispered instructions when she forgot which rope to haul, or the correct way to tie off a line. She returned the favour whenever she could, all previous disagreements long forgotten.

Only Ithgol remained aloof and friendless. Yashni had made some tentative efforts to talk to him but the Kyrg responded to her advances with stony silence. Zastra, like the rest of the crew, wanted nothing to do with him. He was a bully and a thief, who had stolen their food and water and would have let Yashni drown rather than get his clothes wet. Worse than that, he was a Kyrg.

He found no friends amongst his own kind; indeed he was singled out as a daily target of Burgal's brutality. He took his beatings wordlessly, talking to no one and refusing to ask for help as he struggled with his new tasks. This meant he often fell foul of some rule he had not yet grasped. Koltan would assign him extra deck scrubbing duties or cleaning out the head, the most hated and menial of tasks. Captain Dastrin took pleasure in launching regular, well-aimed kicks at the Kyrg whenever he was kneeling on the deck with scouring brush in hand.

'That's the only way to treat animals,' he would say. If Ithgol hadn't been a Kyrg, Zastra might have felt sorry for him.

By the time they had been aboard for three Moonscrossings, most of the new crew members had reached a basic understanding of what was required of them. There were some days when Zastra performed her tasks well enough to escape the strap altogether. Occasionally, she even began to find pleasure in her work. In mild conditions the ship was a beautiful sight, sending up plumes of spray as it skipped across the surface of the waves, but when the winds became fractious, changing direction and strength without warning, it was different, as the large sails fought against their bindings like untamed beasts. At such times, the deck of the ship became a dangerous place, even for the most experienced hands. On one watch, a sudden squall came upon them and Koltan gave the order to reduce sail. Jerenik, Zastra and Ithgol were sent aloft to reef the mainsail. Ithgol, clumsy as usual, didn't get his line tied off quickly enough and the squall hit the exposed sail and tore it in half. The Kyrg received yet another beating and all three of them were ordered to repair the sail in their off-duty time.

'You seem to like getting beaten, Kyrg,' muttered Zastra as she picked out a large sail needle. 'Why don't you stop being so stupid and listen to our advice for once.'

Ithgol merely grunted.

'Three Moonscrossings and you still can't reef properly. You've been making bad choices right from the start. Like attacking that mindweaver. You must like getting beaten.'

'I didn't want her in my head.'

'Can't think you've got anything worth hiding in that tiny little brain of yours,' Jerenik remarked, tugging his needle through the tightly woven sailcloth.

'Why aren't you with others?' Zastra asked. With the notable exception of Ithgol, the Kyrgs did not take any part in the handling of the ship, spending their time wrestling with each other and practising fighting with their serrated scythals. Ithgol made no response. He either didn't know, or wasn't going to tell her. He continued sewing in silence. He made a very neat job of it, rather to Zastra's surprise. When they had repaired the sail to Koltan's satisfaction, they were released.

'Not you.' Koltan threw a pail and scouring pad at Ithgol's feet. 'Captain Dastrin wants the foredeck sparkling.'

Ithgol grabbed the pail as if he might crush it, but did as he was bid. On her way to her bunk, Zastra passed Zarvic, who was showing Yashni how to splice a damaged line.

'Zarvic, why do we have all these Kyrgs on board if they aren't going to help,' she asked

'They are warriors. You'll see, when we get some action.'

'Action?' Yashni's hands shook so much that she dropped her end of the rope. Zarvic raised an eyebrow.

'You don't think we just sail up and down the coast, do you?'

'Have you had to fight much?' Zastra asked. The Southlander grinned.

'Only once, but it was a beauty. A pair of Southern Kyrginite galleys came upon us from out of a sea mist and tried to board the ship.'

'Kyrginites? I don't understand. Don't the Kyrgs fight for Golmeira now?'

'Our allies are the Northern Kyrgs. The Southern Kyrgs, or Skurgs, as we call 'em, are a different beast. They come from the Sand Islands, hundreds of leagues to the south, in the coldest reaches of the Golmeiran Sea. When the fancy takes them, they sail north to attack our merchant ships. They're a terrible lot. Cannibals, some say.'

'Cannibals?' Yashni went white.

'Sometimes they don't even wait until you're dead. Apparently our friendly northern Kyrgs hate their southern cousins something harsh. Burgal and his lot will come in useful if we meet any more Skurgs, I can tell you. Hey, watch out there!'

Some of the crew were attempting to lower the foremast spar. The top reef flapped lose and a sudden wind-gust slapped into the stray piece of foresail with surprising force, whipping the lines from the hands of the sailors. The sail and spar swung across the deck with frightening speed, spinning towards Jerenik and another crewman who were standing against the side rail. Zarvic and Zastra raced towards them, but it was clear they would never make it in time. A squat body jumped in front of the swinging spar. It was Ithgol. The thick wooden beam thudded into him with a sickening smack and its wild movement was momentarily halted. Ithgol grunted, straining as the wind filled the fold of sail and pressed the spar deeper into his body. His feet began to slip.

Another wind-gust and he would be swept overboard. Zastra and Zarvic grabbed the vangs, ignoring Koltan's shouts as they fought to get the spar under control. Others joined them and between them they wrestled the spar safely to the deck

'Useless flecks,' shouted Koltan, using his strap on anyone who had the misfortune to be within range. 'We could have lost the whole spar and its rigging.'

'And it would have taken me with it,' muttered Jerenik. 'Not that Koltan would care about that. I guess even Ithgol has his uses.'

Zarvic slapped Ithgol on his back.

'Well done, fella.'

The Kyrg grimaced.

'You should go see the healer,' Zastra said. 'That spar hit you pretty hard. You might have a broken rib or something.'

Ithgol bent down to continue his deck scrubbing. Zastra picked up a brush and joined him.

'Don't need help.' Ithgol coughed. A gob of blood splattered onto the deck.

'You're making more mess. Go and see Tijan. I'll deal with this. We'll all get in trouble if Dastrin's precious deck isn't spotless.'

Ithgol snorted. Zastra didn't know if that was directed at her or their captain.

'Do I have to make you?' This elicited another snort, this time clearly directed at her. It was followed by a grimace.

'Look, Ithgol, you should know by now that I don't like to give in, especially to a Kyrg. I'll keep nagging at you until you get those ribs checked out.'

Ithgol eyed her for a moment, then flung down his brush and stomped off in the direction of the hatch. Zastra gave a small nod of satisfaction. Tijan, the healer, had a sickroom on the lower underdeck. When she had finished scouring the foredeck, she went below. Ithgol was nowhere to be seen. Tijan scowled at her.

'What now?'

'Did Ithgol come and see you?'

'The Kyrg? Three broken ribs to set and bind. He refused to take a draught for the pain and then declined a week's bed rest. No one ever declines bed rest.'

'He'll be all right, though?'

'Not sure I care. Probably. Now unless you're ill, get out and leave me in peace.'

After the incident with the spar, Ithgol's presence was better tolerated, among the crew at least, if not by Dastrin and the officers. He still refused to let anyone help him. Not that the crew had time to spare. There was a never ending list of tasks. In addition to their regular chores, everyone had to take a turn as lookout, which meant a stomach churning climb up the main mast to perch atop a horizontal bar nailed below the masthead. The lookout had to straddle the mast, one leg hanging down either side. The motion of the ship was amplified at this height and the first time Zastra took her turn she'd had to concentrate hard not to vomit. Being sick on the deck was another excuse for a beating. Once she had got used to the way the mast moved, she even began to look forward to taking her turn. Sitting on the lookout perch was easier than riding a swaying jula tree and she relished the rare opportunity to be alone with her thoughts.

The cold winds of autumn strengthened into the bitter gales of winter. Zastra's hands stung from handling the frozen ropes. The crew were given woollen jackets to go over their vests, but even so they were always cold. Unable to sleep as she lay shivering in her damp clothes, Zastra's thoughts often turned to the Border Mountains. She reached for the tiny fragment of firering that she kept in the pocket of her trousers. She missed Findar enormously. Etta and Dalbric too. She despaired of ever seeing them again and hoped that the yaya-root was helping Etta to stay well. There had been no chance of escape. Whenever they reached a port, the *Wind of Golmeira* anchored at some distance from land and none of the new recruits were allowed ashore. She thought again about Dobery and his idea that she could lead an uprising against Thorlberd. How ridiculous that seemed now. She had been trapped into working for her uncle rather than fighting against him.

Zastra's black mood seemed to be shared by the whole crew. Some, like Jerenik, shared her homesickness. He had run away from home because he considered his parents' lives too dull. They were farmers and he had opted for the more glamorous life of a thief. He claimed to be an excellent pickpocket yet his pickings had been slim.

'I should have stayed at home,' he complained. 'No one has anything worth stealing these days. I got caught and they turned me over to the soldiers. Look at my poor hands. They froze to the rope last watch.' He displayed his palms, red raw and oozing blood. 'We shouldn't have to work in these conditions.'

'I dare you to ask Dastrin for a holiday.' Zarvic's teeth chattered. 'Although even the punishment barrel is frozen solid, so I don't know what they'd do to you.'

'Our captain would think of something,' Jerenik remarked grimly.

'Listening to you whining is punishment enough,' growled Ithgol. 'You soft Golmeirans should try a few winters in the Northern Wastes.'

'What *do* Kyrgs do in the winter?' Jerenik cocked his head to one side. 'Besides snuggling up with a she-caralyx or some other beast for a bit of warmth?'

Ithgol raised one corner of his mouth, giving the appearance of a silent snarl.

'I supposed they kicked you out for talking too much. Is that why the other Kyrgs hate you?'

Ithgol grabbed Jerenik by the collar of his jacket and shoved him against the side of the hull. Jerenik held up his hands in surrender.

'Okay, I'll shut up. No need for violence.'

Ithgol dropped him to the floor. Jerenik straightened his woollen jacket.

'I forgot that Kyrgs don't have a sense of humour.'

At that moment, Yashni came below decks. Jerenik turned to her.

'What about you, Yashni? How did you end up amongst this fine company?'

'My father sold me to the soldiers to pay for a cask of spirits.' Yashni rummaged in the bunk she shared with Zastra and retrieved her jacket. 'I hate this stupid ship, but I've nothing to go back to.' Zastra reached out to squeeze the girl's shoulder.

'Cheer up.' Jerenik clapped his hands. 'There's spring to look forward to. If we don't all freeze to death first. Zarvic told me four of Koltan's watch died of frostbite last year.'

'Is that your way of cheering us up?' Zastra asked. 'If so, you need to work on it.'

'Get real, mountain girl. There's no point fooling ourselves. It'll be a miracle if we survive the winter.'

Chapter Seventeen

Kylen scoured the valley to make certain no one was watching before she lowered her body flat and wriggled under a limestone shelf that jutted over a dark slit in the mountainside like a spearhead. It was one of the many secret entrances to the underground network of passageways and caverns that made up the Caves of Karabek. Since Thorlberd's invasion three years ago, the caves had become an increasingly important refuge for her people. She had released Breeze – the caves were no place for a fellgryff. He had been reluctant, his intelligent brown eyes pleading as she pushed him away. They had been together for more than a year and had formed a strong bond, but he would have to fend for himself now, as would she. She hoped they would meet again, but knew it was unlikely. The fellgryff would have to roam far away to find good grazing. She would have to tame another fellgryff next time she needed one. She crawled forwards. Lights were forbidden in the outer passages and she reached into the darkness, searching the stone walls with her fingers for the secret signs carved into them to guide her way. She could sense the weight of the mountainside above her head. Running beneath the earth to hide like a cowardly scrittal was not the Sendoran way, and it felt like failure. No, it *was* failure. Unopposed, the Kyrgs had swarmed across Sendor's northern territories, burning villages and killing Sendorans without mercy. Kylen had fled before the onslaught, warning her people to pack up their essential belongings and run for their lives. She had ordered her team to split up and spread out across the region to warn as many as possible. She just hoped Hylaz and the others had made it back to the caves safely.

She followed a passageway that led deep within the mountain until it opened out into a vast cavern, hollowed out by an underground river. Jula lamps were set against the wall, orbs of orange light that struggled to penetrate the gloom. The ceiling of the cave was lost to darkness. Kylen was shocked to see how packed it was with exhausted refugees.

'Lady Kylen,' one of them whispered as she passed by. 'Mendoraz's girl. She'll take care of us.' But others just hung their heads, or looked away. Hope was as weak as the guttering light of the lamps.

There was a stirring at the far end of the cave. A young boy ran towards her, zig-zagging through the crowd, a flush of excitement across his face. Despite her weariness, Kylen couldn't help but smile.

'Zax!'

Her brother rushed towards her and threw himself into her arms.

'Hylaz said you were coming. What took you so long? He's been back for two days.'

'I guess he's got longer legs than me. Where is he?'

'He's bringing the biggest vizzal you ever saw. I killed it, sis.

Well, me and Hylaz killed it together really, but it was my spear that got it first.'

Kylen noticed a thin ribbon of blood running across Zax's forearm

'You're bleeding.'

'Don't fuss. It was only that my spear snapped before the vizzal was quite dead, so it kicked me. Then Hylaz shot it.'

'Hylaz!' Kylen called sternly. A vast frame emerged from the dimness at the back of the cave, a fat vizzal slumped across his shoulders.

'My Lady.'

'How did you allow Zax to be hurt?'

'It happened just as my little master told it. I had my bow on the beast the whole time, but the lad deserved the chance to prove himself. The scratch will teach him to be more careful in future.'

'Tonight we feast!' proclaimed Zax.

'I'm not sure about feast.' Kylen rubbed the top of his head tenderly. 'You did well, but look around. We have many mouths to feed. You wouldn't object to sharing your trophy?'

'No...' Zax looked a little disappointed, but quickly brightened up. 'I'll just have to go and kill another ten vizzal, won't I?'

'It's too dangerous. There are Kyrgs just behind me.'

Zax screwed up his face.

'Stop treating me like a child. I'm nearly twelve.'

'My Lady, I'm glad you are safe,' Hylaz said. 'General Alboraz has also returned today and has requested an audience with you.'

'Requested? That's unusually polite.'

Alboraz was grey with exhaustion, his face covered in dirt and sweat. His arm was in a dirty sling and there was a nasty gash across his forehead that had barely healed.

'You're hurt?' Kylen didn't hide her astonishment. Alboraz was renowned as one of the best fighters in Sendor, famed for never having a scratch on him. The general bowed and presented her with his sword. It was caked in dried blood.

'Lady Kylen, I have failed Sendor. I await my just punishment, by the ancient rites of our land. The Golmeiran army has triumphed. I gave the order to retreat. I did it to save my men and women from certain death, but because of my decision our land is lost. I accept my fate willingly.'

Kylen reached out and took the sword from him. She turned it once in her hands, feeling its weight. A good sword. Heavy, but well balanced. Old, but well kept. Which made its current, bloody state all the more shocking. She took out her cleaning rag and began to wipe away the blood.

'General Alboraz, if I were to condemn you, I would condemn myself, for I made the same choice.'

She finished cleaning the sword and returned it to him, hilt forwards.

'I too would prefer to have died in battle. But our resistance would have died too and Sendor along with it. In these caves are the last of our people. While we live, there is a chance we can fight back. Your duty is to take back this sword. One day, I swear to you, it will be needed. And on that day, I would wish to have you by my side.'

Chapter Eighteen

Despite Jerenik's forebodings, the *Wind of Golmeira* made it through the winter. Only two of the crew had been lost, one to a wasting sickness, the other swept overboard in a storm. Everyone was heartily glad when spring arrived and along with it periods of calm weather during which the crew's battles with wind and rigging were temporarily suspended. Dastrin had no use for idle hands and took the calmer weather as an opportunity to train the crew in ship to ship combat. *Wind of Golmeira* carried two great catapults that were broken into pieces and stored in the hold. To make the ship ready for battle, the catapults had to be brought up on deck and assembled. Each catapult had a crew of ten, responsible for ratcheting back the giant arm and loading the cradle at the end with a cargo of rocks or bales of straw drenched in jula oil, the latter to be set alight and flung at the enemy. The new recruits were not entrusted with anything as vital as the catapults. Their role was to fetch more rocks from the hold or stand by with buckets of sand or water pumps, ready to douse any fires caused by an enemy ship with its own flaming missiles.

Everyone was tested for their ability to fight. Zastra, not wishing to draw attention to herself, deliberately aimed for the edge of the target with the crossbow rather than the middle and pretended she didn't know how to use a sword. However, what she considered poor performance with the crossbow was still far better than most and she was picked to be stationed in the rigging as a sharpshooter. She dreaded the call to action, hoping it would never come. The idea of fighting on behalf of her uncle made her sick to the pit of her stomach.

The calmer seas of spring brought more ships out into the Sea of Golmeira. Fishermen and traders mainly, but then word came that Skurg galleys had been spotted in Golmeiran waters. The *Wind of Golmeira* headed south to investigate. Yashni and Zastra were swapping shifts when there was a hail from the lookout.

'Two... um, or maybe three sails to the southeast.'

'Is it two or three, idiot?' yelled back Lieutenant Jagula. There was a short pause.

'Three,' came the reply.

'So many?' exclaimed Yashni.

The crew were ordered to prepare for battle. The catapults were assembled and the crew given weapons.

'That's how you know it's not a practice,' remarked Zarvic. 'When they give you real weapons.'

Jerenik took a stone and began to sharpen a short-bladed sword.

'Scared we'd mutiny, are they?'

Zarvic looked around nervously. 'Don't ever speak that word. It's death even to mention it.'

'Then we'd better find another name for it, hadn't we?' Jerenik winked at Zastra. She eyed the crossbow bolts that she had been given. One was bent, so she discarded it. She pondered Jerenik's words. *Mutiny. Was it possible?* Many of the crew had been forced into service against their will. Plenty of the older hands, even those who had volunteered, were unhappy. Few of the Golmeirans liked having Kyrgs on board and Dastrin's harsh regime, supported by the likes of Koltan and Burgal, hadn't won him any friends. Yet mutiny would be dangerous. If they failed they would certainly be put to death. Her thoughts were interrupted by Jagula.

'Everyone to their positions. Those are Skurg galleys. We'll see some blood today.'

Zastra shuddered. Not just at the words but at the evident joy with which they were spoken. She finished loading her crossbow to its maximum capacity of three bolts. She would be able to release three shots in quick succession before having to pause and reload. There was to be a sharpshooter at the top of each mast. Zastra was stationed at the least important rear mast, which was significantly shorter than the other two. As she climbed, she looked across the water to the approaching Skurgs. Three galleys, each with a single square sail bloated with a following wind, were heading directly towards them. The prows of the galleys shimmered. As they closed, Zastra saw that the shimmering came from the sunlight reflected by the brandished weapons of row upon row of Skurgs. The wind carried the sound of their war cries. On the deck below, Zastra's crewmates were scurrying about. The catapults were primed and ready but Zastra knew that they would have to tack the ship to bring them to bear. There would be no time to move the spars round the front of the masts and so they would simply tack the ship and allow the sails to press against the mast. It was not an efficient manner of sailing, but needs must.

She knew she would have to keep her wits about her when the huge spar swung round. When the wind caught the sail on the opposite tack, it would give the mast a severe jolt.

'You there, sharpshooters.' The call below was from Lieutenant Jagula. 'Remember your orders. Look for the leaders and don't miss!'

Zastra wiped her sweaty hands on her thighs. The order to tack came. She clung to the masthead, keeping well clear of the stays and braces as they were released to allow the spar to creak around. She clung on as the mast lurched violently as the sail pressed against it. With an ear-splitting *whumph* the catapults were released. Zastra ducked instinctively as a flaming bale of straw whizzed past her. Both fireballs landed just short of the trio of galleys and the Skurgs ploughed forward unchecked. The catapults were reloaded and the next volley sent into the air. The galleys were closer now and both loads hit their targets, to cheers from the deck below. The huge spar swung round again as the *Wind of Golmeira* moved back onto its normal tack. The catapults were swung round to bear in the opposite direction. This time showers of rocks were sent skywards. The Skurg galleys were so close that Zastra could hear the splintering impact of the rocks on the wooden planking. The sail of the second galley crumpled and its prow swung around sharply. A dark cloud of smoke rose from the rearmost galley and a flame snaked up its mast. The sail melted away from top to bottom as the fire consumed it. More cheering broke out from Zastra's crewmates below, but quickly died as the leading galley closed to ram them. The angry red faces of the Skurgs became distinct as they waved their serrated blades in the air. Unlike their own Kyrgs, who lined the prow of the *Wind of Golmeira*, the Southern Kyrgs had grey hair, although they did not appear to be particularly old. Worryingly, they appeared to be in the prime of health.

With a tweak of the rudder the *Wind of Golmeira* avoided a head-on collision and the two ships passed alongside each other's bows, the galley lying much lower in the water. A swarm of grapnels flew up from the smaller ship and as they bit and the lines pulled taut, the *Wind of Golmeira* juddered and swung round clumsily. Zastra instinctively tightened her grip on the masthead to keep her perch but her crewmate on the main mast was not so fortunate. Unseated by the rapid deceleration he was cast helplessly to the deck below.

'Sharpshooters!' the cry came from the quarterdeck. Zastra scanned the galley beneath her. A Skurg guthan with a bronze helmet and a tattoo across half his face surged to the front, shouting commands. Zastra took careful aim. Just as he was poised to leap aboard the *Wind of Golmeira* she fired, aiming for the gap between his helmet and jerkin. The bolt struck home and the guthan fell, but other Skurgs poured past his body. Zastra loosed her second and third bolts as quickly as she could, not even sure where they landed. She reloaded and took aim at the seething mass of Skurgs but by now most were on the deck below her and mixed in with the Golmeirans. A small group of her crewmates had been pushed back against the bulwarks. Zastra recognised Jerenik and Zarvic with Yashni cowering behind them. They were heavily outnumbered. Zastra slid down the forestay using one hand, ripping the skin from her palm with the speed of her descent. She landed so hard that the impact dislodged her crossbow. She had no time to retrieve it before a large Skurg charged towards her, his scythal raised above his head ready to strike. She yanked the short sword she had been given from the scabbard on her back and thrust at the onrushing Skurg, her wrist jarring at the impact as he fell upon her blade. Another Skurg followed. There was no time to think, no time to remember the fencing moves she had been taught all those years ago at Golmer Castle. Survival was about short, brutal moments and instinctive reactions. Through a small gap in the heaving bodies, Zastra caught a glimpse of Zarvic and Jerenik, pressed back by a tide of Skurgs. There was no sign of Yashni. Zastra edged towards them, hacking with her sword, but she found herself shoved aside as their own Kyrgs, Burgal and Ithgol at the head, ploughed their way through. A heavy blow to her head knocked her to her knees and sweat or something worse dripped into her eyes. A cry went up and there was a sudden lull in the fighting. The Skurgs had been repelled. Jagula, blood streaming from a gash to her bicep, grabbed Zastra beneath her armpit and pulled her to her feet.

'Head up novice. It's not over yet. Get that crossbow back up the mast. Now!'

Jagula swung her round roughly and pointed towards the second galley. Its mast was gone, but it was being powered towards them by two banks of huge oars, rising and falling in unison. The *Wind of Golmeira* was trapped, tied fast to the first galley. Zastra retrieved her discarded crossbow and clambered up the main mast. Below her the deck was cleared and the catapults readied once more. The galley was barely a hundred paces away when the first catapult fired. The rocks rained down on their target in a deadly shower. A section of oars spiked upward and others snapped, sending the rhythm into chaos. The second catapult fired and another volley of rock landed, inflicting stomach-turning devastation upon the galley deck. Yet still it came on, drifting towards them. Zastra saw a Skurg issuing orders, re-organising his remaining troops into a compact group. He was at the limit of her range but she fired anyway. Her target slumped to the ground and the other Skurgs looked around uncertainly. They were still in disarray as the galley ploughed into the quarterdeck of the *Wind of Golmeira*. Burgal and his band of Kyrgs were ready and they burst upon the disorganised foe. Zastra let off two more bolts and again slid down to the deck. From her left a grey-haired Skurg sprang towards her. She swayed out of the way, kicked out a leg and tripped him to the ground. She had the tip of sword against her opponent's neck, but hesitated as the large artery in his throat pulsed against the metal. An object flashed past her head and suddenly the Skurg was dead, the hilt of knife protruding from his throat. Zastra turned to see Captain Dastrin clenching his fist.

'Do not hesitate. Death is all they deserve.'

A cheer broke out on the deck behind her. The fight was over. They had won. As the sounds died down, Zastra stared across the length of the deck. How had she not noticed that it was covered in blood and bodies? She rushed to the side of the ship as nausea overtook her and she was sick into the ocean.

Chapter Nineteen

Jerenik came across the deck to Zastra, flushed and sweaty.

'We showed them beasts, eh? I reckon I killed at least four. Nice shooting, mountain girl. I saw how that Skurg guthan went down. Didn't know you were that good.'

Zastra puffed out her cheeks. 'Lucky shot.'

Mata, the Watchmaster for the second Half of the crew, was standing nearby.

'You showed some good sharpshooter skills today,' she said. 'Layna isn't it?'

Zastra nodded weakly. Mata looked down at her sympathetically.

'The first battle is always tough. Remember, it was them or you. Skurgs show no mercy and don't ask me what they do with the bodies of their enemies.'

The Watchmaster look as if she would have said more, but she was called away by Lieutenant Jagula. Jerenik started to clean his sword, whistling a triumphant tune. Zastra remembered the last time she had seen him, backed against the bulwarks by a crowd of Skurgs.

'I saw you with Zarvic and Yashni. Are they all right?'

'Zarvic's dead. As for Yashni, I've no idea. She didn't seem to be enjoying things much.'

'There wasn't a lot to enjoy. Poor Zarvic, he deserved better. He was a good fellow.'

'Oh, cheer up, will you? Don't it feel good to be alive?'

Zastra didn't like to agree, but she had to admit to a feeling of strange exhilaration. Or perhaps it was just relief. Whatever it was, it was mixed with sadness for the death of Zarvic and her other crewmates. And where was Yashni? There was no sign of her on deck, so she went to search below. She found the girl in a dark corner of the healer's room, curled into a tight ball.

'Yashni, are you hurt?'

The girl did not move. Zastra looked her over but could see no sign of injury.

'It's all right.' Zastra reached gingerly towards the girl. 'It's over now.'

A muffled sob emerged from the darkness.

'It's not all right. It'll never be all right. I'm... I'll never be able to... I can't...'

'Hush now,' whispered Zastra. 'Not everyone is suited to fighting. Don't be upset.'

'But they'll know. Dastrin will find out and throw me in the barrel for being a coward.'

A shadow fell across them both as the dim light of the jula lamp was blocked by a tall figure. It was Watchmaster Mata.

'What's going on here? I'm to make a note of the injured for Captain Dastrin. What's the status of this one? I can't see any wounds.'

Yashni scrunched up even tighter.

'Please,' Zastra entreated. 'It's not her fault.' Mata studied them both for a moment before kneeling down and pushing Yashni's shoulder back so she could see her face.

'Yashni, isn't it? She's on my watch.'

Zastra nodded. Mata stood back.

'Well, Yashni, Tijan needs someone to help him with the wounded. I can say I ordered you down here to assist. But I need you to get up. Right now.'

Yashni unfurled slightly, her moist eyes searching for Zastra's. Zastra nodded encouragingly. Mata held out her hand. 'Come with me,' she said firmly. Yashni allowed herself to be led across the room towards the healer. Tijan did not stop what he was doing, but listened as Mata whispered something in his ear. He nodded brusquely and thrust a bundle of bandages into Yashni's hands. Mata returned to Zastra.

'You'd better get back on deck. There'll be a lot of work to do and you don't want Dastrin to think you're shirking.'

'Thank you. I—'

'Keep your thanks.' Mata cut her off tersely. 'Not a word about this. Up you go, or you'll be for the barrel.'

In many ways, the aftermath was worse than the battle itself. There was much to be done and none of it pleasant. One of the Skurg galleys had drifted away – a floating bonfire – and was left to its fate. The other two ships were searched for anything of value and then Dastrin ordered them to be sunk. The dead Skurgs were unceremoniously thrown overboard. Any wounded amongst the Golmeiran crew were taken below to await the attentions of the overworked Tijan. The bodies of their own dead, the dark skinned form of Zarvic among them, were placed in sacks weighted down with rocks and then also tipped overboard. Dastrin allowed no words to be said, nor any grief to be shown for the dead, his only concern the state of his ship. No one was allowed a moment's rest until the decks had been scoured clean and repairs completed to the quarterdeck, where the impact of the second galley had caused considerable damage. With their numbers reduced by the absence of the wounded and the dead, the system of alternate Halves was temporarily suspended. All worked together until the ship was back in some kind of order. Zastra and her crewmates moved around like ghosts, following orders in a daze of exhaustion.

It was two days before Koltan allowed his Half to take a break. Zastra sought out Yashni. She found her below decks, helping a man with a broken arm eat a bowl of porridge. She smiled shyly as Zastra came towards her. The crew had each been given a small square of toffee, a reward arranged by Mata for their hard work. Zastra snapped her piece in two and gave half to Yashni.

'How are you doing?'

'Busy.' Yashni accepted Zastra's offering gratefully. She had dark circles under her eyes but her voice and body were full of energy. She barely had time to chew a mouthful of toffee before there was a call from another bunk. Yashni dashed across to tighten some bandages and then fetched the thirsty patient some water. A Kyrg with a heavily bandaged head grunted in pain and Yashni adjusted his pillow and mixed him a draught of medicine, talking to him in soothing tones until he was calm and drank it all down.

'Looks like you've found your perfect job.'

'Maybe.' Yashni flushed. 'Tijan has said he'll ask if I can be assigned to him as his assistant. I do hope they'll let me.'

'Then I hope so too.' Zastra looked around. 'You'll be more use here than scrubbing decks.'

Yashni bowed her head.

'Thank you for... you know.'

'It's nothing.' Zastra waved away her thanks. 'Anyway, it's Mata you should thank, not me.'

'Yashni, I need more bandages over here.' Tijan glared at them from the far side of the room.

'Is he always that grumpy?'

'Oh yes.' Yashni dashed to a nearby chest and filled her arms with clean bandages. 'But he's a dear really, if he takes a liking to you.'

The healer glared across at Zastra.

'Unless you're wounded, get out! Or should I tell the captain that you need more work?'

'I guess he doesn't like me yet,' muttered Zastra. She did not wait for Tijan to repeat the command. Her cot was waiting and she felt as if she could sleep for a week.

Chapter Twenty

Once the *Wind of Golmeira* was repaired to Dastrin's satisfaction, the crew resumed their usual duties, split again into alternate Halves. The first morning back in their normal routine, Zastra responded to the gong that signalled the beginning of her shift as usual, but was stopped by a large hand against her chest. It was Koltan, impassive as always.

'Lieutenant Jagula wants to see you.'

'Me? What for?'

'No questions. Jump to it.'

Jagula, next only to Dastrin in power and authority. *What did she want with her? Had she found out about Yashni somehow?* Perhaps she would question Zastra about what had happened. Zastra determined she would say nothing. Jagula's cabin was a tiny box with a burlap curtain for a door, squeezed between Dastrin's large quarters in the quarterdeck and the officers' mess. Zastra had never been there before and wasn't sure how she was supposed to announce herself. She could hardly knock, neither could she barge in unannounced. She settled for a loud cough. The burlap curtain was snatched back and a knife was at her throat before she could move.

'Oh, it's you. Come in then, don't skulk about.' Jagula lowered the knife and Zastra followed her into the tiny cabin. There was barely enough room for them both, and Zastra had to tilt her head to one side to prevent it hitting the ceiling.

'I saw your shooting. You are good. Better than good.'

'Just lucky.' Zastra's heart began to race. Did Jagula suspect something?

'False modesty disgusts me. It is lying by another name. You seem to have a good head under pressure. Something you'll need if you are going to become a Watchmaster.'

'A what?' Zastra jerked back in surprise and grimaced as the back of her head connected with a low beam.

'Watchmaster Mata tells me you can read. Is that true?'

Zastra nodded, rubbing her head ruefully. Some of the crew had received letters the last time they had put into port and Zastra had offered to read for those who could not. She didn't know how Mata had found out, but it was hard to keep anything secret amongst the crowded decks.

'Good. Watchmaster Mata has offered to tutor you. Your training starts immediately. Dismissed.'

Zastra headed back up to the deck in a daze. Before her eyes had adjusted to the light after the darkness below decks, Koltan shoved a scourer into her hand, together with a bucket.

'Don't think that now you're Jagula's new pet you can shirk your duties. When you've finished scrubbing the quarterdeck, the head needs flushing out.'

Cleaning the head was the most unpleasant of all the crew's

tasks and generally reserved for Ithgol. Zastra guessed that Koltan was less than pleased by her sudden promotion.

'Have fun.' Jerenik grinned at her. 'Don't know what you did to annoy Jagula, but it must have been bad.'

Zastra told him what had happened. Jerenik slapped her hard between her shoulder blades and chuckled.

'Well, if this is how they reward you for good fighting, I might just let the Skurgs kill me next time.'

Zastra's lessons with Mata had to be crammed into her free time after her shift with Koltan had finished. Koltan's displeasure at Jagula's decision did not lessen, and Zastra became extremely familiar with the fetid stench of the head. Mata began by teaching her the basics of sailing and navigation. It was much more complicated and difficult than Zastra could have thought, but she found it interesting and learned quickly. She began to understand the meaning of Koltan's hitherto incomprehensible commands, that tacking and wearing, rather than being ways to make the crew suffer, were manoeuvres that had to be timed and handled to perfection. Slowly and patiently, Mata taught her the secrets she herself had learned from many years at sea. How and when to trim sail, how to increase the speed of a ship by changing the weight balance, or by trimming the jib and more besides. One area where Zastra seemed to naturally excel was in judging the strength and direction of the wind. She could sense a change almost before it was upon them and knew instinctively the best point of sailing to get the most out of the ship. Sometimes, it felt as if she were back in the mountains, riding a Jula tree.

'The wind is like family,' Mata would say. 'One moment it is all smiles and friendly embraces, but it can turn in an instant. You must love it but remember that it can hurt you too.'

Zastra could hardly believe it when Mata complimented her on her grasp of mathematics.

'Not many of our crew can even add up, let alone understand the basics of geometry. I'm impressed.'

Zastra tried not to smile. Sestra, her old teacher at Golmer Castle had always berated Zastra for her lack of attention, particularly in maths classes. Zastra was surprised by how much she remembered, even after all these years. However, they soon reached the limit of what Sestra had taught her and Mata became distinctly less impressed as Zastra struggled with the more complicated navigational calculations. She found it next to impossible to work out the tidal effects of the twin moons, vital to guiding the ship safely in and out of the various coastal harbours, and she spent all her spare hours poring over charts and learning tables of numbers by rote. Mata insisted she become familiar with the entire southern landscape of Golmeira with its distinctive landmarks and dangerous reefs. In spite of herself, Zastra enjoyed learning what Mata had to teach. The first time she was put in sole charge of helming the ship through three or four tacks was an exhilarating experience. Mata was a good teacher and her love of the sea and store of knowledge were vast. Ever since her kindness to Yashni, Zastra had liked and respected the seasoned Watchmaster. Although she gave out punishment when necessary, she never seemed to enjoy it in the way that Burgal and Dastrin did. When Zastra struggled with the principles of using the stars for navigation at night, instead of a beating, Mata would provide extra homework to fill the gaps in Zastra's knowledge. Before long, she had been entrusted with handling the ship for an entire watch. Despite

Koltan glowering at her the whole time, the watch passed uneventfully. As Zastra headed below for a well-earned rest, her Watchmaster grabbed her arm.

'It's all very well, flitting about near the Golmeiran Coast. Wait until you hit the Southern Reaches. That'll knock the cockiness out of you.'

Chapter Twenty-one

The *Wind of Golmeira* journeyed back and forth along the long coastline of Golmeira. For the most part, their task was to protect merchant vessels from Skurgs and other pirates as they trafficked goods along the major trading route to the Far Isles, which lay hundreds of leagues east of Golmeira. Any large vessel that wished to exit the Sea of Golmeira at its eastern edge would generally pass through the narrow and treacherous Lodaran Straights, which lay between the inhospitable desert land to the east of Sendor and Southland, the vast island that supplied the rest of Golmeira with horses and grain. It was possible to sail round the southern tip of Southland, but such a journey took several days, even in good weather, and most traders could not afford to waste the time. Each end of the straights was guarded by one of Thorlberd's vessels. All ships, even those of the Golmeiran fleet, were forced to halt and be boarded for inspection before being allowed to pass through. Mata, the most experienced sailor in the crew, was generally charged with navigating their passage. Zastra had studied the charts and Mata had made her redraw them over and over again until she had by heart the location of the many hidden rocks and rogue currents that made the narrow channel so dangerous to the untutored. Yet still she watched in awe as Mata took personal charge of the helm, barking terse instructions to the men and women at the sails as they picked their way through the dangerous waters using only a tiny flap of the rearsail and the jib, a small triangular sail that sat at the very front of the ship, attached to the bowsprit.

Once through the straights and out into the open waters to the east, they made for the Far Isles. A round trip could take a quarter of a year, especially if the weather turned ugly, which it often did. The crew had to be particularly wary for the four days of Moonscross, when the twin moons, Horval and Kalin, came into alignment and the seas grew ugly and unpredictable. It was wise at this time to seek shelter at one of the island ports that were scattered along the route. Mata explained how these outposts, independent of Golmeira and Sendor, made their living from fishing and from the trade convoys. Each island differed in the architecture of their buildings and the style of clothes worn by the inhabitants. The only thing they had in common was the friendliness of their people, who would wave at them from the shore or from their small fishing vessels whenever they passed. If ever the *Wind of Golmeira* dropped anchor, they would row out to them and shout greetings and news about the sea conditions. Zastra wished she was allowed to talk to them. Mata reckoned these Outlanders, as she called them, knew more about sailing than anyone in the Golmeiran fleet. However, only officers were allowed to leave the ship. Burgal and his Kyrgs stood on constant guard whenever they were near land to ensure none of the crew tried to escape.

Their frequent trips along the trade route gave Zastra plenty of opportunities to practice reading her charts, and her shipcraft began to improve as she helped guide the *Wind of Golmeira* in and out of the island settlements. As they made land at one such port, easing themselves in at high tide to avoid grounding on a sandbar that was clearly visible through the clear waters of the bay, Zastra overheard Dastrin and Jagula complaining about the anchorage fees and costs of supplies.

'I'm sure Lord Thorlberd will turn his eye to these settlements,' remarked Dastrin.

'I hope it is soon. They are ripe for the plucking,' agreed Jagula. 'Just the sight of a migaradon would send these people jumping into the sea in fear. I wouldn't mind a nice beach house, when I retire.'

They began to tot up what they thought the island was worth and how much reward money they would get for capturing it. Jagula even picked out which house she would like for herself. Zastra felt sick just listening. A group of children were playing on a nearby beach, and seeing her watching, they waved and shouted. She raised her hand in acknowledgement, but with a heavy heart. She fervently hoped that these children would never have to face Thorlberd's army and his mindweavers, or worst of all, the terrible flying migaradons. They wouldn't stand a chance. She vowed to do everything in her power to ensure that such a thing never happened.

The bustling port of Mynganard on the westernmost of the Far Isles was always a welcome sight after the long voyage from Golmeira. Elegant whitewashed houses with roofs of green tiles crowded the gentle slopes that surrounded a wide semi-circular bay. Dastrin, no doubt in return for a bribe, allowed a group of handpicked Far Islanders to come on board the *Wind of Golmeira* to sell their goods. These tradespeople were open and friendly, well fed and plump. The crew were poor enough, but whenever they docked at Mynganard, Dastrin distributed a portion of their yearly pay and many of the crew were tempted by the wares on offer. Wine was particularly popular, although banned by Dastrin, and several barrels made their way on board for consumption. It seemed that many of the crew thought the punishment barrel a fair price for a night of inebriation and a sore head.

Those who did not choose to spend their money on the delights offered by the traders of the Far Isles were give a written receipt, which could be exchanged at any Golmeiran Payment Office for money. The few members of the crew who could read and write were in demand at this time. Everyone liked to have independent confirmation that Jagula had written the right amount of money on their receipts, and many wanted them sent to a Payment Office near their homes. Their families would know to collect them and exchange them for money. At such times, Zastra found herself busy checking the slips of paper and writing out addresses for her crewmates. She sent her own receipt to the Payment Office at Kirkholme, with a brief note asking for a message to be left with Miray, the cloth merchant. She hoped Miray would be honest enough to pass the message on. Etta and Dalbric would need the money and the receipt would tell them that she was at least alive. It was the best she could manage. Escape had proven impossible. It seemed the only way to leave the *Wind of Golmeira* was in a bag, weighted down with rock and destined for the bottom of the ocean.

Chapter Twenty-two

The sun was setting over the Karabek Mountains. Kylen crouched silently in the darkness, just beyond the edge of the cone of light that filtered in through a small circular opening above her. The calls of the Kyrgs were muffled by the rock, but she could still hear them. They had been crawling all over that part of the mountain like scrittals all day, ever since a band of exhausted refugees had been careless enough to be spotted as they searched for the secret entrance to the caves. The circle of light was briefly obscured by a pair of ankles. Kylen withdrew further into the shadows, but the ankles moved on. Another pair of legs followed close behind and paused in front of the opening. There was a strange snuffling sound and a low grunt. The circle went dark and Kylen found herself staring into the red face of a Kyrg. She froze, as did the Kyrg. He yelled in excitement and began to paw at the turf that surrounded the entrance, ripping a hole in the mountainside. Kylen retreated back into the network of passageways. She did not bother to be quiet. She wanted the Kyrgs to follow her. She felt a thrill of satisfaction as they scrambled after her, stupid as a herd of blind goats. All passageways save the one leading to the pre-arranged ambush site had been blocked off. The Kyrgs didn't know it, but they were heading to their death.

It was pitch dark, but she had practised the route several times and ran her hand lightly against the wall as she jogged forward. She could hear the heavy boots of the pursuing Kyrgs. The air suddenly became cooler and fresher as the narrow passage opened into a cavern. She stepped to one side and yelled a warning. The Kyrgs, sensing a kill, began to run, their boots pounding against the ground as they piled into the cave, where her loyal Sendorans were armed and waiting.

Kylen felt no pity. The Kyrgs had butchered hundreds of her people during their invasion. They were receiving their just rewards. Besides, it was important to send a message to any Golmeiran or Kyrg who dared enter the Caves of Karabek. And that message was death.

Once the slaughter was complete, Kylen and her Sendorans retreated deeper into the caves, blocking the passage behind them. That particular entrance had been compromised and could never be used again. As they reached the main cavern, someone piled into Kylen's side. Reflexively, she dropped to one knee and let her attacker fly over her shoulder before she pinned him to the floor. Warm flesh squirmed beneath her.

'Gerroff! Let me go.'

'Zax?'

Kylen stood up with a laugh. Her brother jumped up, red faced.

'You left me out, again!' he protested. 'You always leave me here, like a baby.'

'You aren't ready. Look how easily I took you down.'

'I'll never learn, unless you let me practise on real Kyrgs.'

'This isn't a game. A Kyrg won't let you up to have another try if you don't kill him first time. Where is Alboraz?'

'He's worse than you are. He won't even let me scout near the surface.'

Kylen remembered that she had only been a year older than Zax was now when her father had ordered her to safety, rather than let her fight at Golgannan. It still burned. Maybe it was time to let her brother experience something of battle. A Sendoran soldier should be blooded early. She went in search of Alboraz. Zax followed, pleading his case the whole time. She found the general in discussions with one of his lieutenants.

'Another entrance has been discovered,' she reported, 'but we dealt with it.'

Alboraz unfurled a map. 'Show me.'

Kylen indicated the entrance and Alboraz marked it.

'They are persistent, I'll give them that. But the caves serve us well. The underground lakes give us plenty of water. If only we had more food, I think we could hide here for years.'

'I can hunt,' Zax piped up.

'It's too dangerous, lad.'

'At least let me fight. Let me prove myself.'

Alboraz's dismissive grunt angered Kylen.

'Zax has a point. It's time he had his first taste of real fighting. Next time one of our entrances is discovered, he could lead the ambush. There would be little risk, especially if we double our numbers.'

Alboraz shrugged.

'If you think it wise, my Lady.' Kylen chose to ignore the contempt in his tone and Zax spent the whole day discussing the ambush, and what tactics they should use. Although his excited chatter made her smile, Kylen couldn't help hoping it wouldn't be too soon.

Chapter Twenty-three

It was midsummer and the *Wind of Golmeira* returned from a trip to the Far Isles, re-entering the Sea of Golmeira, as usual, via the narrow Lodaran Straights. As they sat anchored next to the guard ship to await inspection, Mata asked Zastra to take them through the channel.

'I think you are ready. Take it steady. We're in no hurry.'

Zastra gulped and positioned herself at the helm. She was so nervous that the first order she tried to give died in her throat. It didn't help that both Jagula and Dastrin were on deck, watching closely. She was sure Dastrin was hoping she would fail. Koltan was rubbing his hands and taking loud bets on her crashing the ship into the side of the channel.

'They need to hear you,' Mata said quietly.

Zastra cleared her throat and started calling out her orders. The crew knew the dangers of the Lodaran Straights well enough and did not hesitate to obey. The foresail and mainsail were reefed and they picked their way forward only by the jib and a partly reefed rear sail. Mata stood to one side, offering only an occasional touch of the rudder and whisper of advice as needed. Zastra had successfully negotiated half the passage and was beginning to feel more confident when a treacherous current surged against their prow. The ship veered sharply to port and headed straight towards a jagged rock formation that rose upwards from the sea close to the edge of the channel. Zastra ran to the starboard beam and peered over the side. Dastrin strode towards her.

'What in the stars are you playing at, girl? Alter course immediately!'

'Not yet.' Zastra held up her palm. If she recalled Mata's charts correctly, there was a submerged reef nearby and if they turned too quickly she would run the ship aground.

'How dare you—' Dastrin's face went puce. Luckily, Jagula interjected.

'She's right, Captain.'

'Aye.' Mata nodded in agreement.

Zastra scoured the choppy waters and then she saw it. A patch of green water, passing close to their hull on the starboard side. The instant the reef was behind them, she returned to the helm. The rock formation loomed ahead, worryingly close. She just hoped there would be enough room to turn the ship. It was fortunate the wind was with them.

'Stand by the jib and prepare to loose the foresail,' she cried. 'Lively now!' The crew needed no urging, leaping to their lines. Zastra spun the wheel and the ship heeled round as neatly as if it were tied to an anchor, the jib filling with wind and drawing the bowsprit around just as the foresail was sheeted into place to drive the ship forward. The treacherous rock formation passed by to their left, so close that Zastra could almost reach out and touch it. Breathing heavily with relief she took them back to the middle of the channel and they negotiated the remainder of the passage without incident.

'Watchmaster Mata, Lieutenant Jagula, my cabin. Now.' Dastrin did not sound pleased.

'That's your glory days over, mountain girl.' Jerenik, as usual, had appeared from nowhere. After a short time Mata emerged from Dastrin's cabin and beckoned Zastra to follow her to the officers' mess.

'Do you feel ready to take us west?' she asked, pulling out a pair of charts.

'You'd trust me to do that? I nearly ran us aground just now.'

'But you didn't. You kept a calm head and we made it through safely. That's the main thing.'

'What about Dastrin?'

Mata gave a thin smile.

'Lieutenant Jagula and I persuaded the captain that you deserved another chance. You had best prove us right. We make for the Western Spur.'

Mata pointed towards the edge of one of her charts where the Sea of Golmeira was bounded by a range of tall volcanic peaks known as the Smoking Giants.

'What lies beyond?' Zastra asked.

'No one knows. The Smoking Giants themselves are too dangerous to even set foot upon, with their slopes of boiling rock. The sea around the Spur is always angry and the heat from the Giants means the shoreline is constantly shrouded in mist. Many a ship has misjudged its position in the fog and foundered. If the wind changes to easterly in those parts you're doomed. It can feel as if the Spur is a living beast, sucking you towards it. If it ever appears on your horizon, turn the ship around immediately. Do not hesitate. The last safe point is the Pyramid Isle, here.'

Mata pointed to a small dot on the map, far south of the Golmeiran coast and close to the Spur.

'Is that where we're going?'

'Yes.'

'Why? What's there?'

'You'll find out soon enough.'

Zastra knew better than to probe further. She might be trusted with navigation, but Dastrin shared tactical information with only his officers. She pointed to the bottom edge of the map.

'Where does the Spur end? Can we sail around it?'

'If it has an end, it has never been reached. Ships that pass beyond the edge of this chart do not return. The further south you go, the fiercer the winds become. Strong enough to stop your breath and the waves are like mountains.' Mata shuddered. 'I was once aboard a ship that was blown into those waters by an evil storm. I have never been so scared, either before or since. Only a lucky change in the direction of the wind saved us. It sent us back into calmer waters and I've never wished to go back.'

At first, Zastra was pleased to be trusted with the helm and the navigation but the weather conspired to make the journey difficult. They had to fight for every inch of progress against a fractious headwind. A blanket of heavy cloud lay sulkily across the heavens, refusing to allow her to calculate their position from the stars. She was left to make her best guess using shadows cast by the pale light of the sun. Mata made no comment and offered no help as Zastra issued her course corrections. As her confidence evaporated, Zastra began to wonder if Mata's insistence on leaving her to do things for herself would go as far as allowing her to crash the ship into the Smoking Mountains.

It was with huge relief and no little satisfaction that she heard the lookout call out that the Pyramid Isle was in sight, if a little further off their port beam than she had calculated. It was well named; its steep sides rose to a sharp point, forming a triangular outline against the grey, overcast sky. As if to taunt her, the head-wind died down and gentle breeze from the northeast quarter allowed her to lay the ship on direct course. As the island loomed larger, Zastra suddenly felt uneasy.

'Something is missing. It's too quiet.'

Mata nodded grimly. 'There are no birds. There would normally be flocks of seabirds around an island like that, yet there are none.'

Zastra took out her telescope and peered toward the island.

'What could have scared them away?'

A dark object rose from the tip of the pyramid. It was so big that it looked as if part of the island itself had split off. The shape shivered and sprouted wings. Zastra felt a familiar feeling of dread.

'A migaradon.'

'Aye,' Mata confirmed. 'We've brought supplies. The island itself cannot provide enough food. Migaradons are always hungry.'

'Koltan, get that signal up!' cried Jagula. At the prow, Koltan fumbled with a stack of wooden signal panels. Each square had a different symbol, painted black against a white background.

'Hurry man. Before it attacks.'

Koltan slotted four different symbols into a large metal grid and lowered it over the side of the ship, locking it into position between two brackets. The grid could be hung on either side of the ship as required. On this occasion, the grid faced the oncoming migaradon.

'Are we sure it's the right signal?' Zastra was not the only one who appeared concerned.

'We'd best hope so,' remarked Mata drily. 'Or we'll not survive the day.'

Jerenik and Yashni had never seen a migaradon before and they stared in open mouthed astonishment as it flew towards them, its angry metallic shriek hurting their ears. The crew froze as the dark shadow swept over the ship, the relief noticeable as the creature passed harmlessly overhead.

'What is it doing here?' Zastra asked.

Mata shrugged. 'I hear that Grand Marl Thorlberd has stationed many such creatures around the Sea of Golmeira. He wishes to control the seas as he does the land.'

She ordered Zastra to guide the ship into the narrow inlet that served as a harbour on the Pyramid Isle. The water was deep, with no shoals and sandbanks to worry about. That was a relief. It would be disastrous if they ran aground so far from the mainland and with only a migaradon for company. However, the entrance to the inlet was extremely narrow, barely twice the width of the ship, with black rocks rising steeply on either side. Mata watched closely but offered no advice as Zastra ordered the sails be trimmed until barely a hand's width was left to take the wind and she eased the ship through the entrance to tie up against a wooden jetty. It was the first time the ship had touched land since Zastra had joined the crew. She guessed that Dastrin had no worries about the crew escaping. There was nowhere for them to run.

'Unload the supplies,' ordered Jagula. A gangway was lowered amidships and Zastra and the others were ordered to carry an assortment of boxes and crates ashore.

'It must eat a lot.' Jerenik sighed as he deposited one of four large jars of syrup on the jetty. 'I was hoping these would be for us. You can't get a better breakfast than fresh rolls and syrup.'

Zastra dumped her own jar beside his.

'Since we've been on this ship, we've been given nothing to eat but porridge and salted goat. What made you think they would suddenly start giving us fresh rolls and syrup?'

'I can dream, can't I? Maybe if we killed that... that thing? Then the food would be going spare.'

'Go ahead,' suggested Mata drily. 'No one has ever defeated a migaradon in battle, even when fighting for their lives. But no doubt your hankering after food will provide a better incentive. Just remember that its hide cannot be pierced by any weapon and the rider is a mindweaver who can control your thoughts and freeze you in your tracks.'

'Porridge it is, then,' Jerenik said, with another sigh. They were interrupted by a call from the lookout.

'Sail to the north,' she called. A small triangle of brown could just be made out on the horizon, framed between the steep sides of the entrance to the bay. It was moving erratically.

'What in the stars are they doing?' Mata wondered aloud.

Dastrin took out his telescope and trained it on the vessel. He licked his lips. 'No signal. This should be interesting.'

Zastra took out her own telescope. 'It looks like a fishing boat. Small, single sail, no obvious weapons. It can surely mean no harm.'

'That doesn't matter,' Dastrin snapped. A harsh shriek cut through the air and the migaradon launched itself upwards. The fishing vessel tried to spin round but something was wrong with the rudder and it could only crab sideways as the migaradon closed. The beast circled once and then dived down, snapping the mast between its claws like a twig. The little boat rocked violently. One of the sailors was gesticulating and another jumped overboard in panic. The migaradon stove in the side of the boat with one swipe of its huge tail.

'Lower the yacht!' cried Mata. 'There may be survivors.'

Zastra was already tugging furiously at the ropes that held the yacht in place.

'Stand down!' ordered Dastrin. 'If they don't have the signal, they are responsible for their own fate.'

Mata looked about to argue the point, but Dastrin silenced her with a look. Zastra refused to believe that Dastrin wouldn't help the fishermen. She loosened one rope and moved the next, before she was hauled away by Burgal.

'Please!' she begged. 'They'll drown if we don't help them.'

'One more word and you'll be in the punishment barrel.'

Once more, Dastrin trained his telescope on the fishing boat, licking his lips in anticipation. Zastra shrugged off Burgal and strode towards the captain. She was determined to make him listen. Before she had gone two paces she was lifted off her feet. A strong arm gripped her waist and a hand pinched her windpipe, smothering her angry protest. Starved of air she ceased struggling and found herself deposited unceremoniously on the foredeck. Livid at such treatment, she spun round to confront her attacker.

'The punishment barrel is not pleasant,' Ithgol remarked.

'I don't care,' she croaked. 'Don't you see what he's doing? He's a monster.'

She felt someone grab her arm. It was Mata.

'Be silent,' the Watchmaster hissed. 'You can do nothing. The Kyrg has saved you certain punishment.'

'I didn't ask him to. Those poor sailors...' Zastra tried to wrestle herself free. Mata maintained her grip.

'It's no good. Captain Dastrin will not let us save them.' Zastra took a couple of breaths to try and calm herself. She was shaking with anger.

'How can you stand it?'

'Because I must. I have a wife and family in Golmeira. They depend on the money I send. I will not risk their living for a futile gesture. You must learn to accept what you cannot change.'

'No one should ever accept such things,' Zastra muttered bitterly.

'Go and relieve the lookout until you have calmed down. That's an order.'

Mata shoved her towards the mainmast. Jerenik slapped her on her back as she made her way past. 'You and the Kyrg best friends now? That was a nice hug he gave you. I didn't know you were so close. Tell me, when's the wedding?'

'This isn't funny, Jerenik. We can't let this happen again. We have to do something.'

'Anytime you come up with a plan, mountain girl, I'm in.'

Chapter Twenty-four

Ixendred set down his pen and re-read the last lines of his report. With the help of the Kyrg mercenaries his push into Sendor had been successful and the rebels had been forced to retreat to the Caves of Karabek. Sendor was at last under Golmeiran control. His only concern was that he still hadn't captured the experienced General Alboraz or either of Mendoraz's children. They were almost certainly hiding within the caves but every time they found an entrance, the Sendorans were waiting in ambush and by the time he sent reinforcements, the entrances had been blocked off. It was impossible to pin down his enemy. As he was pondering how he could explain this to Grand Marl Thorlberd without looking weak, his tent-flap was yanked open.

'Writing to my father, Ixy? There's really no need. I've already sent a message telling him of our success.'

And taking credit for it all, no doubt. Ixendred put down his pen.

'We still haven't captured Kylen or Zadorax. Your father will not deem this mission a success until they are caught.'

'It's only a matter of time. I've got a plan which will succeed where you have failed.'

Ixendred strove to maintain a polite tone in the face of such insolence.

'Much as I admire your enthusiasm, Rastran, your father holds me responsible for your safety. I shall not allow you to endanger your life in some ill thought-out scheme.'

Rastran grinned with an air of knowing superiority.

'I have a new weapon, just arrived from Murthen Island. Something so deadly that even the legendary Caves of Karabek will be no obstacle.'

'Weapon? What weapon? Why has no one told me of this?'

Rastran merely smirked.

'I order you to tell me.'

'Remember your place, Ixy. You do not make demands of the Grand Marl's son.'

Ixendred slapped his desk with the palm of his hand.

'It is *you* that must remember your place. Your father put me in charge of this mission, not you. You obey *my* orders.'

'Not any more. You have failed. I told my father as much.'

'I'll bet you did.'

'I'll need just two troops. One of ours and one of the Kyrgs. We have discovered another entrance to the caves and will attack tonight. You can watch if you'd like. It will be a valuable learning experience for you. Although I'd advise you to keep a safe distance.'

With a triumphant smirk, Rastran left the tent. Battening down his anger, Ixendred questioned all his captains and lieutenants about Rastran's plans, but none admitted to any knowledge. In the end he dismissed the youth's comments as arrogant bluster. To make certain, he gave explicit orders that no troops were to leave camp without his permission before he retired to bed.

In the middle of the night he was jerked awake. The ground beneath his thin mattress was shuddering. Staggering up, he pulled back the flap of his tent. Across the valley a great fire illuminated a cloud of dust that spread upwards to block out the light of the stars. A gaping hole had been torn in the side of the Karabek Mountains. In the light of the blaze, he made out bodies in strange, unnatural poses scattered across the rocks. Most were wearing uniforms of the Golmeiran army. Ixendred hastily pulled on his own uniform and strode from the tent.

'What's going on?'

The nearby soldiers looked at him wordlessly, stunned expressions on their faces.

'Well?' barked Ixendred. One of the soldiers roused herself.

'L-lord Rastran's new w-weapon,' she stuttered. 'I had no idea...'

She gaped at the ruined face of the mountain. The sound of marching feet, muffled and ragged, signalled the return of Rastran and the remnants of what had been two troops. He swaggered into the camp, followed by a handful of Kyrgs and Golmeiran soldiers. Ixendred looked with dismay at their torn uniforms and pitifully small numbers. Less than a quarter had returned. He strode up to Rastran and placed his palm on his chest, forcing him to stop.

'What in the stars have you done, boy?' He was shaking with fury. Rastran tried to throw him off, but Ixendred would not be moved.

'Get your hands off me, Ixy. I have shown those savages the

strength of Golmeira and I've finally captured one of Mendoraz's brats. Bring him here.'

A fair-haired boy, no more than twelve years old, was dragged forward.

'This is the boy Zadorax. I know his face. He once soiled the grounds of Golmer Castle, he and his animal of a sister.'

'She was too much for you,' Zadorax said defiantly. Rastran shoved him to the ground.

'What was that?' demanded Ixendred.

'I told you. Weren't you listening? It's my new weapon. Sintegrack it's called.'

'What happened to my men and women? Where are the rest?'

'We misjudged the power of the sintegrack.' Rastran shrugged. 'Some slowcoaches were caught up in the blast. Don't worry, they can be replaced.'

'A life is not to be surrendered so lightly, boy.' Ixendred ground his teeth so hard his jaw ached. 'Each is someone's son or daughter.' Even as he uttered them, he saw that his words were wasted.

'I've finished listening to you, Ixy.'

Rastran signalled towards a lieutenant. 'Make arrangements to take the prisoners down to Castanton and put them on the next ship bound for Murthen Island. They will prove useful for our experiments.'

'What experiments?' Zadorax tried to look brave, but his voice wavered.

'Wait and see.' Rastran smiled unpleasantly. 'You can be certain that your sister will follow shortly, as soon as my next batch of sintegrack arrives. Not even the Caves of Karabek will save her.'

Chapter Twenty-five

The *Wind of Golmeira* put in briefly at Port Castanton. Dastrin ordered the release of more of the crew's wages and Zastra realised with a shock that it had been more than two years since she had been pressed into service in her uncle's fleet. She wondered whether Fin would even remember her. The thought of escape was never far from her mind, even more so after the events at the Pyramid Isle. The word mutiny, once mentioned by Jerenik, had never again been spoken in Zastra's hearing but Dastrin was an unpopular captain and his distinct lack of presence whenever there was any fighting had not gone unnoticed. Only fear of the barrel, or worse, kept the crew in line. Zastra longed to act, but didn't know who to trust. Except for Jerenik, it was impossible to tell who might be willing try and take over the ship.

Dastrin returned from a trip ashore and ordered the *Wind of Golmeira* to head south. No one knew where they were going or why. They sailed well beyond their normal range. Some of the more experienced crew members began nod and mutter to themselves in a knowing manner.

'Looks like we are heading for the Sand Islands of the Southern

Kyrgs,' Mata remarked as she and Zastra plotted their daily location.

'Why in the stars would we do that?' Zastra had no desire to
meet more Skurgs. It appeared Mata was correct however, as their
course continued to take them directly towards the Skurg homeland, driven by a helpful wind from the northwest quarter. It grew
noticeably colder as they ventured further south. At last, a cry
from the lookout indicated that land had been sighted and two
islands emerged on the horizon, one behind the other. They lay
across the ocean, long and flat, each with a raised bump almost
like a head at the eastern edge. The one at the rear was much larger
than its neighbour and was shrouded in haze, looking almost like
a large shadow cast by the smaller island.

'I always think they look like a pair of sleeping lizards,' said
Mata. 'A baby and its mother.'

Dastrin ordered the *Wind of Golmeira* to retreat and take station
just out of view of the reptilian islands. They tacked back and
forth across the same stretch of water for another two days.

'I don't like this,' muttered Jerenik. 'Why are we waiting around
in Skurg territory like fishbait?'

The rest of the crew seemed to share his feelings and the mut-
terings and unrest increased as the days went by. Finally, Dastrin
called the officers to his cabin.

'About time,' remarked Jerenik.

'What are you in such a hurry for?' Yashni asked. They rarely
saw her since she had gone to work with Tijan, but she had been
released when the healer had been called to Dastrin's cabin with
the other officers. 'Surely you don't want to attack the Skurg
homeland?'

'I don't like sitting here waiting for Skurgs to decide how

they're going to cook us,' Jerenik returned. 'What's going on, d'you think?'

'We'll just have to wait and see, I suppose.'

'Or maybe not.' Jerenik winked and disappeared down one of the hatches that led to the lower underdeck. Yashni stared after him.

'Where's he going?'

'Who cares?' Zastra shrugged. 'Enjoy the peace and quiet while it lasts.'

The timbers of the ship creaked and groaned as they sailed up and down on the now familiar tack. Zastra's eyelids began to droop and she dropped into a doze. She was roused by the bell that summoned all hands. Rubbing her eyes, she followed the rest of the crew to assemble before the quarterdeck, finding Ithgol and Yashni in the crowd.

'Where's Jerenik?'

'Close,' Ithgol sniffed. 'I can smell him.'

A dirty face poked up from the hatch amidships. It was Jerenik. He slunk over to join them.

'Where have you been?' Zastra wrinkled her nose in disgust. 'You smell as if you've been rolling around in the head.'

Lieutenant Jagula called for quiet and Dastrin addressed the crew.

'The Skurgs have stolen something from one of our ships. We have orders to take it back. We should have been joined by reinforcements. As they haven't bothered to show up, it looks as if we must complete this mission alone. Since we know little of the island's defences we will send an advance party, under cover of darkness. Know this. This mission must succeed. I will not accept failure.'

The crew broke up and Koltan informed Zastra, Ithgol and Jerenik that they were to join the advance party.

'Bet our brave captain won't be joining us,' muttered Jerenik.

'Shh,' whispered Zastra. 'You'll get us in trouble.'

'We're already in a world of trouble, mountain girl. I overheard some of our esteemed captain's discussion with the officers. There's more to this mission—'

'You there,' cried Jagula. 'Quiet down or there'll be trouble.'

Zastra was ordered to Mata's cabin before she could find out what Jerenik meant. Mata was not one of those going with the advance party but she looked grave nonetheless.

'Be extra careful tonight,' she said. 'Be ready for anything.'

She informed Zastra that she would be tasked with navigating the boats to the landing point on the island. They went over the route and the navigation plan but Zastra found it difficult to concentrate. Mata's concern and Jerenik's cryptic remarks made her wonder what they were getting into. As if attacking the Skurg's home was not dangerous enough, there was clearly something they weren't being told. She couldn't shake the feeling that their luck was about to run out.

Chapter Twenty-six

The *Wind of Golmeira* had two boats; the yacht with a sail and a large dinghy powered by five pairs of oars. Both were lowered into the sea and packed full of sailors. Dastrin had used the cover of darkness to take the *Wind of Golmeira* closer to the lizard-shaped islands. The boats were to make it the rest of the way. As they pushed off, Zastra noted that Jerenik had been right. Captain Dastrin had not joined them.

Under the close attention of Lieutenant Jagula, Zastra used the light wind to guide the yacht toward the islands. There was little moonslight but she used an occasional glimpse of the stars through gaps in the cloud to keep their course. The dinghy kept close by, rowlocks muffled and the oars placed into the water with unusual care to avoid making any splashes. If the Skurgs heard them coming they would be dead as soon as they hit land. Their only hope lay in stealth. An occasional whispered exchange kept the boats together.

'Are you sure you're steering right, girl?' muttered Jagula after they had been sailing for some time with no sign of land. 'It'll be the barrel for you if you get us lost.' Jagula seemed unusually tense. Zastra glanced up at the sky. She believed she was still on the course that Mata had planned for her but there had been no gap in the clouds for a while. If the currents were even a little stronger than she had accounted for, they could be in trouble. Then, to her relief, she heard the welcome sound of waves lapping against a shoreline. She just hoped it was the correct island. As the hulls of the boats scraped onto a shelf of shale, Zastra strained her eyes and ears for any indication that they had been seen.

'Our flekk of a captain set us down too far away,' someone whispered. 'After rowing for so long I'm too tired to move, let alone fight. All so he's at a safe distance.'

'Quiet down,' Jagula snapped in a hoarse whisper. The boats were pulled up and hidden as best they could manage in the dark and then Jagula led them along the shoreline and up a sandy incline. It was almost impossible to see anything but Jagula seemed to know the route. The sandy surface beneath their feet changed to solid stone as they climbed and the slope began to level off as Jagula ordered them to halt. There was no shelter and a chilly wind swept around them, gritty with sand. Zastra began to shiver as the sweat from the uphill march grew cold against her skin. Her woollen jacket provided little protection, so she huddled up next to Jerenik, grateful for the warmth of another body.

'I n-never knew you c-cared, mountain girl.' He blew into his cupped hands to warm them.

'Someone needs to stop your teeth clattering, or the Skurgs'll wake up and wonder what the racket is.'

As dawn began to break over the horizon, Jagula gave the order to move forwards. They were at the top of a hill that sloped down towards a large wooden dome. The dome was surrounded by a wide circle of grass, itself enclosed by a tall fence of wooden stakes sharpened to points at the top. There was no sign of life.

'This is going to be easy,' said Jagula, testing the sharpness of her sword with a dirty thumb. She ordered them to advance. The fence was too high to scale but they had come prepared with axes and a gap was soon made. Cries from within the stockade indicated that their chopping had roused the inhabitants and, as Jagula urged them through the gap, they were confronted by a semi-circle of grey-haired Skurgs, teeth bared.

'They don't look pleased to see us,' remarked Zastra.

'Maybe they don't like getting up so early of a morning,' Jerenik suggested.

Jagula snorted. 'There's barely enough to keep me busy. They didn't even think to bring their scythals.' She drew her sword. 'With me!'

She sprang forward. Jerenik grabbed Zastra by her wrist. 'Don't be at the front,' he muttered. By the time she had shrugged him off they were towards the rear of the charge. She sprinted to catch up with her crewmates, noting with surprise that the Skurgs had not run to meet them. In a most un-Skurg-like manner, they lobbed a few small objects in their direction before turning and running away. One of the objects, a small brown sack, landed on the ground a few paces in front of her and she noticed a plume of smoke tailing behind it. As she ran past it, the ground exploded beneath them. Her eardrums screamed in protest and she smacked into the ground as dirt rained down on her back. As she lay stunned, a large rock landed inches from her head. She wiped the dirt from her face, her ears filled with a high pitched ringing. All around her the grassy carpet had been torn away, leaving craters of mud. Acrid smoke filled the air. Beside her lay a body, unmoving. It was Jerenik. Blood streamed down his face and dripped from the end of his nose. She shook him vigorously but he could not be roused. As the smoke cleared, Zastra saw that she was surrounded by the bodies of their crewmates. Many were missing limbs. A mound of mangled flesh wore Jagula's black uniform, two silver pips on a crumpled sleeve. Zastra eased herself to her feet only to be bowled over by one of her crewmates.

'Run!' he screamed wildly. 'Back to the boats!' The surviving members of the crew needed no further urging and made for the gap in the stockade, running or staggering as best they could. As Zastra stared at their receding backs, another of the strange missiles landed on the ground some distance to her left. It sat innocuously for a moment, before vanishing in a huge flash and crash of noise. It was supplanted by a large hole in the ground and Zastra was bowled over once more. She shook her head to try and clear away the dreadful ringing in her ears and pulled the motionless Jerenik up and onto her shoulder. He was heavier than he looked and she could only stagger towards the gap in the fence, certain the Skurgs would overtake her at any moment. She forced herself into a shuffling run, her thighs burning with the effort when, all of a sudden, the heavy weight was lifted from her shoulders. It was Ithgol, barely breaking stride as he took Jerenik from her. She ran after him. A small band of Skurgs armed with double-headed axes pursued them, war cries ringing out. Zastra and Ithgol reached the top of the hill together and headed down the incline towards the beach. The remnants of their advance party had already got the dinghy into the water, its oars pounding against the surf in a disordered frenzy. Someone had attempted to launch the yacht, unsuccessfully, and it lay against a line of rocks with its hull stoved in. Ithgol's pace slowed as they reached the beach and his legs buckled in the soft sand. Zastra grabbed one of Jerenik's arms to help him, but by the time they reached the water the dinghy was already three lengths clear of the shore and gathering pace.

'Swim!' cried Zastra. 'We can keep him up between us.'

'I can't swim,' Ithgol growled. He dropped his burden and unsheathed his scythal. 'You go.' He turned to face the onrushing Skurgs. There were six of them. *Too many*, Zastra realised. *Even for Ithgol.* At their feet Jerenik stirred. Zastra stepped over his prostrate body, drew her sword and tugged a knife from her belt. Ithgol issued a strange sort of rattle.

'Just stay out of my way.'

'Ha!' cried Zastra, launching her knife with deadly accuracy at the leading Skurg. Ithgol stepped forward and two more Kyrgs fell to the ground before his swinging scythal. Another rushed at Zastra, his axe whistling past her ear as she swayed to one side and impaled him on her sword, the force of his charge forcing her back into the sea. She twisted free and turned to find Ithgol standing over the fallen bodies of the remaining Skurgs. Zastra hailed the dinghy but the crew couldn't, or wouldn't, hear her. The white sails of the *Wind of Golmeira* appeared on the horizon and the dinghy gathered speed and headed towards it. Ithgol spat into the sand.

'Golmeiran cowards.'

'Quite a few Kyrgs too, saving themselves as fast as they can,' remarked Zastra. 'Come, on, we'd better find cover. If we're lucky the rest of the Skurgs will think we've escaped with the others.'

There was a groan at their feet. Jerenik sat up and dabbed his bleeding head. 'What did I miss?'

'Tell you later.' Zastra examined his wound, a nasty gash above his hairline. 'Can you move, do you think?'

'My head hurts.'

'Don't complain,' Ithgol growled. 'You're lucky this one saved you. I would have left you. If you can't help yourself, you're a danger to your comrades.'

'I couldn't just leave him there to be killed, or worse. Why did you help, if that's what you believe?' Zastra protested.

'You were unhurt. Honour demands that I help uninjured comrades. Even stupid ones.'

Zastra snorted in disbelief. 'What does a Kyrg know of honour?'

'Will someone tell me what in the stars is going on?' interjected Jerenik.

'Looks like we're stranded, but at least we're alive. For which, although I hate to admit it, we have Ithgol to thank.'

'Keep your thanks. Use your breath to walk.'

They dragged Jerenik between them.

'Keep by the water's edge,' said Zastra. 'It'll wash away our tracks.' Every so often she glanced backwards but no more Skurgs appeared.

'Must have been the sintegrack,' muttered Jerenik. 'Those little bags. I overheard Dastrin giving the orders. Some new weapon that the Skurgs stole from us. Dastrin was desperate to get his greedy little hands on it.'

Zastra whistled softly. 'Such a powerful weapon would make Thorlberd completely invincible. No wonder he wanted it back.'

They rounded a headland and were at last out of sight of the landing beach. Jerenik slumped to the ground. Blood still oozed from the gash in his head and his face was grey. Zastra tore a strip of material from the bottom of her vest and wrapped it round his head to staunch the flow.

'Stay down,' Ithgol commanded in a low voice. He crawled towards a large clump of sand grass and used it as cover to observe the landing point. A few moments later he returned. 'A group of Skurgs came and picked up the bodies of the others, but they've gone now.'

'Good.' Zastra tied off her rudimentary bandage, ignoring Jerenik's complaints as she pulled the knot tight. 'Let's hope they think we've all escaped.'

Out to sea the white sails of the *Wind of Golmeira* flickered and disappeared over the horizon.

'They're leaving us behind!' Jerenik's voice rose in alarm.

'Let's not panic,' said Zastra. 'Dastrin told us the mission couldn't fail. Once the reinforcements arrive they may try again.'

'So, we should just wait 'til they come?' Jerenik tested his bandage gingerly. 'That sounds rather dull don't it? Why don't we sneak in and steal the sintegrack? Then, when Dastrin comes back, we threaten to blow up the ship unless he lets us go. What d'you think, mountain girl?'

'I think that whatever brains you had have fallen out of that hole in your head.'

'Why? I know you want to escape too. It's been written on your face ever since they caught us.'

'That may be so,' admitted Zastra. 'But threatening to blow up the ship isn't exactly a great plan, especially as we would be on it.'

'Mmm. Suppose you have a point.'

'I would rather we destroy this sintegrack, or whatever you call it. It's evil. You saw what it did to Jagula and the others. Dastrin can't be allowed to get his hands on it.'

Ithgol grunted in agreement. 'It's a coward's weapon. Killing at a distance.'

Jerenik's eyes lit up. 'I like it. With the noise we'd make, Dastrin'd have to come back to see what was going on. I'm not so sure the cowardly flekk will come back otherwise.'

'The question is, how? Bearing in mind that two boatloads of us couldn't get through the defences last time and there are only three of us.'

'I have an idea,' offered Jerenik. 'A plan of genius, I believe.'

Ithgol snuffled scornfully.

'Let's hear it,' said Zastra.

'Wait 'til night then bluff our way in. Our not-so-friendly Ithgol here can pretend to be one of them. We find the sintegrack and set it alight. Don't suppose either of you have a firering?'

Zastra dug around in one of her pockets until she found the piece of Hedrik's firering. It looked tiny in her palm, discoloured where it had split off from the fragment she had left behind with Findar. Jerenik reached for it and her fingers closed around it instinctively.

'Even if we can find the sintegrack, how do we make sure we don't blow ourselves up with it?'

'I can't be expected to think of everything. You're the Watchmaster-in-waiting after all.'

Zastra scratched her head, but couldn't find a way around the problem.

'Let's go have another look at that compound,' she suggested at last. 'Maybe seeing it will give us some ideas.'

They skirted inland until they found a vantage point overlooking the rear of the Skurg stockade. The Skurgs were rebuilding the fence, dragging bodies of the Golmeirans inside the wooden dome. Zastra tried not to think about what would happen to them. She pointed towards a small stone square lying in the ground at some distance from the dome.

'What's that?'

'Don't you have your navigation telescope?' Jerenik asked.

Zastra rummaged around in the pockets of her trousers and brought out her small telescope with a cry of satisfaction.

'I forgot I had this.'

'Are you sure you didn't get a bang on the head too?'

Zastra opened out the telescope and trained it on a pair of Skurgs who were heading towards the stone square. Each carried an armful of small brown packages.

'They've got the sintegrack.'

One of the Skurgs lifted the stone and disappeared into the ground, followed by his companion. They re-emerged a few moments later, empty-handed.

'That must be where they keep it.' Zastra snapped her telescope shut. 'Makes sense. They don't want to accidentally blow up their home.'

'That makes it easier,' said Jerenik. 'There's no lock I can't pick.'

'It might work. They'll think they've got the better of us. I doubt they'd expect another attempt tonight. I've got an idea to get us past the stockade, but it's risky. Are you sure you're both in?'

Ithgol grunted. Zastra took that for assent. Jerenik grinned.

'Beats just sitting here,' he said.

Chapter Twenty-seven

It was a long wait for night to fall. Jerenik began to fidget.

'I'm bored.'

Ithgol hissed at him, but he would not be silenced.

'I'm starving to death here.'

'I'll kill you myself if you can't be quiet.'

'Typical Kyrg. Always offering to kill something. If only you turned your violent urges towards something we could eat. A nice vizzal perhaps? There must be something to hunt on this wretched island.'

'Fine.' Zastra stood up. 'I'll go.'

Ithgol rose with her.

'I will join you. If I have to stay here, I will kill him.'

'I would help,' offered Jerenik, 'but I should probably rest. I could have brain swelling.'

'As if your head could possibly get any bigger.' Zastra adjusted his bandage, and reassured him that his brain was very much still inside his skull.

'I'll enjoy the peace even if we don't find anything,' Zastra remarked as they left Jerenik behind. Ithgol responded with a low rattle of agreement.

The sandy island was dry and there was little vegetation, none of which looked edible. Ithgol crouched down and snuffled the air. He froze and then followed an invisible trail that led towards a flat rock. Zastra sniffed the air too, but all she could detect was the faint saltiness of the sea. With a rapid flick of his wrist, Ithgol lifted the rock and impaled a small yellow lizard with the tip of his scythal blade.

'Is it edible?' Zastra asked suspiciously.

'Not delicate enough for your stomach, Golmeiran?'

Zastra didn't think the lizard looked very appetising, but her belly was grumbling.

'One's not going to be enough.'

Ithgol began sniffing the air again.

'Can you really smell them?'

'Kyrgs often track by scent. Our womenfolk are best at it.'

'Womenfolk?' It had never crossed Zastra's mind that there must be female Kyrgs. She wondered whether they were as ugly as their menfolk. They ventured deeper into the island, where the terrain became increasingly rocky. Ithgol sniffed out three more lizards. Close to the base of a steep hill, they found a large stream and the Kyrg used his strength to lift rocks from the stream bed, unearthing some green-coloured shellfish. As he lifted a particularly large stone, a river snake as long as his leg was startled out of its slumber. Zastra speared it with her knife.

'That should do even for Jerenik.'

'Don't be so sure. He eats even more than he talks.'

'I would say that was impossible, but I've seen him at breakfast and I think I'd have to agree with you.'

They headed back. To break the silence, Zastra asked a question that had been in her mind ever since her first day aboard the *Wind of Golmeira*.

'Why don't the other Kyrgs like you?'

Ithgol didn't break stride.

Zastra sighed. 'Between you and Jerenik, there's one normal person. He never stops talking, and you never say anything.'

'You wouldn't understand.'

'How can I understand if you don't tell me? Look, you saved my life, which in my view makes us friends. Friends talk to each other.'

Ithgol slowed his pace and half turned towards her.

'You would be friends with a Kyrg?'

Zastra shrugged. 'It surprises me as much as it does you, but... yes, I suppose I would.'

Ithgol pulled up.

'I am *Mordaka*. Outcast. If I ever return to the Northern Wastes, I will be put to death. The others know this and only their obedience to your Golmeiran officers stops them killing me.'

'What did you do?'

'Tried to save my sister's life.'

He set off again, covering the ground quickly. Zastra was forced to jog to keep up, but even so she began to lag behind. They were halfway back to where they had left Jerenik when he stopped to take a drink from his flask. Zastra had lost her own flask during the attack and she eyed his longingly. He passed it to her.

'Look at you, sharing things,' she said with a grin. The water was pleasant against her parched throat but she took only a few sips. Apart from the stream where they had caught the snake they had seen no fresh water.

'A Kyrg is taught to show his strength. Food is scarce in the Northern Wastes, and the weakest are sacrificed before winter comes. We call it the Culling.'

'That's awful.'

'When you've only food for a hundred people, you must choose, else all will starve. Death at the culling ceremony is an honoured sacrifice.'

'What if someone refuses?'

'A Kyrg obeys orders from higher ranks without question. No one has ever refused.'

'Why do you choose to live in such a barren place? If you lived in more fertile lands there would be no need for such brutal ceremonies.'

Ithgol let out a strange sound, half bark, half laugh.

'Kyrgs were a peaceful race until we were forced out of our ancestral home in the Helgarths by your Grand Marl Fostran. He banished us to the Northern Wastes.'

'Peaceful? Don't be silly. The story of Fostran fighting off a pack of Kyrgs single-handed is one of our best known legends.'

'Tales told by victors are often twisted. What weapons did the Kyrgs carry in this story?'

'Axes, scythes and pitchforks.' Fostran's battle with the Kyrgs had been Zastra's favourite among all those about the legendary Warriors of Golmeira. She knew all the details by heart.

'Exactly. Farm tools.'

'But you attack our people in the Helgarths,' she protested. 'Hardly the act of a peaceful race. There are other stories too—'

Ithgol broke in angrily.

'We are not Skurgs,' he snapped. 'We steal only what we need to survive.'

'So you have never... um, eaten people?'

He emitted a low growl. 'Long ago, the Skurgs lived with us, our brothers and sisters of the grey hair. They were a small clan. It is said that the first winter after Fostran banished us, the Skurgs chose to feed upon their own, rather than starve. And so they were cast out.'

'What happened with your sister?'

'She had a fever. She would have recovered in time, but the summer hunting had been poor that year. Stores were low and she was one of many Jelgar chose for the Culling.'

Ithgol kicked at a loose pebble and watched it skid off into the distance.

'She accepted her fate. I could not. I made her flee with me, but the winter that year came early. She did not survive.'

The flow of words was interrupted by Jerenik, who had come looking for them, shading his eyes against the evening sun. 'Where've you been? Did you find anything to eat?' He made a grab for the bag but Zastra yanked it out of his reach.

'We'll have to wait until dark. We don't want the Skurgs to see the smoke.'

'Come on, it's worth the risk. My stomach is eating itself.'

'Wait,' growled Ithgol, reverting to his old, monosyllabic self. Only when it was fully dark did they dig a pit and light the fire. The lizard flesh was pungent and unpleasant and the river snake proved to have more bones than flesh so their hunger was only partly satisfied. Jerenik began to fidget again.

'How much longer do we just sit here? I'm freezing to death.'

Ithgol growled at him and Zastra did not feel the need to add anything. The sound of chanting came to them on the night air.

'Celebrating their victory,' muttered Ithgol. Zastra shivered, recalling the horrors of the morning. She was more determined than ever that neither Dastrin nor Thorlberd would get their hands on the sintegrack. They could kill thousands at a time with such a weapon. She wrapped her arms around herself to try and keep warm. A question rose in her mind.

'Ithgol, how did Burgal know you were an outcast?'

Ithgol held out his left arm, palm upward. A line of circular tattoos, of different designs and colours, ran up the inside of his forearm. 'A tattoo is added each year, for those that are not culled. I have not had one since I ran away and so my treachery is clear.'

'I wondered what they were. Why are some different colours?'

'Colour represents rank. See where mine change from orange to green? That was the year I was promoted to the second rank.'

'Why don't you just tattoo yourself as a guthan?' suggested Jerenik. 'Red ones like Burgal has? I could do it for you.'

Ithgol grabbed Jerenik's throat in one hand.

'That would be the deepest dishonour. Only a thief like you would suggest such a thing.'

Zastra tried to pull him away, but Ithgol's arm was like a block of stone. Jerenik's face began to go purple and his eyes bulged.

'Let him go, Ithgol. We mustn't fight amongst ourselves.'

Ithgol released Jerenik with a shove. Jerenik shot the Kyrg an evil look. *Somehow, I have to get them to work together,* thought Zastra. *I just wish I knew how.*

Chapter Twenty-eight

'My Lady, surely you can't be serious?'

'We are used to achieving the impossible, Hylaz,' Kylen responded, but even she frowned as she examined the Golmeiran encampment. There must be thousands of soldiers, well organised, with tents in neat lines and sentries patrolling every entrance and exit. General Ixendred was an effective adversary. They had sneaked past several intelligently placed sentries to get even this close.

'We can't even be certain Lord Zadorax is here.'

'Where else could he be? We know that Rastran was responsible for that... that outrage.'

Kylen shuddered as she recalled that night. Even from her position deep within the caves she had felt the earth tremble. One of their people had managed to stagger back to tell her about the terrible weapon, and describe the crowing Golmeiran who had taken her brother prisoner.

'I'm certain we will find that cowardly flekk here. The supply wagon we captured yesterday was full of wine and other delicacies. Only someone like Rastran would demand such luxuries.

Now, if only we knew which is his tent.' She continued to scour the encampment.

'Even then, how can we hope to get into the camp unnoticed? Let alone out again.'

'We have to try. I should never have agreed to let Zax be part of the ambush. If he hadn't been so close to the surface, he would still be safe.'

Hylaz sighed heavily. 'What do you need me to do?'

At the edge of the Golmeiran camp a sentry leaned against a large rock and watched a lopsided wagon loaded with barrels inch towards him. It was driven by a large man with a bent back and a thatch of grey hair that looked as if it had not been washed in years.

'Halt. Let's see your papers.'

'Eh?' The waggoneer scratched his disgusting hair and a couple of insects flew out. The sentry took one step backwards, trying not to gag.

'Papers.'

The old man patted his chest and began to rummage around his filthy rags. At last he produced a dirty scrap of paper.

'Provisions for Lord Rastran.' He gave a damp sniff. The sentry examined the papers.

'You're late.'

'Had to fix the wheel.' The sentry inspected the cart. The front wheel was made of recently hewn wood, raw and unfinished. He stepped back and pointed out a large cabin of freshly cut wood. 'That's Lord Rastran's residence. He'll be pleased to see you.'

The old man nudged the cart forwards.

'Good work,' came a whisper from inside one of the barrels. 'But check your wig. I think it's slipped.'

The man planted a large hand on the top of his head and rotated the grey wig in a small circle.

'How's that, my Lady?'

'Hideous. But it'll do. Let's give Lord Rastran his special delivery.'

No one paid them any attention as they parked the wagon in front of Rastran's residence. Hylaz dealt quickly and silently with the two guards that stood outside. It was a solid structure; Kylen reckoned it must have taken a whole troop many days even to dig the foundations in such stony ground. *What a waste of time and effort.* She supposed Rastran wouldn't lower himself to sleep in a tent like the rest of his army. They entered the cabin. Kylen recognised Rastran instantly. He was taller than she remembered, but still had the same black hair and insolent manner. He was alone, seated on a chair with his feet resting on a table.

'How dare you—' His face contorted with shock as Kylen swept his chair from underneath him and pinned him to the floor, her knee on his chest.

'G-guards!'

'They're taking a break,' Hylaz informed him. 'Golmeirans have such weak heads.'

'Where is he?' Kylen demanded. 'Where is my brother?'

Ixendred was busy auditing his army's provisions. A dull, but complicated task. He had asked not to be disturbed and was therefore extremely irritated when one of his captains poked his head through his tent flap.

'Can't you see I'm busy?'

'Apologies, Master at Arms, but I think something is going on in Lord Rastran's quarters.'

'His quarters? You mean that ridiculous little palace he had built? I'd quite happily burn it down. You know he had wood sent from Golmeira to build it? Sendoran trees weren't good enough, apparently.'

'There seems to be some kind of disturbance.'

'I couldn't care less what our princeling is doing. Sort it out yourself.'

The guard hesitated.

'The last soldier who went into Lord Rastran's quarters without invitation was whipped for impertinence.'

Ixendred sighed. It probably was just Rastran playing his usual games, but he had learned over the years never to assume anything. He was responsible for Rastran's safety after all.

'I suppose we'd best go and check.'

'We need to leave, my Lady.'

'Not now Hylaz, I'm busy.' Kylen redoubled her pressure on Rastran's chest. 'Tell me where my brother is.'

The door to the cabin burst open and Ixendred and three Golmeiran soldiers barrelled in. They stopped short at the scene in front of them. Ixendred dropped into a polite bow.

'I see Lord Rastran has visitors,' he remarked. 'Lady Kylen, I presume?'

'Tell me where my brother is, or Thorlberd's pup will die.'

Ixendred gave an open handed gesture.

'Go ahead. You'd be doing me a favour.'

A stifled cry of rage emerged from beneath Kylen's knee.

'You really want me to kill Thorlberd's eldest son?'

'It would rid me of an inconvenience. Although I would have to kill you in retaliation. Whereas if you lay down your weapon I'll spare your life. I have twenty more guards outside. You cannot escape.'

'I don't fear death.'

'That is quite evident. Attacking our camp with just one companion is not the act of someone who values survival.'

Rastran glared up at her and then his eyes narrowed. 'You will pay for this, Sendoran bitch.' Kylen reasserted her downward pressure.

'Your mind-meddling doesn't work on me. Or had you forgotten?'

She eased the tip of her sword into Rastran's neck and drew a bead of blood.

'H-he's been sent to Murthen Island,' Rastran stammered.

'Where's that?'

'I d-don't know. The location is a secret.'

Kylen twitched her sword by a fraction. Rastran's words came out in a high pitched flood.

'It's in the Sea of Golmeira, somewhere southeast of Castanton. That's all I know.'

Almost before he had finished, Kylen and Hylaz exchanged a quick nod and together sprang through the open window. Ixendred stepped over Rastran.

'Seize them!' he cried.

Kylen jumped on the cart and sparked the horses into life while Hylaz scrambled into the back. There was no sign of the twenty soldiers they had been expecting. Ixendred had been bluffing. The Master at Arms and his three companions burst from the cabin door. Hylaz began to heave the contents of the cart at them. The Golmeirans were forced to dodge the heavy barrels that bounced and rolled into their path.

'Have some wine,' cried the big Sendoran, flinging a barrel towards Ixendred. 'Compliments of Sendor.'

The barrel burst as it hit the ground, drenching their pursuers in dark red liquid. Relieved of its heavy load the cart sped up as it thundered towards the edge of the camp. The perimeter guards were sent diving out of the way as the horses charged through.

'Horses!' cried Ixendred, wiping the red wine from his face. 'Fetch me our fastest horses.'

Unfortunately for Ixendred, the horses were stabled at the opposite side of the camp and by the time they had been brought the Sendorans had disappeared into the mountains. Rastran emerged from his residence to confront Ixendred.

'I shall not forget your treachery.'

'Do not confuse tactics with betrayal,' Ixendred returned. 'I was trying to distract her.'

'You would have let her kill me.'

'I wanted her to believe that. Or to keep her guessing at least. You're alive aren't you?'

Rastran dabbed a finger to his neck. His fingertip came away with a red smear of blood.

'I want them found. Send the whole army after them if you have to.'

'Absolutely not,' Ixendred snapped. 'If we scatter the army about these mountains, they will be easy pickings for any Sendoran with a crossbow.'

'I insist you do as I command.'

'Have you forgotten your father's instructions? I am in charge here, not you.'

Rastran screwed his features so tight that his skin, already pale, became as white as chalk.

'Very well. I will go to Murthen Island myself and see to the punishment of that brat Zadorax personally. If his sister comes for him, this time I shall be ready.'

'Try not to enjoy yourself too much.' Ixendred didn't bother to hide his repugnance.

'I'll take the Bractarian Guard with me. I don't trust the Kyrgs.'

Ixendred clenched his jaw but made no protest. The Bractarian Guard were his best soldiers but it would be worth it to be rid of Rastran.

Chapter Twenty-nine

The singing had long since ceased. The crescent moons passed their zenith and Ithgol and Zastra agreed it was finally time to move. They approached the stockade cautiously. Ithgol set his back against the wooden spikes and planted his feet. Zastra clambered onto his shoulders, reached for the top of the fence and pulled herself up. Jerenik followed. Zastra had seen some acrobats perform a similar move when she was a child. She and Jerenik wedged their feet between the sharp points at the top of the stockade and crouched down to grab Ithgol's hands.

'He's too heavy!' gasped Jerenik as they heaved the Kyrg upwards. They pulled so hard that they overbalanced and landed inside the stockade in an inelegant bundle of arms and legs.

'Oof!' grunted Ithgol.

'Great plan, mountain girl.'

'We made it, didn't we? Is everyone all right?'

Zastra took the silence as affirmation. A small patch of light illuminated two Skurgs seated next to the stone trapdoor. Ithgol marched over. In the dark, he looked no different from them. The

Kyrgs stood in greeting and he cracked their heads together with a sickening thud. The Skurgs collapsed silently to the ground.

'Time to work my magic.' Jerenik bent down to examine a large keyhole in the middle of the stone slab.

'Or we could just use this.'

Zastra removed a chain from around the neck of one of the Skurgs. It carried a large key which fitted into the lock. Beneath the trapdoor, wooden steps led down into the darkness. Zastra took up the lamp and made her way down into a square bunker. Directly in front of them was a solid wooden door, with two more on either side. All the doors were locked and the trapdoor key did not fit any of the locks.

'*Now* it's time for your magic.'

Zastra stood back and Jerenik produced a pair of thin metal implements, each with a hook at the end. After moment's fiddling he had unlocked the door opposite the steps. The door creaked as they opened it. A loud yell made them jump.

'Who's there?' It was a female voice, strident and angry. 'I demand you let us out.' A fist pounded on the door to their left, breaking the silence of the night.

'Hush!' whispered Zastra urgently. 'We are not your gaolers. Who are you?'

'Who are *you*?' came the riposte, none too polite.

'Someone who could help you escape, if only you keep your voice down and tell me who you are.'

'Golmeiran, are you?' asked the voice, a little more evenly. 'You sound like it from your accent. Border regions?'

Zastra couldn't help a little inward smile. She had worked hard over the years to disguise her natural accent with that of the mountains.

'Aye,' she said.

'We're Golmeiran sailors, kidnapped by Skurgs. Can you get us out?'

Jerenik looked nervously up the stairs. 'We're wasting time.'

'I'm not leaving anyone locked up here when we set fire to the sintegrack,' Zastra insisted. 'They wouldn't stand a chance.'

'I suppose you're right.' Jerenik began to tackle the second door, while Zastra and Ithgol entered the first room. It was piled high with small cloth bundles. Zastra picked one up and examined it. A waxed string protruded from the bag.

'They must set fire to this string, like a candle wick.'

An idea began to form in her mind. She tugged the string from some of the parcels and began to splice them together. 'If we make a longer string it might just give us time to get away.'

Jerenik finally succeeded in opening the second door. Five men and two women stumbled out, shading their eyes against the light of the lamp. Jerenik turned his attention to the final door and soon had it open. It contained just one prisoner, his face bruised and swollen.

'Yerdan,' cried one of the women, rushing over to help him. 'What have they done to you?'

'Nerika, is that you?' croaked the man. 'They told me they'd killed you all.'

'Time for reunions later,' said Zastra curtly, gesturing them up the stairs. The prisoners did not need much urging.

'You two as well.' Zastra nodded at Jerenik and Ithgol. 'I don't know if this string idea will work. There's no point in risking all our necks.'

'Aw, you really do care, mountain girl.' Jerenik's teeth gleamed in the dark.

'I just don't want your stupid face to be the last thing I see if this goes wrong.'

'I will do it.' Ithgol made a grab for the string.

'No. It's my plan. Besides I can run faster than you. You're not exactly built for speed. Stop wasting time and go.'

Zastra waited until the others had reached the top of the stairs and then scraped her knife along her fragment of firering, taking care not to cut into her fingers. A shower of sparks dropped onto the ground and the end of the spliced string caught fire. The flame moved towards the mound of sintegrack with surprising speed. She turned and sprinted out of the passageway, taking the stairs three at a time.

'Run!' she yelled, discretion no longer necessary. They had just reached the perimeter of the stockade when the earth trembled and roared as though enraged by its violation. The ground was yanked from beneath their feet and the sky burst into a brilliant fireball. Winded, Zastra scrambled to her feet. They had barely managed to get beyond the edge of the blast. The Skurg dome had not been so lucky. Half of it had collapsed into a crater larger than the hull of a ship and fire was licking at what remained of the wooden structure.

She felt a strong grip on her arm and realised that Ithgol was dragging her through the splintered remains of the fence. Jerenik whistled.

'That was some fire-fountain. You nearly killed us all.'

The woman called Nerika rounded on them.

'Whose stupid idea was it to destroy the sintegrack?'

'If you had seen your crewmates torn apart by it, you would want it destroyed too,' Zastra argued.

'You can thank us anytime you like,' Jerenik remarked. 'You know, for the rescue.'

The woman stared at them, aghast. Realisation dawned on Zastra. 'You came to steal it, didn't you? You wanted it for yourselves.'

The woman did not deny it.

'Look!' One of the other prisoners pointed out to sea. Dawn was breaking and three ships were closing on the island.

'Is it Justyn?' Nerika asked eagerly, but her companions shook their heads. Zastra recognised the lead ship as the *Wind of Golmeira*. The dual flag of the Golmeiran hawk alongside Thorlberd's gecko flew atop the mainmasts of each vessel. Dastrin had returned, with reinforcements.

'I suggest we run,' said Jerenik. A large bunch of very angry looking Skurgs had stumbled from the burning dome and were gesticulating towards them. Jerenik nudged Zastra in the ribs.

'They don't look very pleased with you.'

'With us, you mean,' returned Zastra. 'Come on, let's go.'

They made for the beach. The three ships anchored close to the shore and dropped their boats. Yerdan made a grab for Zastra's sword but she saw his move and ducked under his arm, hooking her leg between his and tipping him over. He looked up to find the tip of Ithgol's scythal laid against his throat.

'Please,' Nerika begged through gritted teeth. 'We mustn't be caught.'

The boats were closing on them, but were not yet as close as the Skurgs who had bunched together at the top of the beach.

'We don't have much choice.' Zastra drew her sword. 'Tell me quickly, are you with Lord Justyn?'

Nerika nodded.

'We'll tell Dastrin that you are merchant sailors captured by

Skurg pirates. You must say nothing about us destroying the sintegrack or we'll all be done for.'

'Hey,' Jerenik protested. 'I didn't agree to risk my life for these ingrates.'

'Shut up, Jerenik. Together we might have enough for that mutiny you were bragging about. Ithgol, are you with us?'

Ithgol grunted. Zastra was getting used to interpreting his different types of grunt and she took this one for agreement.

She turned back to Nerika. 'We were all pressed into service and have no desire to serve Dastrin or Thorlberd. We—'

'Down!' barked Ithgol. They ducked as a volley of crossbow bolts whistled over their heads. They stayed down as Golmeiran sailors and Kyrgs rushed past them and piled into the Skurgs.

It proved a one-sided battle and the Skurgs were quickly overpowered. Zastra and the others were taken aboard the *Wind of Golmeira* to face an irate Captain Dastrin, who demanded to know what had happened. Zastra bent her head deferentially.

'We were captured after our attack failed. They locked us up with these Golmeiran merchants. Then there was this terrible noise and the earth shook so much that the door of our jail caved in. We saw your sails. Thank the stars you came back.'

'Are you telling me that the sintegrack has been destroyed?'

'Sintegrack?' Zastra feigned innocence. Dastrin glowered at each of them in turn.

'Who are you?' he narrowed his eyes at Nerika.

'We're from the *Daydream*, a trader out of Castanton. We were carrying a cargo of tobacco back from the Far Isles when a storm blew us off course and into Skurg waters.'

'Why didn't they kill you?' Dastrin queried. 'They usually kill everyone. He turned back to Zastra. 'You too. Why are you even alive?'

'They wanted information about the Golmeiran fleet,' Yerdan interjected. 'Of course I had none but they tried pretty hard to make me tell.' In the full light of morning his bruises stood out clearly and he could barely stand. Mata stepped forward to grab him before he collapsed.

'Someone take this man to Tijan.'

'I am most displeased.' Dastrin glowered. 'Failing in your mission and allowing yourselves to be captured. It is unacceptable. I have a mind to have you all put in the barrel. However, we are shorthanded after the heavy losses incurred by the advance party. Burgal, show them my displeasure.'

Zastra's arms and back stung as Burgal and his Kyrgs set about them with their straps, but she knew better than to protest. Jerenik and Ithgol also took their punishment in silence.

'You new people are now members of the Golmeiran fleet.' Dastrin proceeded to give his usual lecture to Nerika and the others. Jerenik leaned towards Zastra as she rubbed the stinging red marks on her arms. 'The sooner we take over this ship the better. I've had enough of that flekk Dastrin and his punishments.'

Chapter Thirty

Zastra was eager to talk to Nerika again but it was difficult to find any time alone. Her first opportunity came a few days after they had left the Sand Islands, when they were both sent up the main-mast to grease the sheaves. Nerika lost no time in bringing up the subject.

'What's your plan? When are we going to take this ship?'

'We can't do anything with these two other vessels for company. I've tried to find out how many in our company would join us. Dastrin isn't popular, but we have to be careful. If it gets back to him that we've even mentioned mutiny we'd be killed without hesitation.'

'I can't afford to wait. Me and Yerdan are known to quite a few folks in Thorlberd's fleet. We're fortunate none of them are on this ship. Lucky, too, that there's no mindweaver on board.'

'I'm happy to listen to suggestions.'

Nerika dipped a rag into the pot of oil that Zastra held for her and began to smear it around the sheaves. 'We'd be heavily out-numbered and those Kyrgs are good fighters.' She nodded in the direction of Burgal and his charges.

'We have Ithgol.'

'He's only one and I wouldn't trust him. He's a savage.'

'That's not true,' Zastra insisted. 'I trust him. If he says he'll fight with us then I believe him. Our only chance is when we're given weapons. They keep them locked away in the hold and only Dastrin has the key. We have to wait for our next engagement and be ready to seize any opportunity.'

'Hey there, Layna,' came a shout from below. 'Are you done yet? Because the bilges need pumping.'

Zastra groaned. 'Ever since we rescued you, I get all the lousy jobs.'

'Don't blame me. Losing the sintegrack certainly annoyed your Captain Dastrin, and that was all your own doing.'

Days passed and still the *Wind of Golmeira* stayed in formation with the other vessels. They couldn't stage a mutiny when two ships were ready to come to Dastrin's aid. Zastra continued to try and recruit mutineers. Six of her Watchmates had agreed to take part but others she approached had refused, too scared even to listen. Luckily, they did not inform the officers of Zastra's plans. One person she desperately wanted to recruit was Mata, but it would a huge risk even to ask the question. If Mata did not agree to join them, she would be bound to report Zastra, especially now she had been promoted to lieutenant in place of Jagula. Yet, with her years of experience, Mata would be a valuable ally and Zastra sensed that she had no fondness for Dastrin and the way he ran his ship.

Zastra was still being schooled in the arts of sailing and navigation. One afternoon, Mata took her to the top of the mainmast to observe the other two vessels. This was Zastra's chance. As she wondered how to approach the subject, Mata pointed to the near-est ship.

'See how the *Lodara* sits too far forward, dipping her prow into the sea as if she were trying to dive in? Her captain should shift more weight towards the rear so that she sits up more. He could get a twenty percent increase in downwind speed at least.'

Zastra took a deep breath.

'Do you think Dastrin is a good captain?'

Mata frowned.

'Doesn't matter what I think. It's my duty to obey. I made that vow when I joined up.'

'But you chose this life. Many of us have been forced into it. It doesn't seem fair.'

'Aye, it used to be that you joined the fleet because you wanted to serve. I did, like my mother before me. Folks shouldn't be forced to do things they don't want to. I love the sea. It has been my home since I was a young girl and I can't think of anywhere I'd rather be. I've always been proud to protect and serve Golmeira.'

'Are you still proud? After the way Dastrin let those fishermen die at the Pyramid Isle?'

Mata chewed her lip thoughtfully.

'What if we refused to fight for him?' Zastra asked tentatively.

'He'd have you killed.'

'Not if we took the ship.'

Mata stared at her, open mouthed. 'Do you know what you are suggesting? It's suicide. Even if you succeeded, what would you do then? Thorlberd would hunt you down and I don't like to think what he'd do to you.'

'We could join with Lord Justyn. Take on Thorlberd, rather than just run.'

'Lord Justyn? Pah! I saw the tip of his sails once and he couldn't run away fast enough. Justyn doesn't scare Thorlberd. No, Layna, put this mad idea out of your head before it gets you killed.'

'But—'

'Not another word or I'll have to report you. You've a good career ahead of you in the fleet as long as you put aside this foolishness. What ho? What's this?'

Mata stiffened and squinted at the northern horizon. Zastra followed her gaze and made out a tiny white blur, too small and too low for a cloud. Mata cupped her hands and hailed the deck.

'Sail to the north!'

They scrambled down the rigging. The white blur closed, transforming into a single-masted courier that flew towards them, coming about with an elegant flourish to fall into line with the convoy. Almost before the little ship had completed its turn, it dropped a boat and the captain was rowed across to the *Wind of Golmeira* to exchange brief words with their captain. Dastrin immediately ordered Mata to signal the other ships' captains to come aboard. Zastra glanced meaningfully at Jerenik. He winked in acknowledgment and waited until Koltan's back was turned before disappearing below decks.

The meeting was a long one. Eventually the captains left Dastrin's cabin and returned to their ships. The courier headed back towards Golmeira and Dastrin ordered Mata to set a course to the east. The *Obala* and the *Lodara*, followed their lead.

'Where are we going?' Zastra asked Mata.

'Somewhere in the south-eastern corner of the Golmeiran Sea by our heading. And yet no land is charted there.'

Zastra's attention was distracted by Jerenik, who was strolling with apparent nonchalance towards the prow of the ship. A rotten stench clung to him. She joined him with a polishing cloth in hand. As they made a show of cleaning the copper rails Jerenik made certain no one was close by before he spoke.

'Special mission,' he whispered. 'A convoy is headed for somewhere called Murthen Island. Our beloved Grand Marl does not think the present escort of two warships is enough to protect his precious cargo. We are to be reinforcements.'

'Murthen Island?' Zastra creased her forehead. 'Never heard of it.'

'Ain't you supposed to be a wondrous navigator?'

'Are you sure you heard right?'

''Course. I ain't deaf.'

'Where do you go?'

'Down into the bilges and then back towards the rudder. There's a small gap that you can slip through as long as no one changes course. I can squeeze upwards til I'm right beneath Dastrin's cabin. I used a hand-drill to make a small hole in the floor so I can hear what's going on.'

'No wonder you stink.'

'I'm just lucky my natural charm makes up for it. I wonder what this precious cargo is. Even Dastrin doesn't seem to know. It's all very secret.'

Koltan came towards them and Zastra and Jerenik redoubled their polishing. Koltan inspected their work closely, pointing out several patches where the shine was not up to his standard, before he was pulled away by the sight of Ithgol making a mess of a bowline.

'How many have you got?' whispered Zastra.

'Eight,' he returned. 'You?'

'Six, not including Ithgol. With Nerika's six that only gives us twenty. That leaves us considerably outnumbered. It's so frustrating. I know how much everyone hates Dastrin but they are all too scared to do anything.'

'It don't look good.'

'We have to try. Next time they give us the weapons I'll be in the mast with the crossbow. That'll give us an advantage. We must hope that others join us when they see we mean business. Do you know anyone who's good at sewing?'

Jerenik raised a questioning eyebrow. 'I don't see how needlework is going to get us out of this mess. Unless you think Dastrin can be bought off with a bit of nice embroidery. What were you thinking?'

'A flag.'

'A flag? I don't see how that will help but Ithgol is pretty handy with a needle.'

'Speaking of Ithgol, I think it's time he got some new tattoos.'
Jerenik chuckled.

'He'll not like it.'

'Use some of that natural charm you keep boasting about.'

That night a squall came, short but brutal. All hands were roused to lower the spars and pump out the water as wave upon wave crashed over the deck and threatened to overturn the ship. The rain drove down viciously, adding to the confusion. Zastra joined Mata at the helm to offer her assistance.

'We must run before the wind!' Mata yelled, struggling to make herself heard over the howling gale. 'If we try to turn, we'll broach. We must hope there's no land in our path or we'll run aground for sure.'

Mata ordered the crew to swap out the normal jib for the storm jib. It seemed a precious small piece of material to stake their lives on but too large a sail would split with the force of the gale and leave them without any means to direct the ship. The rudder fought them hard and it took Mata and Zastra's combined strength to keep the ship before the wind. They lost sight of the *Lodara* and the *Obala* as the swells grew higher and heavy storm clouds blocked out the moons and the stars. Mata, ever the teacher, showed Zastra how to feel the sea with the rudder, paying no heed to the huge waves that swept over the quarterdeck railings and slammed into them. It was terrifying, exhilarating and exhausting all at the same time. Hour after hour the ship ploughed through the dark, uncharted sea, the crew hoping that only open sea lay in their path.

Chapter Thirty-one

Morning came and the storm disappeared as if it had never existed. Two of Zastra's crewmates could not be found, most likely swept overboard by one of the huge waves that had burst across the deck. Off to windward lay the *Lodara*, largely unscathed. The outline of the *Obala* was just visible in the distance, its rear mast snapped off at the base. It took several hours for the three ships to regroup and reset their course, adjusting to the slow pace of the damaged *Obala*.

'Sail to the south.'

'South?' Dastrin's eyes narrowed. 'Are you certain? The convoy should be coming from the north.'

'Aye, Captain,' came the reply. 'Two ships. One of them's in trouble. Broken spar.'

'I suppose we should see what's occurring.' Dastrin snapped his fingers. 'Signal the other ships to investigate. We shall follow. Make ready for battle.'

Nerika walked past Zastra. 'I recognise those ships,' she whispered. 'They belong to Lord Justyn.'

'Then this is our chance.' Zastra's heart began to race. The crew were given their weapons and Zastra gave Jerenik the signal. It was time to take the gamble of their lives.

Dastrin positioned the *Wind of Golmeira* at the rear of the line, with the *Lodara* at the front. *How typical of our brave captain,* Zastra thought, as she climbed up to her new position at the head of the foremast. Even the damaged *Obala* was sent on ahead of them. She peered round the peak of the foresail and looked back towards the rear mast. Ceran, one of their co-conspirators, had been stationed there. She didn't have to worry about him. The woman at the mainmast could be a problem. She would have to keep an eye on her. The *Lodara* began to engage the enemy, its catapults spewing fire and rocks into the air with great enthusiasm. One of Justyn's ships was sending piles of burning material towards the *Lodara* in return. Zastra checked her crossbow. All three bolts were loaded and ready.

On the deck below, Nerika and her fellow rebels strode towards Dastrin. Jerenik, Ithgol and the rest of their mutineers surrounded the Kyrgs. This was the moment.

'We refuse to fight for the dictator Thorlberd,' cried Nerika in clear, ringing tones. 'Dastrin, you are relieved of command.'

Even from her position high in the foremast, Zastra saw the colour drain from Dastrin's face. He looked around desperately for Burgal. The Kyrg issued an angry roar and rushed at Nerika, flailing his scythal. Zastra took aim and fired. Burgal collapsed to the floor. Another Kyrg made to follow and Zastra shot a bolt through his foot. He howled in pain as his foot was pinned to the deck.

'Anyone else who moves will be shot,' said Nerika.

'Shoot her down,' squawked Dastrin gesticulating wildly towards the other sharpshooters.

The archer in the mainmast turned her crossbow towards Zastra. Ceran in turn pointed his bow at her.

'Drop it,' he yelled. The woman looked from one to the other and obeyed, her bow shattering as it hit the deck.

'You'll never get away with this,' stammered Dastrin. 'I'll have you all put to death.'

Nerika stepped towards him. There was a flash of metal and, with a vicious jab, she stabbed him in the ribcage. He slumped to the deck.

'Kill all the officers!' she cried. Zastra's eyes widened in shock. This was not the plan they had agreed. The crew shifted uneasily and the Kyrgs adopted their fighting crouch. The small band of rebels and mutineers were heavily outnumbered. The situation did not look good. Zastra slid down the backstay and sprang onto the deck.

'Lieutenant Mata!' she cried. The new lieutenant was staring down at Dastrin's body in open mouthed shock. 'You are now officially captain. Order the Kyrgs to stand down before more blood is shed.'

The Kyrgs inched forward, aggression rattling in the back of their throats. 'Hold your positions,' Mata commanded. The Kyrgs stopped in their tracks, just as Zastra had hoped. Ithgol had been right about Kyrgs and their slavish obedience to the chain of command. Zastra took advantage of the moment of calm.

'Listen to me,' she cried, jumping up onto the lid of the punishment barrel to address the crew. 'We have all fought together as friends and crewmates. We do not wish to fight you. But I will not serve a Grand Marl who rules by fear and tyranny and makes us his slaves. Those ships over there belong to Lord Justyn, who stands against Thorlberd. We can join him. This is your one chance, here and now, to escape from servitude to a murdering tyrant.'

'Who are you to tell us what to do?' came a distrustful shout from the midst of the crew. She thought of what Dobery had said to her, back in the mountains. *If you have the courage to reveal yourself.* Zastra filled her lungs, striving hard to keep the fear and doubt from her voice. Everything depended on them believing in her. Trusting her.

'I am Zastra. Daughter of Leodra and Anara, and heir to the throne of Golmeira.'

A ripple of shock spread across the carpet of heads. 'I am living proof that Thorlberd's reach is not yet so powerful.' She gained confidence as they listened. 'He tried to kill me and failed. There is still hope. I do not say it will be easy, but here is where we must make our stand. If not for yourselves, then for your children. To fight so they have a future free from oppression and tyranny. Who has the courage to join us?'

A cheer broke out and spread across the deck. A large chunk of the crew broke away to join the small band gathered behind Zastra. Inexpressively moved, she saw that only about a dozen of the Golmeiran crew had not joined them. They lowered their weapons and surrendered.

'Take them to the forward hold and lock them in. The Kyrgs too. We will release them when we find a safe place to land.'

'These Kyrginite animals do not deserve to live,' cried Nerika. Several of her comrades nodded in agreement and one of them raised a crossbow.

'Stop!' Zastra commanded. 'We will not begin by murdering defenceless prisoners. Especially those who have fought by our sides with courage and honour. Take them below.'

Ithgol and Jerenik ushered the Kyrgs below before anyone else could protest. Nerika grabbed Zastra's elbow.

'You're making a mistake.'

Zastra shrugged her off.

'Mata, will you take command of the ship? You have the skills and experience.'

'No, Layna. You have made your bid to lead these people and you must follow it through.' Mata looked bemused. 'Or Zastra, should we call you? You're the captain now. But I will helm the ship for you.' Barking out a series of orders, Mata coaxed the crew back to the sails.

'What's our heading, Captain Zastra?' she sang out, loud enough for the whole crew to hear.

'We will assist Lord Justyn. Attack the *Obala*.'

Jerenik appeared carrying a large piece of cloth.

'Time to raise the flag, Captain?'

Zastra nodded and Jerenik unfurled the cloth. Ithgol had made a fine job of it. The hawk of Golmeira stood proud alongside the eagle of Leodra's house. Zastra felt her throat catch as the flag was raised up the mainmast and her crew roared with approval.

The *Obala* had no idea of the danger coming from the rear. At the front of the line, the *Lodara* was in a bad way. Two of her sails and part of her foredeck were ablaze. The smaller of Justyn's ships was mastless and listing badly. Zastra had Jerenik distribute strips of red ribbon for her crew to tie round their arms to identify them-selves. Their bowsprit rammed into the rear quarter of the *Obala*, and the ship ground to a sudden halt. Zastra drew her sword and raced to the prow.

'With me!' she cried, shocked at her own boldness. She leapt for the deck of the *Obala*. Ithgol led the rest of her crew across behind her. Zastra found herself face-to-face with the *Obala*'s captain, a dark-skinned woman who was wearing an expression of shock. It seemed to be the favoured look of the day.

'Stand down in the name of Leodra,' cried Zastra. 'Any on this ship who oppose Thorlberd, stand with us!'

The captain drew her sword and laid into her strongly. For some reason that Zastra couldn't understand they had plenty of room and time to fight. Her opponent was left-handed and had both strength and skill. Zastra drew on everything she could remember of her training back at Golmer Castle, but it was not enough and the woman pressed her back towards the taffrail. Zastra would soon have nowhere to go. Parrying another strong thrust she stepped forward and struck the woman hard on the nose with the palm of her hand. Her opponent staggered back. Sensing her advantage Zastra charged, diving low to avoid a swishing blade. She grabbed the woman's legs and knocked her off her feet. It was an ugly tactic but effective. Her opponent's head struck hard against the base of the rearmast. As she lay stunned, Zastra pinned her hand to the deck with her right foot and held her sword against her throat. The *Obala*'s captain had no choice but to surrender.

Zastra stood back, slowly realising why they'd had so much space to fight. Everyone else had formed a circle and watched. Ithgol had made use of the distraction to take command of the Kyrgs. Zastra acknowledged his nod. The tattoo trick must have worked, the Kyrgs believing Ithgol to be a high ranking guthan. A grey-haired man dressed in the grey vest and half trousers of a crewman stepped towards her.

'By what right do you use the name of Leodra?' he asked.

'I am Zastra. I have every right to use my father's name.'

A man in a lieutenant's uniform barged through the crowd. 'Who gave you permission to speak, Brindik?' He shoved the grey-haired man aside. 'No upstart pretender shall challenge the rule of Grand Marl Thorlberd. Crew of the *Obala*, with me.'

'I refuse,' shouted Brindik. 'And there's many like me. Come, my friends. This is our chance.'

He stepped behind Zastra and drew a pair of knives. About twenty other Obalans shuffled to join him.

'Look around you, Lieutenant,' Zastra cried. 'You are outnumbered and the Kyrgs are with us. Do not do anything stupid to get yourself and your crew killed.' Raising her voice she addressed the remaining Obalans. 'Anyone who wants to stand against Thorlberd can join us. If you do not feel able to do so, you have my word you will not be harmed as long as you give up your weapons and surrender.'

More men and women emerged from the crowd and stood behind Zastra and Brindik. The rest lowered their weapons and were led below, together with their Kyrgs, who obeyed Ithgol without question, even as he led them into a locked cage. Zastra was relieved beyond measure that they had not needed to kill any Golmeirans. Their plan to avoid bloodshed could not have worked better. There was no time for self-congratulation. The *Obala* was on a direct heading towards the larger of Lord Justyn's ships and the angry mob on its deck had no idea that they were on the same side of this fight.

'Nerika!' she called. 'Where is Nerika?'

'Here!' Nerika dashed to the *Obala*'s prow and waved vigorously, yelling across to the other ship. For a moment, it appeared she would not be able to make herself noticed, but then a man pushed through the crowd and returned Nerika's wave. He was good looking, despite the veins of grey running through his sandy hair. A broad smile of disbelief spread across his face. He shouted something and his crew lowered their weapons. The two ships converged and Nerika climbed across and rushed forward into arms open wide in welcome. Yerdan was poised ready to step across after her. Zastra stopped him with her arm.

'Is that Lord Justyn?'

Yerdan grinned as if at a secret joke before stepping over. Zastra assessed the situation. Brindik had taken control of the *Obala*. Over on the *Wind of Golmeira* Mata was striding around giving instructions to the few members of crew left on board. The *Lodara* was burning, a floating torch from which men and women were leaping into the sea in a desperate attempt to escape the flames. Some were struggling to stay afloat. Zastra walked over to Brindik and waited for him to finish giving orders to two of his crewmates.

'Looks as if you've got everything under control here,' she said. 'Do you need any help?'

'We could do with more hands. Nearly half of my sailors are locked up below. We don't really have enough to run the ship.'

Zastra beckoned Ithgol and Jerenik.

'Take our crew back to the *Wind of Golmeira*, but leave ten with Brindik. I don't think we can spare any more or we'll be short-handed ourselves. I hope that will be enough?'

Brindik frowned. 'It'll have to do. What's our next move? You have a plan, I hope?'

Jerenik grinned. 'Plans are boring. We prefer to make it up as we go.'

Zastra gave him a frosty glare.

'Um, right, back to Mata,' he said. 'Can't stand here chatting all day.'

Zastra turned to Brindik. 'I hate to admit it but Jerenik is right. We just took our chance when we saw it. These ships belong to Lord Justyn. I intend to see if we can come to some arrangement. Will you come?'

'I've enough on trying to organise this lot. They don't all agree that I belong in charge so I'll have to knock some heads together. Still, it beats serving a traitor. My son was in your father's army and was killed the day your uncle took power. I will go along with what you decide, Zastra.'

Zastra nodded curtly.

'Lower some boats to pick up the poor souls from the *Lodara* before they drown. Offer them the choice to join with us or else be locked up with the others.'

'Right. Not sure how we'll cope with so many prisoners in our small hold.'

'We'll think of something,' Zastra said, although in truth she had no idea how they would deal with that problem. Taking a deep breath she went forward to where the prow of the *Obala* touched up against Justyn's ship. Its name, *Darkhorse*, was engraved into the side. A large shape loomed beside her. She shook her head.

'I thought I told you to go back with Jerenik.'

Ithgol merely cocked his head towards the *Darkhorse* and they stepped across together. An old man with a dark blemish across his left cheek fairly skipped across the deck towards her, amazement filling his face.

'Zastra? Can it really be you?'

'Dobery!' she cried in joyful astonishment.

Chapter Thirty-two

Kylen scanned the jetty. Castanton had always been a busy port and it was no different now Thorlberd was running things. The most easterly harbour within Golmeira, it was the last stopping point before the Straights of Lodara for vessels making the long voyage to the Far Isles. Two large warships were laid up for repairs, dwarfing the smaller trading vessels. Barquentines from the Far Isles, their hulls painted in bright colours, stood out like spring flowers amongst the dark hulls of the Golmeiran ships. The stone jetty was covered with cargo of all shapes and sizes, being unloaded or taken aboard. The air was heavy and damp, laced with the pungent odours of drying seaweed and rotting fish. They had been able to smell Castanton long before they reached the outskirts of the port. Their journey from Sendor, following the winding route of the Borderline River, had been long and arduous. It was too dangerous to travel via the river itself, since it was constantly patrolled by armed Golmeiran barges, so they had been forced to hack their way through the thick bamboo forest that grew right up to the banks of the mighty river that formed the border between Sendor and Golmeira. As if the bamboo wasn't enough of an obstacle, the forest floor had been infested with prickly vine weeds, snagging and scratching their skin even through their clothes.

'Come, Hylaz,' she said. 'We've lost enough time on our pleasant jaunt down the Borderline valley. We need to find a vessel to take us to Murthen Island. Assuming anyone knows where it is.'

She pulled a cap out of her bag and positioned it carefully on her head.

'How do I look?'

'Like a thief and a crook. You'll fit in very well here, my Lady. No one will recognise you.'

'Unless you continue to call me my Lady,' she remarked. 'Now, put that awful wig on. We don't want any Sendoran hair on display.'

Hylaz began to rummage around in his small backpack as Kylen strode towards the jetty.

'Oy. Wait up!'

Kylen turned in disbelief.

'Oy?'

'Um...You did say I wasn't to call you my Lady.'

Kylen snapped her fingers to hurry him along.

'Come on. Every moment we delay, Zax might be suffering.'

They started with the most run-down vessels. Kylen figured their captains would be eager to earn some ready money without asking too many questions. The first boat they tried was owned by the ugliest woman Kylen had ever seen. She had only two teeth, one in her upper gum and one in her lower. Brown and rotten, the teeth ground against each other as she spoke.

'Nah,' the woman said. 'Not even if I knew wheres in the stars you wants to go. I can smell a Sendoran, even ones looking like a doxy.'

Kylen put a warning arm across Hylaz's broad chest. She looked at the silver chain that had been thrust back into her palm.

'You can't be after more? Unless your cabins are lined with silks and you serve honeyed vizzal each night for supper.'

The woman showed her gums in what might have passed for a grin.

'You could offer me five times as much, I'd not take you. Grand Marl Thorlberd 'as said no Sendorans to leave the mainland. It's my 'ead if theys catch me. An' I quite like my 'ead.'

'I expect she's the only one who does,' muttered Hylaz as they continued down the line of ships, but the answer, although not always so rude, was the same. No one would take them.

'It's hopeless.' Kylen flung herself to the ground by the side of a warehouse. 'Even if someone was prepared to take us, no one knows where this Murthen Island place is. Or if they do, they aren't admitting it.'

Hylaz sat down beside her. Kylen racked her brains, trying to think of a plan. Two drunks, unable to gain entry to a closed tavern, tried to catch her eye, but she ignored them and they shuffled away. A trading vessel pushed off and disappeared around the headland. Night drew in and lamps were lit. The drunks returned and one of them aimed an insult in their direction. Kylen paid no attention, engrossed in watching two fat Golmeiran ships being loaded up. Only a handful of crates had been taken aboard each vessel before the gangways were drawn up. *Small cargo for such large trading ships.* On the nearest ship, a dark figure in black robes emerged from the shadows of the quarterdeck and into the circle of light cast by a small jula lamp. *A mindweaver.* As Kylen watched, another black cloak entered the patch of light. *Two mindweavers.* One of the drunks weaved across her line of sight, blocking her view. Kylen motioned him away. He seemed about to argue, but then the tavern doors opened and he and his partner staggered into its welcoming embrace. Kylen nudged Hylaz, who was snoring gently at her side.

'Ugh?'

'Something on that transport is important enough to need two mindweavers to protect it. What could it be, do you think?'

Hylaz rubbed his eyes and tried to stifle a yawn. When the two mindweavers were joined by a third, Kylen was even more certain something important was occurring. Mindweavers were a rare breed. To see three together outside a castle was unheard of. As the pale arc of remaining daylight disappeared over the horizon, the gangway on the trading vessel was lowered again. A line of shadows shuffled along the quay and started up the gangplank. Chains clanked. As they reached the deck of the ship, the jula lamp cast a faint glow on a line of prisoners. Most had fair hair that reflected the orange cast of the lamp. Kylen gasped.

'Sendorans. Hylaz, I'm sure of it.' She watched for a while to make certain, her mind racing.

'I've got an idea.'

'We can't possibly rescue them, my La... um...'

'I wasn't thinking of rescue. They can only be going to one place.'

'You can't mean...?'

'I don't ask you to join me, Hylaz, but I have to get to Zax. That ship must be headed for Murthen Island and I intend to be on it. Take a message back to Alboraz, to let him know where I am.'

She scrambled up and ran towards the ship.

'For Sendor!' she cried, jumping at one of the guards and yanking her away from the prisoners. As the other guards rushed to their companion's aid, Kylen made sure she landed some solid punches. She didn't want it to look too easy. In any case, it was always pleasant to make a Golmeiran suffer. But when someone got her in a strong grip, she made only a half-hearted attempt to escape and was soon in chains and shoved into line. There was a grunt and a thud by her side.

'Seems like these two are eager to join our trip,' said one of the guards. 'Must have heard how much fun the Island is.'

'Hylaz?' Kylen hissed. 'What are you doing? I told you not to follow me.'

'My Lady, I know I'm supposed to obey without question, but I can't think of anything more dangerous than telling General Alboraz I stood by while Lord Mendoraz's daughter was captured.'

Chapter Thirty-three

Zastra rushed to greet her former teacher. Dobery had not changed much. Perhaps he was a little thinner than when she had last seen him but his face, far from handsome yet somehow wonderful, had not altered.

'Zastra, my dear, how in the stars did you end up here?'

'It's a strange story,' she said, unable to suppress a smile. Dobery raised an eyebrow in the direction of her Kyrginite companion.

'So it would appear.'

Nerika brought over the man with the sandy hair.

'This is the girl. Claims to be Leodra's daughter.'

'Claims?' Dobery was a picture of indignation. 'Do not doubt it, Justyn.'

'So you are Zastra.' Justyn looked her up and down. 'Master Dobery tells me I should make an alliance with you.'

'Alliance?' Nerika snorted. 'She's just a child.'

'I stopped being a child many years ago, about the time my parents were murdered,' Zastra returned grimly.

Nerika blinked but quickly recovered her composure.

'Perhaps if you'd not been so stupid as to destroy the sintegrack, you might have something to offer.'

'I have two ships under my command. And we did save your lives. Or had you forgotten?'

Justyn raised an eyebrow. 'It sounds as if we have some catching up to do. But the last thing I need is more ships. A flotilla is hard to hide.'

'Hide?' growled Ithgol. 'Cowards hide. The daughter of Leodra might ask what need she has of *you*.'

'Stay out of this, Kyrg.' Nerika rounded on him. 'Unless you wish to be locked up with the rest of your murdering kind.'

'He's with me,' Zastra interjected. 'He has fought many times by my side with honour and courage. We would not have succeeded today without him.'

There was a commotion at the side of the ship. A gig pulled alongside and a young woman with dark shadows beneath her eyes hauled herself wearily on deck. Justyn rushed over to assist her, his face alive with concern. 'Polina. Are you all right?'

'I'm alive, for which I'm grateful,' the young woman responded. 'We lost some good men and women, including Captain Fogan. He was crushed beneath the rear mast when it collapsed. As you can see, all our masts are gone and the hull is leaking in a hundred places. We can hardly pump the water out fast enough. For the moment the *Caralyx* is helpless.'

'I'm sorry about Fogan. He was a good sailor and an even better man. How long before you can sail?'

'At least a day, maybe more.'

Justyn frowned.

'That's not good. We can't just sit here and wait for Thorlberd's fleet to pick us off.'

Zastra coughed.

'Might I make a suggestion?'

Polina turned towards her and Zastra felt a sudden probe dig into her mind.

'Stay out of my head!' she cried. Ithgol growled and grabbed Polina's throat. Justyn and Nerika both whipped out their swords. Zastra felt the probe withdraw.

'Easy, everyone,' she said, striving for composure. 'Ithgol, stand down.' Ithgol reluctantly released Polina, who stared at Zastra in puzzlement.

'Are you a mindweaver?'

'No, but I can tell when someone is prying and I don't like it.'

Dobery raised his hands in a gesture of calm.

'Zastra, this is Polina, a fellow mindweaver, as you have discovered. We are all friends here.'

'Friends don't go peeking into private thoughts.' Zastra was in no mood to be forgiving.

'I like to know what I'm dealing with. I don't trust strangers, especially those that ally with Kyrgs,' Polina remarked stiffly.

Dobery coughed diplomatically.

'Zastra, I believe you were about to make a suggestion.'

Zastra took a breath and re-ordered her thoughts.

'Polina, do you think the *Caralyx* will be able to stay afloat?'

'I believe so,' the mindweaver replied.

Zastra gestured towards the *Obala* and the *Wind of Golmeira*.

'Our ships are undermanned at present. We could transfer all our prisoners to the *Caralyx* and divide its crew amongst the other vessels. If the *Caralyx* cannot sail, the prisoners will be no danger to us. Sooner or later they will get picked up, or else limp to shore.'

'It would be safer to kill them all,' protested Nerika. 'They'll tell Thorlberd all about us.'

'And say what? That Lord Justyn is still free and I am alive? This he knows already. I will not agree to the murder of surrendered prisoners.'

'What say you, Dobery?' Justyn turned to the old man.

'It is a good plan.' Zastra's old teacher gave her an encouraging smile. 'We cannot guard all these prisoners safely and I know that you, Justyn, would not slaughter defenceless men and women.'

'Very well. But I insist Nerika be given command of one of your ships, if my people are to be in your crews.'

Despite her growing dislike of Nerika, Zastra didn't think she could protest.

'The *Obala* has no captain at present,' she conceded. 'I'll talk to Brindik and if he has no objection, then neither do I.'

'Let's see to it,' said Justyn. 'The sooner we head back to Uden's Teeth, the better.'

'Uden's what?'

'A refuge. Somewhere Thorlberd doesn't know about.' Justyn beckoned one of his crew. 'We need to regroup.'

Ithgol snorted. 'Running and hiding. Is this all Golmeirans do?'

Justyn gave him an icy glare.

'Do you think we can beat Thorlberd, with all his fleet? Not to mention mindweavers and migaradons. I will not throw away the lives of my men and women just so you can avenge your parents, Zastra. To survive takes all our strength.'

'An old friend once told me that survival alone is not enough.' Zastra glanced sideways at Dobery. 'I'm not saying that we should march on Golmer Castle tomorrow. But today I learned that many would stand against Thorlberd, if given hope. If they see there's something to believe in. Dastrin's mission was to protect a cargo of great value to Thorlberd, headed for somewhere called Murthen Island. We should find out what is so important that Thorlberd sent three ships to protect it.'

'Murthen Island?' mused Dobery. 'I've heard that name before, although it seems to be a great secret. Thorlberd sends his best scientists and most powerful mindweavers there. I've had no luck finding out what goes on there, or even where it is.'

'If it is more sintegrack, or anything like it, we would do well to know about it,' Zastra insisted.

'So you can destroy it again?' Nerika remarked bitterly. 'It's hardly worth the risk.'

'Pol, what do you say?' Justyn addressed his mindweaver who frowned thoughtfully.

'It does seem like an opportunity we should not let pass by,' she conceded.

Justyn turned to Zastra.

'By a small majority it seems we are in favour of this plan, such as it is. Let's see to the repair of our ships and offload the prisoners onto the *Caralyx*. Then, Zastra, you set course and we will follow. Let's hope you know what you are about.'

Zastra's first action was to speak to Brindik about Nerika taking charge of the *Obala*. He made no objection.

'They respect me, right enough,' he said, 'but because I've been one of the crew, they don't see me as a captain.'

Zastra sent word back to Nerika and then she and Ithgol returned to the *Wind of Golmeira*. The crew cheered them as they came on board, slapping Zastra on her back and thanking her for their release from Captain Dastrin. Even Ithgol received a few nods of acknowledgement. Mata had been busy in their absence, making sure the ship was ready to sail. On Zastra's instructions, she oversaw the removal of the prisoners to the *Caralyx* and took the opportunity to requisition the *Caralyx*'s yacht to replace the one they had lost at the Skurg sand island. Ithgol and Jerenik installed themselves in Burgal's old quarters while Zastra found herself in Dastrin's cabin. As the door closed behind her, she sank into a chair, not even noticing how comfortable the stuffed leather was compared with her old bunk on the foredeck. She was suddenly weary. It seemed an age since they had sighted Justyn's ships and made the decision to mutiny, although less than a quarter of a day had passed. Their desperate gamble had paid off and they had won. She thought of Justyn's parting words. Did she really know what she was about? She was now responsible for all those who had agreed to stand with her. Responsible for their lives and maybe even their deaths. Weariness came upon her like a heavy cloak draped around her shoulders. She was glad that no one came to disturb her. Anyone coming through the door in those moments would have seen right through the illusion that she had worked so hard to create.

Chapter Thirty-four

When all the ships were ready to sail, Lord Justyn invited their captains to supper in the cabin of the *Darkhorse* to discuss tactics. Zastra brought food and wine from Captain Dastrin's personal stores, which Justyn accepted graciously. He proved to be an excellent host, polite and attentive. In contrast, Nerika said barely a word to her. Zastra didn't mind that one bit. She spent most of the evening catching up with Dobery.

'I was afraid I'd never see you again. I felt how angry you were, back at Steepcrest, when you tried to stop me going back to Five-peaks.'

'I'm sorry I attempted to force you, my dear.' Her old friend patted her hand. 'You did what you felt was right and put your family first. I cannot argue that you were wrong. We must all follow our own path and your instincts have always served you well. How in the stars did you end up on one of Thorlberd's ships?'

Zastra told him how she had been forced into the fleet and of her adventures since. In turn he related how he had decided to join Lord Justyn and so got himself work on one of Thorlberd's supply ships, hoping the rebels would attack it.

'It was the easiest capture we ever had.' Justyn chuckled as he speared a large strip of salted vizzal. 'Two ships, so we thought we were in for a battle. Pol induced one captain to order his crew to lay down their weapons and we took them easily. By the time we turned our attention to the other ship, Master Dobery had... what's the word?'

'Persuaded?' suggested Dobery.

'Quite so. Dobery had persuaded the crew to lock the captain away. We took their supplies and let them go.'

'How many are you?' Zastra asked.

'Just what you see, plus two other ships. We also have some friends in Golmeira, but it has become increasingly dangerous for us to go ashore.'

'Only four ships?' Zastra was unable to hide her disappointment.

'We were more, but Thorlberd's fleet has hunted us down without mercy. We have lost many good friends over the years.'

The mood darkened. Justyn ordered the next course to be brought in.

'Where were you based when my uncle took power?' Zastra asked. 'I don't remember a Lord Justyn.'

Polina leaned forward.

'He's not a real Lord,' she said in an exaggerated whisper. 'But don't tell anyone.'

'I don't think it's a secret any more.' Justyn smiled ruefully. 'I was an ordinary soldier in the guard of Seacastle. Our Marl, Krysfera, was a mindweaver and a brave woman. She held out long after the other castles had fallen, hoping someone would come and help us. We were punished for our resistance. Thorlberd sent three migaradons and a whole bunch of mindweavers who overpowered Krysfera, sending her mad, and then forced the guards to open the gates. At that point, we knew it was all over and many of us made for the sea. I'm not proud to say it, but I fought my way aboard the last ship just as it set sail. That ship was the *Darkhorse*. We left Seacastle burning behind us. The *Darkhorse* was so crowded that people began to panic and fight amongst themselves. Captain Fogan saw my uniform and asked me for help. We invented Lord Justyn to try and create order from the chaos. Pol was on board too, saw what we were about and helped reinforce the story in people's minds. Since then, 'Lord Justyn' has become quite famous. We have gained recruits who wouldn't have spared a moment for plain old Justyn, soldier of the guard. Still, it has been tough. We'd never had survived this long without Uden's Teeth.'

'Uden's Teeth?' Zastra queried. 'You mentioned them before, but I've never heard of them. They aren't on any of the charts.'

'That's because no one knew about them. It was only blind luck that we found them. Three of Thorlberd's ships had us trapped against the Western Spur. We fled south towards the storm reaches, but couldn't shake them off and they forced us closer and closer to the Spur until we were deep into the mist, where the spray from the sea merges with the steam from the Smoking Mountains. We could hear the surf pounding on land and we were sure we would run aground. Through a sudden gap in the fog, we spied a channel leading into the spar itself. We had no choice but to enter. We heard our pursuers break up against the rocks behind us. The channel was too narrow to allow us to turn round so we continued on, even as we felt the bottom of the ship scraping against the channel bottom. Later, we realised how lucky we had been. It had been high tide, and only then is the channel deep enough for a ship to pass through.'

'Where did the channel lead?'

'The other side of the Spur and a blue-green sea as calm as a lake. A few days' sail from the channel we came upon a string of uninhabited islands, several with fresh water. The land was suitable for growing crops and filled with native animals, many unknown to us. It has proven a safe haven, too far beyond the borders of Golmeira for even a migaradon to reach. Every now and then we venture back to Golmeira when we need supplies, such as firedust and healing herbs, which Uden's Teeth do not supply.'

'Why the name?' Zastra spooned some honeyed yellow root onto her plate.

Polina gave an embarrassed laugh. 'It's my fault. My grandfather was called Uden. His teeth were crooked and, foolishly, I said that the islands reminded me of his smile. The name stuck.'

The rest of the evening was spent in a further exchange of stories, until all the food was eaten. Zastra had not enjoyed herself as much in a long time. She lingered over her hot chala and was disappointed when at last the party broke up. She signalled for the dingy to collect her, knowing that all that awaited was her lonely cabin.

Chapter Thirty-five

Zastra scanned the empty horizon for the hundredth time.

'Where are these ships? I begin to wonder if Murthen Island even exists.'

'If they're out there, we'll find them,' Mata said in a low tone as she joined Zastra at the prow. 'A piece of advice. Try not to show your doubts to the crew. They like to think their captain knows everything.'

'But that's impossible.'

'You'll be amazed how far bluff and confidence can get you. Trust me, a crew is a simple beast and likes clear directions, not worries and doubts. They are ready to follow you, but you must lead with confidence.'

It hadn't occurred to Zastra that the crew would be listening to every word she said and vowed to be more careful in future. They were interrupted by a cry from the lookout.

'Signal from the *Darkhorse*.' There was a pause, and then another cry. 'Sail to the north.'

'About time.' Zastra strode to the side of the ship and pulled out her telescope.

The *Darkhorse* changed course to pursue the strange vessel. Zastra ordered the *Wind of Golmeira* to follow and together with the *Obala* they converged on a large fishing boat. Justyn called out to the boat to ask if there were any islands nearby.

'Nah,' called back a stout woman who appeared to be in charge. 'They's no islands round here, 'cept the Mongrels. We's from there usselves.'

Zastra knew the Mongrels, a pair of low lying islands about a hundred leagues north of their current position.

'Are you certain?' shouted Justyn. 'Is there nothing to the southeast?'

The crew of the fishing boat looked at each other and whispered nervously.

Ithgol banged his fist on the bulwark. 'Tell us what you know,' he bellowed. 'Or I'll eat you for supper!'

The woman started back in terror and then pointed south by southeast.

'I dunno 'bout no island, but they's a patch of sea yonder where boats disappear, an' ain't never seen n'more. Some say they's an awful monster lives in the clouds that eats boats whole and spits 'em out. Why don't you go see, 'stead of botherin' us poor fisher folk?'

'Sounds like a migaradon,' Zastra remarked. 'Perhaps we are close after all.'

Justyn seemed to agree and signalled the convoy to continue in the direction indicated by the fisherwoman. A day later four sails were sighted, line astern, on a converging course. The convoy displayed Thorlberd's gecko-and-hawk standard. Zastra ordered the same flag to be raised up the main mast of the *Wind of Golmeira*. Mata assembled the secret signal they had found amongst Dastrin's papers and lowered the grating. The subterfuge seemed to work. The convoy reduced sail and allowed them to close. Zastra walked round the deck, giving quiet instructions to her crew as they prepared for battle with as little show as possible. The catapults stayed below decks. They wanted to capture Thorlberd's precious cargo intact, not destroy it, at least until they knew what it was. Her crew crouched behind the bulwarks, armed and ready. Ahead of them the crew of the *Darkhorse* did likewise. They closed to within hailing distance of the convoy and Zastra began to feel a heavy weight pressing down on her mind, trying to control her. She resisted. Dobery leaned over the stern of the *Darkhorse*, cupping his mouth with his hands.

'Mindweavers!' he called. 'They know what we are about.'

A shout came from the one of the two ships in the centre of the convoy. Both were fat trading vessels, designed for carrying cargo rather than speed. *What are they carrying that requires such protection?* The weight on Zastra's mind increased. She sensed that more than one mindweaver was attacking her, but her mental wall held firm. She strode forward. Secrecy was no longer required.

'Prepare to board,' she cried, but one by one, her crew slumped to the ground in an unseeing daze, Ithgol among them. Only Mata and a few others were able to fight the disabling power of the mindweavers. Without sufficient hands to the ropes, the sails slackened and the helmswoman staggered and fell against the wheel, causing the *Wind of Golmeira* to veer sharply to port. The *Darkhorse* forged ahead, on a collision course with the leading cargo ship. Zastra saw Dobery and Polina standing next to each other, fixed in concentration. She guessed they were somehow protecting the crew of the *Darkhorse* from Thorlberd's mindweavers.

Zastra and Mata dragged the inert helmswoman off the wheel and set course towards the rearmost cargo ship. There were precious few of Zastra's crew left to board, but they were committed now. Zastra took up a grapnel. As the bowsprit of the *Wind of Golmeira* ground against the hull of their target, a terrible scream rang out and the weight of the mindweavers' probes was suddenly gone. Zastra ran along the bowsprit and sprang across to the deck of the other ship, landing so hard she stumbled. She drew back in alarm as the planking buckled and popped beneath her feet, almost as if it were alive. *What in stars is going on?* A piece of wood snapped up from the deck and flew past her ear. There was a roar and the crew of the *Wind of Golmeira*, miraculously revived, surged across the narrow gap between the ships to join her. Not a moment too soon. A pack of Kyrgs and Golmeiran sailors charged towards her. Swords and scythals clashed as the groups joined. Zastra parried a blade and struck out, noting that Ithgol had appeared at her side to protect her flank. The deck continued to shiver and break up beneath their feet. A large splinter tore up from the deck and buried itself in the stomach of one of the Kyrgs. He collapsed with a groan. Zastra found it almost impossible to keep her balance as the deck shuddered beneath her feet.

'Zastra...' A desperate plea echoed inside her mind and she knew, somehow, that it was Dobery. Ducking to avoid a swinging scythal, she lunged at a tattooed Guthan. He collapsed to the floor and a gap appeared in the sea of bodies. She could see Dobery gesturing towards her from the other cargo ship, mouthing words that she could not hear. She fought her way towards him just as the hull of the ship she was on ground against Dobery's. The old man reached towards her, his face creased in concentration.

'Help me across.'

Zastra grabbed his hand, supporting him as he slithered awkwardly across the bowsprit.

'We must go below,' he croaked. 'Something is causing this chaos. We must stop it, else we will all perish.'

They made for the amidships hatch which was rattling furiously against a metal padlock.

'Jerenik!' Zastra yelled. His head emerged from between a pair of Kyrginite legs. He got to his feet, colliding with a black cloaked woman just as she fell to the deck screaming, half a plank lodged in her thigh. Dobery laid a hand on the mindweaver's head.

'It is as I feared. There is a strong mind aboard this ship, out of control. This mindweaver tried to tame it and it has broken her.'

Another scream rose up from below. The deck was now peppered with rectangular gaps where planks had burst away from their neighbours. Another fountain of splinters shot upwards, sending them diving out of the way. Zastra grabbed Jerenik and pointed to the padlock.

'Can you open it?'

Jerenik nodded. 'Easy. See it's a basic padlock, I'll use my—'

'Just get on with it.'

'I can't do anything while it's bucking around like that.'

Zastra sat squarely on the hatch and beckoned Dobery to join her. Their combined weight was just enough to suppress the frantic movement. Jerenik got to work and the padlock was soon open. Zastra and Dobery rolled aside and the wooden grating spiralled into the air like a loose sail caught in a squall. Zastra headed below decks, her sword out in front of her. A foul stench clogged her nostrils. Behind her, Dobery clucked in disgust. As her eyes adjusted to the gloom, Zastra gasped in horror. Half of the underdeck was occupied by a huge metal cage, filled with bodies so closely packed they had barely room to move. Some were dead and those that were alive were emaciated and covered in dirt and open wounds. Chains bound them together.

'What is this abomination?' Dobery's face twisted in shock.

'Watch out,' Jerenik yelled from just beneath the hatch. Two black-cloaked figures emerged from the darkness with swords drawn and Zastra's mind was hit with a double blow causing her to stagger backwards.

'I'll handle them,' cried Dobery. Zastra felt the pain lift and she easily fended off the first of the mindweavers, who proved to be unskilled with a blade. She used the hilt of her sword to knock him senseless. The second mindweaver drove towards her. Zastra swayed to one side, tripping her up. Jerenik, following behind, crashed a heavy bucket against the mindweaver's head.

'Let's see what they were protecting.' Zastra stepped deeper into the underdeck. She tripped over the bodies of two more mindweavers, their clothes ripped to shreds, deep cuts covering every inch of their skin. She tried not to think what might have caused such wounds. There was another cage, smaller than the first. Mournful howls were coming from within. Children of various ages pinned themselves back against the bars, trying to get as far as possible from a dismal figure seated in the middle. It was a young girl, on the cusp of becoming a woman. She was a dark-skinned Southlander, her head speckled with bald patches where tufts of hair had been pulled out. Shards of wood swirled in the air around her like shoaling fish. Her wild-eyed stare was fixed on a Golmeiran soldier. The terrified man was creeping towards her, a dagger trembling in his hand. The tornado of wood and splinters stopped circling and launched themselves towards the soldier. He raised his arms protectively across his face and continued towards the girl, even as the splinters ripped his uniform and drew blood. The girl began to scream and the soldier's dagger was whipped out of his hand and driven, blade first, into his chest. The man sank to the ground, dead, and the screaming subsided.

'The girl,' exclaimed Dobery. 'She has the talent of mindmoving more powerful than any I have witnessed. She is out of control with fear. She will surely destroy the ship.'

'Can't you stop her?'

'I don't know how. You've seen what she can do to mindweavers.' Zastra glanced back at the dead mindweavers and their shredded robes. The wild-eyed girl flicked her head towards them, gulped in a lungful of air and began to scream again. All around them, the timbers redoubled their rattling. The ship could surely not survive much more. Some of the other children in the cage were crying, the noise merging with the creaking and cracking of the wood to create a terrible discord.

Zastra approached the open door of the cage. The girl shrank back and the cloud of wooden splinters rose up again to form another protective tornado. The girl's eyes were fixed in terror on Zastra's sword. Seeing this, Zastra crouched down and placed the sword on the ground. Slowly, she removed the dagger she kept in her boot and laid it down alongside the sword.

'I'm unarmed,' she said, keeping her voice calm. 'Don't be afraid. We have come to help you.' The girl shivered, but the scream receded into a whimper and the splinters flew a little less furiously.

'My name is Zastra. What's yours?'

'F-freak. They call me Freak.'

'Come now, what's your real name?'

The girl tugged uncertainly at one of her remaining clumps of hair

'Orika?' she whispered, as if she was uncertain. 'Orika, maybe. I don't remember. I've been called Freak for so long.'

Zastra shuffled to within touching distance of the cloud of flying splinters. There was no way to get through without being cut to pieces.

'Please, Orika, You are going to destroy the ship. Let me help you.'

'They hurt me,' whispered the girl. 'They drowned me in cintara.'

'Orika, I promise I'm not going to hurt you.'

A probe slapped hard against Zastra mental wall, followed by another and then another, in a disordered barrage. It was as if someone was pounding against the door to her mind. As Zastra flinched under the onslaught, Orika's eyes narrowed in suspicion.

'Can't see. You're one of *them*!' Her eyes flicked towards the dead mindweavers.

'No,' pleaded Zastra. 'No, I'm not a mindweaver.'

'Don't... don't believe you.' The girl yanked so hard on a clump of hair that she pulled it out. Her breath became deep and ragged. There was a loud crack and a large fracture appeared in one of the thick timbers that made up the ship's hull.

Zastra knelt down. With a slow exhalation, she closed her eyes and dismantled her mental wall.

'Look again, Orika. You can trust me. I shall hide nothing.'

'Zastra, no!' cried Dobery. 'It's too dangerous.' But Zastra kept her defences lowered. She felt a contact, hesitant at first. Something burrowed through her mind like a living creature, drawn, as if in sympathy, to her saddest memories and thoughts. It was an extremely unpleasant sensation. An image was awakened, clear and terrible, of the event that haunted Zastra most of all. Golmer Castle, the night her parents had been murdered. Silence fell like a thick blanket. Zastra was so busy fighting against the pain of her memories, she didn't realise that the ship's timbers were no longer cracking. The contact with her mind was released.

'They killed my mother too,' wailed Orika. The tornado of splinters fell to the ground and Zastra was able to creep forward and take hold of the girl. Orika buried her head into Zastra's shoulder and sobbed. An ashen face peered through the bars of the larger cage.

'Zastra? Is that you?'

The face, gaunt and dirt-streaked was familiar, but it took Zastra a moment to place it.

'Kylen?'

The Sendoran appeared equally surprised at their reunion.

'We thought you were dead. They told everyone they killed you and the twins when Thorlberd took charge.'

'They lied,' Zastra said shortly. 'What's going on here?'

'They're taking us somewhere called Murthen Island. They've got Zax.'

'What about these children?' Zastra looked at the assorted faces in front of her. 'They don't look like Sendorans.'

One of them, a teenage boy, answered her.

'We are mindweavers,' he said. 'Some of us, anyway. The littluns ain't yet, but they take blood and reckon they can tell if you're going to be a mindweaver when you're older. They make us drink cintara bark to try to make us stronger. Poor Orika had the most.'

Zastra felt the girl shudder in her arms.

'Murthen Island must be where Thorlberd is training the next generation of mindweavers,' Dobery said. 'Using the Sendorans to practice on. I never thought he could be so utterly ruthless. Can someone release these poor folk?'

He gestured towards the large cage and Jerenik set about the locks.

'I'll find out what's going on with the others,' offered Zastra. She left Orika in Dobery's care and emerged onto the deck to find Ithgol and Mata.

'The two warships escaped,' reported Mata nodding towards two sets of sails disappearing to the south. 'We've taken the other transport. It's full of Sendoran prisoners. Most of them are in a bad way. What's going on?'

Zastra explained the situation.

'So, this is the valuable cargo that Dastrin's orders spoke of?' Mata spat out the words. 'It seems there is nothing Thorlberd wouldn't stoop to, to keep himself in power.'

Chapter Thirty-six

Orika had inflicted so much damage on the prison ships that they were sinking fast. Zastra and Justyn divided the Sendorans and the children amongst their own vessels before casting off the doomed transports. The Sendorans were in a terrible state. Many were so thin that their ribcages pushed out against their skin. Their arms and legs were covered in bruises and open sores. Almost half were dead or very nearly so. The horror of being chained to their dead compatriots was etched across the face of every survivor. The *Darkhorse* was so full of the sick and the dying that not a single plank of the deck was visible. Tijan had refused to join Zastra's rebellion and had been left behind on the *Caralyx*, so Zastra called for Yashni to be brought across from the *Wind of Golmeira*. She took charge, calling for anyone with any experience in healing and organising volunteers before beginning to assess the most desperate cases. Justyn, Zastra and Nerika found a small space on the quarterdeck.

'What are we going to do?' asked Nerika. 'The children are deeply traumatised and there are so many Sendorans. We can barely work the ships with all of them lying around the decks.'

There was a commotion at the side of the ship. Kylen hauled herself on board, pushing away hands offered in help. She stumbled across the deck towards them, shrugging off a large Sendoran who was trying to assist her.

'We must attack Murthen Island now.' Her voice was dry and cracked. 'They've got Zax. We must rescue him.' Although she wasn't in as bad a way as most of her compatriots, she still looked in no shape to be standing, let alone fighting.

'Out of the question,' said Justyn. 'Look around you. We have hundreds of wounded and sick to attend to. Not to mention our torn sail and leaking hull. Only the stars know how much damage that poor girl has done.'

Nerika stared at Kylen in open astonishment. 'It would be suicide to attack now, even if we weren't cluttered up with all these Sendorans. We know nothing about the defences of this island. Any attack would be blind foolishness.'

'I'm sorry we're messing up your precious deck. If you're all too cowardly to help, then give me a ship. We'll go ourselves. Zastra, you'll help, won't you?'

Zastra felt for Kylen, but she had to agree with the others.

'I'm sorry, Kylen, but Nerika and Justyn are right. Your people are in no state to fight.'

'Then I'll take a boat and go myself.'

She made for the yacht and began to hack at the ropes holding it in its cradle but the thick cords resisted her weak efforts. The large Sendoran tried to reason with her.

'You too, Hylaz?' She shrugged him off and began attacking the ropes again. Ithgol grabbed her from behind, and paid no heed to her weak struggles as he carried her below. He returned a few moments later empty-handed.

'I've locked her in Justyn's cabin. She has a strong spirit. It would be a shame for her to die needlessly.'

'You did right, Ithgol,' said Justyn. 'I believe she would have tried to swim to Murthen Island if you had not stopped her.'

'Aye, she would at that,' agreed Hylaz. 'Although I don't envy you, Kyrg, when you let her out.'

'Land! On our southern beam,' came the lookout's cry.

An island of yellow sandstone rose out of the sea, topped with a fortress made of the same colour stone. They would have noticed it much earlier but for the distraction of dealing with Kylen and the rescued prisoners.

'That must be Murthen Island,' Zastra remarked. The lookout shouted again.

'There's something in the air, heading our way,' she cried. 'Stars save us, it's a migaradon!'

'Wonderful,' Nerika remarked sarcastically. 'We're all doomed. And for what? A ship full of idiot Sendorans who only want to kill themselves.' She prodded Zastra. 'Nice work, Lady Zastra.'

Justyn shaded his eyes to look at the sky.

'Laying blame won't help us. We must try and outrun it. Migaradons dare not fly beyond sight of land. Return to your ships and make as much sail as you can. If we spread out, some of us may survive. Let's rendezvous a hundred leagues due south of the Pyramid Isle. Go! And good luck.'

Zastra and Ithgol jumped in the yacht and were quickly returned to the *Wind of Golmeira*. Even as the little boat was being hoisted aboard, Mata had made sail and the ship began to head west. The *Obala* was also underway and gathering speed in the opposite direction. The *Darkhorse*, however, was struggling. They were trying to raise a new sail and their prow was still facing towards the migaradon. The ominous speck in the sky was larger now, clear to all. A gust of wind carried its metallic shriek through the air.

'They'll never make it,' Mata cried, as the *Wind of Golmeira* began to pick up speed. 'They have most of the sick Sendorans on board. Yashni is with them too.'

'And Dobery and Kylen,' muttered Zastra, more to herself than to Mata. She gauged the distance between the *Darkhorse* and the rapidly closing migaradon. Mata was right, they wouldn't make it.

'We are the fastest ship, are we not?'

'I should say so.'

'Do you think we could outrun a migaradon?'

Mata chewed her lower lip.

'I wouldn't like to bet on it.'

'But we'd have a chance? Unlike the *Darkhorse*.'

'What are you thinking, mountain girl... I mean, captain?' Zastra had not realised that Jerenik and Ithgol had joined them by the helm. Jerenik smirked. 'Another of your imaginative plans that make themselves up as they go along?'

'I don't believe in leaving comrades behind.' Zastra glanced towards Ithgol who grunted in agreement. 'Can we drop speed just a little, so the migaradon thinks we're struggling?'

'Easy enough,' said Mata. 'But the *Darkhorse* is still the easier target. I doubt we can tempt them.'

'Leave that to me,' said Zastra. 'Call the crew.'

Ithgol and Jerenik rounded up the hands. Zastra leapt up onto the lid of the punishment barrel and scanned the assembled crowd. Many were friends from when she had been a crewmember herself. There were some Sendorans too, barely able to stand but ready to help if they could. She cleared her throat.

'The *Darkhorse* needs our assistance. They cannot outrun the migaradon. I propose we entice the beast to chase us instead. There is no doubt we have the finest ship and crew in Golmeira. If we can't outrun it, no one can. However, this plan will put us all in the way of danger. What do you say? Shall we help our friends?'

The crew roared their agreement.

'I am honoured to serve with you,' cried Zastra. 'Today, we show Thorlberd the true meaning of courage.'

She gave Mata the signal and the sails were slackened off, spilling some of the wind. Their pace slowed noticeably. A subtle touch of the rudder lowered their speed yet further.

'Raise the flag,' commanded Zastra. Her father's colours were run up the main mast and streamed out in the stiff breeze. Zastra took a speaking trumpet and climbed up the rear mast until she was standing on the thin perch of wood that sat above the sail. The migaradon had almost reached the *Darkhorse* and its rider directed the beast downward. The *Darkhorse*, barely moving, was an open target.

Zastra filled her lungs and yelled as loud as she could, the trumpet magnifying her voice.

'Hey... Hey!'

The beast swivelled its flat head and jerked towards her. Its helmeted rider tugged hard on the chains that served as reins to pull it back towards the *Darkhorse*. Zastra waved her sword in the air, suddenly feeling rather foolish.

'I've a message for my uncle,' she yelled.

The head of the rider snapped round and a sharp probe dug into her mind. Zastra let the mindweaver see an image of Golmer Castle and another of herself with her mother and father, before she snapped her mental wall shut. The migaradon wheeled round ponderously and with a strong beat of its monstrous wings, it headed directly for the *Wind of Golmeira*.

That's done it. Zastra signalled down to Mata, who raised her hand in acknowledgement. The crew rushed to the lines. Zastra felt the ship vibrate as the sails were pulled taut and they sprang forward like a bolt released from its bow. Yet the migaradon was closing fast.

Zastra stood tall at the tip of the mast. 'That's right!' she yelled. 'I'm Leodra's daughter. Tell Thorlberd he will have to answer to me for his crimes.'

Zastra felt the mindweaver try again to delve into her thoughts, but she had closed off her mind and was able to resist the attack. She readied her crossbow, silently urging Mata to make the ship go faster. The *Wind of Golmeira* began to heel over, the masts leaning out over the sea. Beneath Zastra's feet was only air and the churning, white tipped water far below. Their prow threw up a huge bow wave as they cut through the choppy surface and she could see Mata and Ithgol battling with the wheel. The migaradon was straining to keep up, but still it closed, an inch at a time. Murthen Island was almost swallowed by the horizon. Behind them, the *Darkhorse* had at last raised a new rear sail and was making progress in a northerly direction.

The migaradon was concerned only with Zastra. As it approached, Zastra raised her bow and aimed for its head. The bolt hit it between the eyes, bouncing off without making a mark. The beast opened its wide mouth and shrieked in derision. Zastra took a moment, raised the bow again and aimed at the rider. Since the migaradon was higher in the sky than her, most of the rider was shielded by the body of the beast. Zastra's bolt shaved the shoulder of the migaradon and the rider ducked. The bolt missed, but in ducking, the rider jerked on the chains pulling the beast up. The migaradon flapped round in an uneven circle before resuming the chase. Zastra had gained them a few moments, nothing more. Soon the migaradon was directly above her again. It dived down. Zastra waited until the last possible minute before she released her last bolt. It struck the sole of the rider's right boot, just visible in its stirrup. Both the rider and migaradon let out a cry of surprised pain. The beast bucked higher into the air with a messy flapping of its great wings. Zastra pulled another three bolts from her jacket and reloaded the crossbow, trying to keep her hands steady.

'Can't you go any faster?' she shouted towards the deck.

'We've giving it everything!' Mata cried.

'I need more.'

She saw Mata take a handful of the crew below decks. There was no time to ponder why Mata had deserted her post. The migaradon was back under the rider's control and its eyes were fixed angrily on Zastra. She was out of ideas. She released three bolts towards the rider but this time the migaradon was ready. As each bolt sprung towards its target, the beast rolled slightly, just enough to protect the rider with its impervious body. The bolts bounced off harmlessly and fell to the sea below. The migaradon was now so close that Zastra could feel its hot, wet breath on her face. A colossal, double-taloned claw swiped towards her, whipping past her head as she ducked out of its reach. The beast squealed with frustrated rage. It swung for her again, lower this time and its claw brushed Zastra's chest as she swayed backwards so hard that she overbalanced. Only the crook of her knees catching on the cross trees preventing her plummeting to the deck below. Suspended upside down, her crossbow flew from her grip and into the sea below. She grabbed the rigging by her head and yanked her legs from the cross trees, swinging her body downwards just as the migaradon snapped the tip of the mast clean off, taking the perch that Zastra had been hanging from with it. Zastra was left dangling from the rigging, swaying helplessly above the waves. Somehow, the ship began right itself and in the process gained more speed. The migaradon strained to keep pace. Zastra whispered a silent word of thanks to Mata and the crew, as she and the migaradon stared at each other. It flew not five paces behind her, but was unable to catch up.

We will hunt you down. The voice echoed in her head, the parting cry of the rider as, with a cry of frustration, the beast wheeled away and headed back towards the point where Murthen Island had just disappeared beyond the horizon. Zastra managed to hook her feet onto the rigging and clamber down, relieved to feel the solid deck beneath her feet. Mata had reappeared.

'I don't know how you did it,' Zastra said, in an undertone, 'but that last burst of speed was what saved us.'

'An old sailing trick. Lose some weight, rearrange the distribution of what's left.'

'Lose some weight?'

'I made the decision that you didn't really need all that nice furniture of Dastrin's. And most of the food and water, I'm afraid.'

'So, having got the crew to risk their lives, I have to tell them the reward for their courage is half rations?'

Mata shrugged.

'Welcome to life as a ship's captain.'

Chapter Thirty-seven

Zastra took the *Wind of Golmeira* towards the agreed rendezvous point south of the Pyramid Isle. They were first to arrive, but within a day, the *Obala* and the *Darkhorse* joined them. Justyn waved from the stern of the *Darkhorse*.

'Glad you made it. We were worried you might have made a tasty snack for that migaradon.'

'Not a chance,' returned Zastra. 'Nice of you slowpokes to finally join us.'

Justyn responded with a good natured salute, then sent Polina across to guide them through the Western Spur. Zastra and Mata paid close attention as Polina pointed out the particular arrangement of three Smoking Giants that served to identify the entrance to the hidden channel. The dense mist that hung over the coastline of the Western Spur meant that once they had used the landmarks to set course, they had to steer through the fog with blind trust that the channel would appear in front of them. They waited until high tide before they followed the *Darkhorse* through. Polina pointed out the locations of hidden rocks and sandbanks, helping them chart a safe course. Only once did they scrape the bottom of the ship, such was Mata's skill as a ship-handler. Still, it was a tense journey, and it seemed an age before they reached the other side. It was worth the wait. The mist and rough seas on the Golmeiran side were replaced by a calm expanse of ocean, stretching out to a distant horizon.

'We've named it the Serene Sea,' said Polina, with a hint of pride.

'I can see why,' Mata remarked. 'It's magnificent.'

The mood of Zastra's crew, brought low by their short rations, lifted as they followed the *Darkhorse* across the calm waters. Two days of perfect sailing brought them to a group of islands, green and fertile, rising out of the sea in a loose semi-circle. They did indeed have some resemblance to a human jaw-line, albeit one with a few teeth damaged and missing. They made anchor in a natural harbour belonging to the largest of the islands. A narrow wooden jetty stuck out from the shore, supported by hundreds of upright stilts. Sturdy wooden huts spread out along a gently curving beach. At the far end of the settlement, a large watermill sat astride a small cataract as it flowed into the bay. On either side of the mill, fields stepped up the hillside, some empty, some full of ripening harvest.

'We named the town Port Krysfera,' said Polina. 'In honour of the Marl of Seacastle.'

Mata whistled in appreciation.

'Impressive.'

Three blunt-ended canoes, hollowed out from large tree trunks, headed out from the shore. They were full of men and women waving in greeting and inviting them to board. Zastra looked down at them distrustfully.

'Are they safe?'

'By and large, as long as you sit very still,' said Polina.

'I'll wait for the yacht,' remarked Ithgol.

'Me too,' said Mata. 'But you should go, Zastra. You don't want to offend these people the first time you meet them.'

Zastra followed Polina's lead, stepping gingerly into the waiting canoe. Jerenik decided to join them, their extra weight causing the canoe to sink lower in the water. Zastra sat bolt upright, gripping the sides of the flimsy craft as she was paddled towards the jetty. It would be highly embarrassing to be tipped up and have to swim to shore – not the way to make a good impression. More people lined the shore, shouting out a welcome. Justyn and Nerika had made it ahead of her and Justyn stepped forward to help Zastra disembark.

'Lord Justyn. Oh, Lord Justyn!' A short man with curly hair and fat cheeks skipped down to meet them. 'Thank the stars you are alive! We have so missed you all.'

'We've a lot to tell you, Pitwyn.' Justyn slapped the man's back heartily. 'How was the harvest?'

'Mighty fine, my Lord.' Pitwyn had a strange little moustache that didn't quite meet the top of his upper lip. The thin line of hair trembled with its owner's excitement. 'The best yet. Marvellous yellow root. And we've discovered a new species of bird that tastes absolutely divine boiled in... I've called it the moccasin bird. The wild birds here don't seem to know how to run away. I've been experimenting with recipes, and I think you'll be... Oh, and you'll never guess, we've finished the bathhouse, it's so... You simply must come and look.' His words tumbled out so fast, it was almost impossible to keep up.

'It is good that the harvest went well.' Justyn gestured towards the ships that filled the bay. 'We have many guests.'

Canoes full of Sendorans were making for the shore. Pitwyn gave a small shriek of horror.

'Sendorans?' he exclaimed. His thin moustache twitched as if he were about to sneeze.

'Yes,' Justyn confirmed. 'And they will be made welcome.'

'Of course, Lord Justyn.' Pitwyn bowed low. 'I just hope they won't lower the tone. Sendorans can be such...'

Jerenik snorted.

'If he thinks Sendorans lower the tone, I can't wait until he meets our friend Ithgol.'

Pitwyn turned his attention towards them. His naked upper lip pursed in disapproval. Zastra realised that she must look a state dressed as she was in her crewmember's attire. Her grey vest and half trousers were salt-stained and faded with wear.

The yacht moored to the jetty and Ithgol joined them. Zastra thought Pitwyn might faint with horror but the curly-haired man recovered his composure when Mata arrived in her lieutenant's uniform.

'Are you going to introduce me to your new captain, Lord Justyn?' he asked, smiling and bowing at Mata.

'I'm no captain,' Mata protested.

Justyn and Nerika shared a complicit grin. Zastra wondered what was so funny as Justyn gestured towards her.

'Zastra, this is Pitwyn, who organises things for us here at Uden's Teeth. A most excellent administrator, responsible for much of what we have built. Pitwyn was once, um, what was it again, Pitwyn?'

'Deputy Chief of Household to the Lady Grinsilla, half cousin to Marl Julan herself,' Pitwyn recited, his back straightening noticeably. 'Only four steps away from royalty and a Lady down to her toenails.'

'Pitwyn, I have the great pleasure of introducing Zastra, daughter of Leodra, rightful heir to the throne of Golmeira.'

Pitwyn staggered back as if a full quarry of crossbow bolts had landed in his ample chest. His mouth sagged into a giant 'O' shape. To Zastra's intense embarrassment, he knelt down before her with a gracious movement and bowed his head so low his forehead almost touched the ground. Jerenik snorted with laughter.

'Oh, to think we have... Royalty. I've always dreamed... But what an honour! If only things weren't in such a terrible state. I've tried, but I'm afraid there's so little... How deeply mortifying. My dear Lady Zastra...'

'It all looks wonderful.' Zastra felt her face flush as she hastily helped Pitwyn to his feet. 'There's nothing to be ashamed of. You have built all this from nothing?'

'Indeed, my Lady. You are so gracious. But it is all rather pastoral... We do now have a bathhouse at least. I'd be honoured to show...You must be in need of a bath. What I mean to say is... Not that you smell anything less than... Oh, my Lady, I'm too unworthy...'

'A bath sounds wonderful.' Zastra tried to ignore Jerenik's silent convulsions. 'But I must see to our guests first and then to my ship and crew. Have you a healer?'

Pitwyn nodded eagerly. 'Oh, yes, my Lady Zastra. We have almost everything you could want. Except for clothing. It is so difficult. We are trying with a loom... Only a little thing as yet, but... Won't you come and see? A royal seal of approval would be so...'

Justyn stepped in to rescue her.

'Zastra is right,' he said firmly. 'We must see to the children and the Sendorans. But tomorrow a celebration is in order, wouldn't you agree?'

'Oh, yes indeed!' Pitwyn's face flushed with joy. 'A feast in honour of the Lady Zastra, what a wonderful... Although you must be gentle with us. It will be but poor fare compared to what you are used to, I'm sure.'

'For the last few years I've eaten nothing but porridge and salted goat, so I shall be glad of anything Uden's Teeth has to offer.' Zastra began to feel distinctly uncomfortable at being the focus of such attention.

'Oh! So gracious. Just like Lady Grinsilla. Royalty always knows how to behave.'

'When he really gets to know you, he's going to be mightily disappointed,' remarked Jerenik.

Chapter Thirty-eight

All the Sendorans were offloaded and tended to. The rescued children, although not starving like the Sendorans, also needed care. The fifteen year-old boy who had responded to Zastra's questions on the transport was among the eldest and one of the few able to talk about his experiences. His name was Waylin. He told how Golmeiran soldiers had come to his village.

'They rounded up all the children and cut our hands with knives.' He opened his palm to display a small scar near his thumb. 'They took some of my blood and put it in a little bottle. Something got them excited and and they took me to some castle. I didn't have a choice. They put me with the others and them black ravens made us drink that horrible brown stuff. Cintara bark. I didn't like it so I spat it out when they weren't looking. I reckons I done the right thing, because after a few days the other littluns were crying out for it like they would die if they didn't have any.'

Waylin shuddered. 'Then they brought Orika. She refused to take it at first, like me, but they reckoned she was special and they forced it down her throat. They got more than they bargained for.'

A bag filled with cintara bark had been recovered from one of the transports. Port Krysfera's healer, a stout, practical woman called Sinisa suggested that the children be given small doses, decreasing daily to try and wean them from their dependence. Dobery agreed that that was the best plan and so it was decided.

The settlers of Uden's Teeth lived in the small wooden huts that lined the beach either side of the jetty. Most of the island was covered in forest, so wood was plentiful. In addition, the settlers had recently finished the construction of two stone buildings, a bath-house and a feasting hall. The hall was a large rectangular building with a sloping roof of oiled wooden tiles. The day after they arrived, Pitwyn insisted on giving Justyn and Zastra a personal tour.

'We finished it last Moonscrescent, but I insisted we wait for you to return before we used it for the first… I knew you could not be long in… After all, you can't have a proper hall without a Lord.'

'Has anyone told him that you're not a real Lord?' Zastra asked in a low voice.

'No one has dared,' returned Justyn. 'But now you're here, I don't think I need worry.'

Pitwyn insisted they make use of the bath-house facilities. For that at least, Zastra was grateful. It had been years since she'd had a proper bath. She submerged herself in the steaming water, washing the salt from her hair and luxuriating in the warmth. Pitwyn had constructed ingenious devices for heating and piping the water, allowing Zastra to keep topping up her bath until an impatient Jerenik poked his head round the curtain to her chamber and asked if she was planning to stay there the whole day. Zastra jumped out, mortified that in her delight she had forgotten that there were only ten baths and hundreds of people waiting.

That evening, as promised, Pitwyn delivered a feast. Two lines of tables stretched the full length of the hall, with benches either side. A large fire at each end served for both cooking and warmth. Although the hall was large, not everyone could fit in at the same time and so the feast was to be taken in three sittings. There was plenty of food and drink for everyone. Zastra's crew, following their enforced period of rationing, ate with as much gusto as the starved Sendorans. The island supplied a variety of interesting fruits, and the roasted forest fowl, its meat noticeably darker than those from Golmeira, was particularly tasty. The settlers had brought with them seeds for yellow-root and onions as well as other Golmeiran vegetables. Most had grown well in the fertile soil.

'Lady Zastra, what say you to our little hall?' asked Pitwyn, who had somehow arranged to be seated next to her. 'Do you find it cosy? I invented a special mixture of bunion wax and sand to fill the cracks and keep out the wind.'

'Bunion wax?' spluttered Jerenik, his mouth full of mashed yellow-root and gravy.

'Pitwyn likes to name all the new plants and animals we find here,' Justyn explained. 'His mother and father were both shoemakers, so many of the names appear to be related to feet.'

'My father was shoemaker to Lady Grinsilla herself, such an... It was because she was so pleased with his shoes that she agreed to take me into her service. A mere serving boy to start with, but then... well, one doesn't wish to boast... The bunion tree is well named, though I say so myself. The wax oozes out of large bumps as if it were...'

'Oy!' Jerenik protested. 'You're putting me off my food.'

'Perhaps he is trying to ensure there is some left for the next sitting,' remarked Zastra, as Jerenik piled more food onto his plate.

'Oh, my Lady Zastra, how witty!' Pitwyn enthused, in a high falsetto. Zastra leaned towards Justyn.

'Do you think we could pretend I was just a mountain girl again?' she pleaded.

'I'm afraid not. I can't tell you how relieved I am that he's found someone more important than me. You know, there were many times I wanted to tell him I wasn't actually a Lord, just to shut him up, but Nerika wouldn't let me.'

Zastra forced herself to maintain a polite smile as Pitwyn continued to make her the focus of his attention. His only saving grace was that he answered most of his questions himself, so she didn't often have to think of a response.

'What clothes do they wear at Golmer Castle these days? Oh, but of course you won't... What I mean is, what *did* they wear? Grand Marl Leodra was a fine figure of a man I believe? Such a... Well, yes indeed, and a large shoe I heard, which is always a good sign, don't you agree? My father always liked a good solid boot. Although a delicate, fine slipper was also a delight to him, the dear old thing.'

Pitwyn began to list all the shoes his father had ever made until Zastra began to wonder if the man had supplied shoes to everyone in Golmeira. She nodded politely and offered up an occasional murmur where some response seemed to be required, while trying to enjoy the food. That, at least, was delicious.

When they had eaten their fill, the first sitting went outside, where hot chala was being served from a large cauldron. The next round of hungry people pushed their way to the tables. The cool night air was pleasant after the heat of the hall. A group of Sendorans were sitting on the ground in a circle, eating out of bowls. A solitary figure paced around the group. Zastra recognised Kylen. With a sigh, she decided to see if she could make peace. She had not spoken to Kylen since she had refused to support an attack on Murthen Island. Kylen was carrying a half-eaten bowl of stew.

'Enjoying the food?' Zastra began, hoping that topic at least would be non-controversial.

Kylen rounded on her.

'It's hard to enjoy food knowing my people are prisoners on Murthen Island. You Golmeirans have no problem feasting and laughing, while others suffer.'

'You can't blame them for being glad to be alive, given what we've been through.'

'What is the use of living, if all we do is sit around? Your Lord Justyn refuses my pleas for a ship.'

'He is right to do so. You and your people are in no state to launch an attack. Have you considered what you are asking of them? How would you even get past the migaradon?'

'We'd think of something, when the time came.'

'That doesn't sound like a great plan to me.'

Kylen flung her bowl away and Zastra was forced to skip aside to avoid being hit in the shins.

'Word has it that you've been hiding out in some cosy mountain village, while your uncle has been enslaving my people.'

Zastra was stung by the words, as well as the contempt with which they were spoken.

'I wouldn't call our life cosy. I hadn't much choice. I had Fin to protect.'

'And I have Zax. Yet you'd rather be fawned over by that nitwit Pitwyn that do something about it.'

'That's not fair.'

'Life isn't fair, particularly for a Sendoran. Or hadn't you noticed?'

Kylen stormed off into the darkness, leaving Zastra feeling foolish and angry. She understood Kylen's pain, but the Sendoran was being unreasonable. Couldn't she see they needed a plan? That she owed her people more than sending them blindly into battle, especially with a migaradon to face. Zastra went to get in line for a cup of chala. Nerika was standing with Justyn.

'Your Sendoran friend didn't seem happy to see you,' she remarked.

'We were friends once. Now I'm not so sure.'

'I hope you persuaded her to drop this mad idea of attacking Murthen Island?'

'You saw how they were treating their prisoners. Those poor children too. Can we really stand by and do nothing?' Zastra nodded her thanks as she was passed a cup of steaming chala.

'Any attack would be risky,' said Justyn. 'We barely escaped this time.'

'It would be impossible,' snapped Nerika. 'I asked Polina to interrogate one of the Golmeiran captains. The island is crawling with soldiers and mindweavers. And that's before we consider the small matter of the indestructible migaradon.'

'There is one among us who has defeated a migaradon, even though she was a child.' Dobery appeared from nowhere, puffing on a pipe of tobacco. All heads swivelled towards Zastra.

'That was blind luck,' she protested.

'Obviously,' snorted Nerika.

Zastra's scar itched uncomfortably as she told them about the cintara-addicted Brutila, a powerful mindweaver who had attacked her from the back of a migaradon. Something Brutila had seen in Zastra's mind had caused the mindweaver to lose control of the beast and crash it into the side of a mountain.

'So I didn't really defeat the migaradon,' Zastra finished with a sigh. 'I don't see how it helps us.'

'Perhaps it does,' Justyn said thoughtfully. 'It tells us that the rider is more vulnerable than the beast.'

'Hmm, maybe you're right. The Murthen Island migaradon was unstoppable, but when I hit the rider in the foot it seemed to hurt them both. Dobery, couldn't you use mindweaving to take out the rider?'

Dobery shook his head.

'We've tried, but when the rider's awareness is merged with the beast it is impossible to penetrate the combined mind.'

'Then I don't see what we can do,' concluded Justyn. 'Without a way to defeat the migaradon, we haven't a chance.'

Chapter Thirty-nine

The second sitting spilled out of the hall and headed for the cauldron of chala. Jerenik and Ithgol came out with them. They both belched loudly.

'Nice,' remarked Zastra. 'Surely you've not been eating all this time?'

Jerenik rubbed his stomach

'I'm going back in a bit. There's seven different types of pudding and I've only tried three.'

'I hope you've left something for everyone else.'

'Hey, it wasn't just me. Ithgol here ate a whole giant bootstrap bird, or whatever it's called. It was supposed to be shared among six.'

Ithgol's attempt at a grunt sounded suspiciously like another burp.

'Besides, I'm sure Pitwyn has it covered. Very efficient fellow, Pitwyn. Big fan of yours, though. He was looking for you. Something about Lady Anara's wardrobe.'

Zastra groaned. 'That's it. I'm returning to the ship. If I have to listen to any more of Pitwyn's fashion-based interrogation, I shall go mad. In any case, we should relieve Mata and the rest of her watch so that they can come and have some food.'

'What about my puddings?' protested Jerenik.

'You've had quite enough. I order you back to the ship.'

Jerenik saluted her with exaggerated smartness. 'Aye, Captain.'

'Remember, now that I am your captain I can make you clean out the head if you get too cocky.'

That wiped the smirk from Jerenik's face.

The yacht touched against the side of the *Wind of Golmeira*. Zastra left Ithgol and Jerenik to haul it aboard while she headed for the lower underdeck. Yashni greeted her with a tired smile.

'Hey, Layna. Oh, sorry... Zastra. I still can't quite believe that you're a Grand Marl's daughter.'

'Don't you start. I've had enough from Pitwyn. How are the patients?'

'The Sendorans are recovering well. They are a strong people. They'd rather split their stitches than lay in bed a moment longer than they have to. Most have gone to the feast. Only those that were really poorly are still here. The littluns are suffering, poor dears. I've given them some of the cintara, like Sinisa suggested, but they always beg for more. It's so distressing.'

'Is there anything more we can do?'

'I've found that a sleeping draught made from lyrabalm helps calm them, but my supplies of that are running low. We could do with getting hold of some more.'

'And Orika?'

'She suffers more than most. She has refused the cintara. You can feel the timbers shivering even now.'

Zastra placed a hand on the hull. The timbers were vibrating in an unnatural way. Yashni nodded her head towards the far corner of the room.

'She'll be glad to see you.'

Orika lay, moaning and sweating. Zastra laid a gentle hand on her shoulder.

'Orika. It's me, Zastra. I've brought you some food from the feast. Much nicer than porridge and halsa paste.'

'N-not hungry.' Orika's teeth were chattering.

'Try some of this. I think it's called red-slipper fruit. It's nice. Not too sweet.'

Orika eased herself up, pulling her blanket tight around her shoulders. She took a large piece of the red fruit and sucked noisily.

'Good?'

'Good.' Orika licked her lips. Zastra sat down beside her.

'How are the dreams? I see the ship is still in one piece, for which we are all grateful.'

'S-sorry. I don't mean it. Please, I don't want to leave. Don't make me leave.'

Orika stiffened in a sudden panic and the ship began to vibrate more noticeably. The wooden bowl with its contents of red-slipper fruit jumped into the air. Zastra grabbed it with both hands. It needed all her strength to stop it flying away.

'Don't worry. I'm the captain, remember. I won't make you leave.'

The creaking of the timbers subsided.

'My head hurts.' Orika grimaced and Zastra looked around for Yashni. Maybe she could give Orika some of the lyrabalm. Orika gripped hold of Zastra's wrist, still shivering.

'Please don't go. I'm cold.'

Zastra pulled the girl towards her and draped the blanket round them both. Orika stopped trembling and fell asleep against her chest. While the girl slept, Zastra couldn't take her eyes off the bowl of fruit. It had given her the beginnings of an idea.

Chapter Forty

The next morning, Zastra eased herself away from the sleeping Orika and took the yacht single-handed in a circle around the bay. It felt good to handle the little craft, sensitive to every nuance of the wind and she lost herself in the pleasure of sailing. Her enjoyment was interrupted by a cry of excitement and she realised she had drifted close to Port Krysfera.

'Oh, Zastra. Oh, daughter of Leodra. There you are!' Pitwyn was scuttling down to the jetty to meet her. She tried to pretend she hadn't seen him, but he cooed even louder and she was forced to return his wave. He was carrying a large bundle under one arm.

'I've had three pairs of shoes made in your honour from the last of my Far Island cloth. I do hope... Won't you try them?'

The last thing Zastra wanted was to spend the day trying on shoes, but she could see no way to avoid Pitwyn's unwanted attentions.

As she slowly brought the boat up against the dock, a fair-haired figure dashed past Pitwyn and came to a standstill, hand on hips, staring at her. It was Kylen.

'About time you turned up. I was beginning to think you'd forgotten our appointment.'

'Our what?' Zastra was confused. She did not remember arranging any kind of meeting with Kylen. The last she recalled, Kylen had been throwing bowls of food at her. Kylen made a tiny jerk of her head towards Pitwyn, who had stopped halfway down the jetty to catch his breath. Zastra eyes widened in understanding.

'Of course, our appointment. So sorry I'm late.'

She skipped out of the yacht. With a couple of quick turns of a rope, she secured it to the jetty.

'Sorry, Pitwyn,' she said, as she and Kylen strode past the forlorn figure. 'It will have to wait. I've a previous engagement.'

Kylen led them round the bay until they were well out of Pitwyn's earshot.

'He's been waiting for you all morning. Look, the poor fellow doesn't know what to do with himself.' The curly-haired figure had placed his bundle down, but hadn't moved from the middle of the jetty. He gazed after them forlornly.

'Where are we going?'

'Does it matter?'

'I guess not,' Zastra admitted. 'Thanks for the rescue.'

Kylen shrugged.

'I owed you one.' She strode on purposefully until they had left Port Krysfera far behind. Zastra struggled to keep up with her until the Sendoran suddenly pulled up short.

'Look. I'm sorry I was so rude last night. I know you are no coward. It's just I'm so worried about Zax.'

Kylen's lip wobbled, and suddenly her shoulders heaved and tears ran down her face. Zastra pulled her into a hug, shocked by the Sendoran's sudden vulnerability.

'It's all my fault,' Kylen sobbed into Zastra's neck. 'I wanted him to be a good Sendoran soldier. I should have kept him safe.'

Feeling rather awkward, Zastra patted her on the back.

'You take too much blame. No one could have predicted what happened.'

Zastra let Kylen cry herself out. At last the Sendoran regained her composure, and pulled away, looking a little self-conscious. Zastra cleared her throat.

'I do understand. The others will too. I promise you, we will do everything we can to get Zax back.'

Kylen chewed her lower lip.

'You said you had been looking after Fin. I'm glad to hear he survived. What about Kastara?'

Zastra hesitated. She couldn't trust anyone with the truth that Kastara was alive. The fewer people who knew, the safer her sister would be.

'Dead,' she said shortly. She had practised the lie in her mind but this was the first time she had spoken the words. A strange shiver ran down her spine.

'I'm sorry. Truly. When did you last see Fin?'

'It seems like forever. More than two years. He's probably forgotten all about me.'

'He may be young, but he will not forget his big sister.'

They clambered over seaweed encrusted rocks until they reached a small beach. A large piece of driftwood had been swept up by the waves. Zastra picked it up and turned it over in her hands.

'I had an idea last night which I think you might like.'

'Why?'

'It's pretty crazy and has very little chance of success.'

Zastra began to outline her plan.

'You're right,' said Kylen, when she had finished. 'I do like it.'

'I thought you were going to agree it was crazy.'

'That too. Come on, let's see what the others say.'

The idea was quite simple in theory. They would take a wooden hatch, sturdy enough to carry Zastra's weight and have Orika use her mindmoving talent to make it fly. Zastra would then be able to attack the migaradon at its own height and get a clear shot at the rider. Justyn advised against it, saying it was too dangerous. Dobery, although concerned about the risk, thought it was worth trying and Nerika remarked that if Zastra wanted to kill herself, it was fine by her. Kylen was impatient to begin at once, but Zastra insisted they allow Orika a few more days to recover before she broached the subject. When she did so, Orika put her hands to her head.

'A migaradon?' she wailed. 'N-No. I couldn't. I can't do it.'

It was not a good start.

'You don't have to fight it yourself,' explained Zastra. 'You just need to get me close.'

'Too dangerous. Too dangerous for you, Zastra,' Orika began tugging anxiously at her hair, which had only just begun to grow back. The ship's timbers began to quiver. Zastra clutched the girl's hands until she calmed down and the ship ceased its trembling.

'Orika, I know I ask a lot of you. But we must defeat the migaradon and I would be in greater danger if I have to face it without your help. Let's at least try, shall we?'

Eventually, Orika was persuaded to give the plan a try. They began with the wooden bowl, which Orika moved up and down in the air with increasing confidence. When she had mastered that, they tried it with a spare hatch cover. Launching the wooden square into the air proved easy but keeping it flat was much more difficult. The hatch kept tipping over and spinning uncontrollably on its axis. When it had clattered onto the deck of the *Wind of Golmeira* for the hundredth time, Kylen loomed up behind Zastra.

'This is useless. I'm going to take one of the ships, with or without Justyn's permission. If we attack Murthen Island under cover of darkness we may have a chance.'

'The darkness wouldn't protect you. They would know you were coming. The place is full of mindweavers, remember. We need to give my plan a chance to work.'

Even as she spoke, the wobbling hatch sliced through the air towards their heads, sending them diving for cover.

'I didn't survive this long to be decapitated by a lump of wood,' Kylen muttered. She called for a canoe to take her ashore. Her place by Zastra's side was taken by Dobery.

'Are you sure about this, my dear?'

'Not you too? Everyone is criticising, but I notice no one else has thought of a better plan. Or any other plan, in fact.'

'I mean, should you be the one to take on the migaradon? If anything happened to you, the Sendorans and Justyn's group will soon fall out. You are the only one that Kylen trusts. This is a risky undertaking. Perhaps you should get someone else to do it. Yerdan seems like a fine fellow with a crossbow.'

'It was my idea,' Zastra insisted. 'I need to do this myself. Yerdan's not bad, but I'm a better shot. You see how Nerika and the others look at me. Even Kylen has doubts. This is my chance to convince everyone I'm not just the spoilt daughter of a Grand Marl.'

'How will getting yourself killed achieve that?'

'Your confidence is truly inspiring,' Zastra said dryly.

'You don't have to prove anything to me. I suppose I'm an old man and I like to worry. Just promise me you'll be careful.'

Zastra picked up the hatch and placed it flat on the deck. She stepped onto it and nodded towards Orika.

'Let's give it a try.'

Her stomach plunged as the wooden square lurched into the air. Flailing her arms, she managed to keep upright as the hatch flew up from the deck and span out over the sea. Just as she began to feel she was balanced, the hatch tipped over and dumped her unceremoniously into the water. Spluttering she rose to find she had landed close to Port Krysfera. As she waded ashore, dripping wet, she noticed Nerika and some of the settlers had gathered to watch and were having a good laugh at her expense. She called for a canoe to take her back to the *Wind of Golmeira*. After five more attempts and five more cold baths in the sea, Zastra was well and truly fed up. She gathered Orika and Dobery into a small huddle.

'I'm s-sorry,' Orika said dejectedly. 'I can do it with just the wood, but it goes wrong when you're on it.'

'Don't worry.' Zastra tried to sound encouraging. 'We'll get there.'

'Perhaps if you let Orika into your mind?' suggested Dobery. 'She may be able to sense how you are balancing and work with you rather than against you.'

Zastra was doubtful. She had secrets she couldn't risk anyone else finding out. Only desperation had induced her to open her mind to Orika when they took the transport. Dobery raised his palm.

'She doesn't have to see everything. You can lock the important things away. Remember how I taught you.'

'It would be nice if we didn't have all these spectators,' Zastra remarked. Orika nodded vigorously in agreement. The crowd on the beach had grown and some had even brought cushions and rugs so that they could watch the entertainment in comfort.

Zastra arranged for the yacht to be lowered and Dobery and Orika joined her as she took the little sailboat out of the bay and round to the far side of the island, out of sight of Port Krysfera. They started to practise. Opening her mind to Orika improved things. The flying hatch no longer seemed to fight against Zastra, and there were moments when she felt almost in control. The main problem was that her defensive mental walls kept snapping back into place, a reflex of her years of training. Once that occurred, she inevitably ended up crashing into the water. By the time the sun began to set, Zastra was soaking wet and shivering with cold. She began to think longingly of Pitwyn's bath-house.

'That'll do for today,' Dobery said. 'We must not put too much strain on Orika.'

Zastra didn't argue. She took the yacht back to Port Krysfera, dropping Orika off at the *Wind of Golmeira* on her way. She noticed a two-masted ship had joined the others in the bay. She left Dobery at the jetty and made her way to the bath-house, over-joyed to find there was a spare bath waiting. She pulled the lever to fill it up and had just placed one foot in the hot water when a figure burst through the linen curtain and into her chamber.

'What the—' Zastra yelped. She plunged into the steaming water in an attempt to hide her nakedness. The intruder stopped short. It was Kylen.

'Oh, um, sorry, I didn't realise you'd be...'

'You didn't realise that I'd be in the bath? And yet this *is* a bath-house.'

I'll just, um…' Kylen flushed. She appeared almost as mortified as Zastra. She quickly averted her eyes and shuffled back behind the curtain. 'Sorry!'

Is there nowhere I can get some peace? Zastra eyed the entrance to her chamber warily, but the curtain remained closed and eventually she reckoned it might be safe to stand up and reach for the soap. With unfortunate timing, Kylen chose that moment to pop her head back round the side of the curtain, making Zastra jump so sharply that her foot slipped on the base of the tub and she fell backwards into the hot water. She surfaced, spluttering, wiping her wet hair from her forehead.

'It seems your bad luck with water continues,' Kylen said with a grin.

Zastra scoured the room desperately for something to cover herself. There was nothing within reach, so she folded her arms across her chest protectively and glared at the intruder.

'What do you want?'

Kylen coughed.

'I only wanted to know when you'll be ready to try this plan of yours. We've had word from Drazan that Thorlberd is sending reinforcements to Murthen Island. We've got to get there before they do.'

'Who's Drazan?' Zastra attempted to regain her composure, but her skin tingled uncomfortably. *Where are those towels?*

'The captain of the *Flower*. Didn't you see it in the bay? The little ship with the two masts. He's been scouting the Golmeiran coast for information. He's a mindweaver, like Polina and Dobery, and he's found out things about Murthen Island.'

'What things?'

'Weren't you listening?' Kylen strode forward, oblivious to Zastra's spluttering protests. 'Reinforcements. For Murthen Island. Due to leave Port Trestra before the next Moonscrescent.'

There they are. Zastra finally spotted a neat pile of towels lying just by the entrance, well out of her reach unless she left the protection of her bath. She gestured toward the pile.

'Chuck me a towel then. I suppose we'd better start out at once.'

Kylen took the top towel from the pile and handed it to Zastra, at least having the decency to keep her eyes directed towards the floor while she did so.

'Um... we can't leave until tomorrow. Mata insists the *Wind of Golmeira* won't be ready to sail before then.'

Zastra froze, one leg on the lip of the tub.

'So this could have waited until after I'd had my bath?'

'I suppose so. Although knowing how long you like to spend in here, it could have been tomorrow before you got out.'

Zastra reached for the bar of soap and threw it forcefully in the general direction of the Sendoran. Kylen skipped out of the way.

'Hey! No need for that.'

'Get out. And tell everyone else to leave me alone, unless there's an *actual* emergency.'

Kylen disappeared and Zastra sank back into the bath and pulled the lever for more hot water. She closed her eyes.

'Oh Zastra? Lady Zastra, have you finished yet? I have something... These new shoes won't try themselves on. You must try them, really you must. They are just the most lovely...' A curly-haired shadow fell across the linen curtain.

'I'm sure she'll be delighted to see you,' she heard Kylen remark pleasantly. 'Do go straight in.'

Chapter Forty-one

Rastran looked complacently out of his window. The sea was flat and calm, uninterrupted as far as the distant horizon. Beneath his position the Bractarian Guard patrolled the walls of the fortress. He hoped his cousin would be foolish enough to attack. What did she have? A handful of ships, crewed by traitorous scum. They wouldn't stand a chance.

There was a knock at the door. Linsak, the chief mindweaver on Murthen Island, begged leave to enter. Rastran smirked. He knew that Linsak, much older and more experienced than him, resented both his presence and the authority he had as Thorlberd's son. He found her ineffective attempts to hide her dislike quite amusing.

'What is it?' he snapped, feigning annoyance. In reality, he was bored and welcomed the diversion, but he liked to put people on the defensive, knowing they dared say nothing in return.

'My progress report, as you requested,' Linsak said, with forced politeness.

'I hope there has actually been some progress this time?'

'Indeed, my Lord. One of our younger mindweavers has revealed an exceptional ability, unlocked by the cintara bark.'

'Well?'

'He was able to crack a sword blade with his mind. Not much as yet, but something we can work on.'

'What use is that? I suppose his ability is limited to metal?'

Linsak nodded. 'As far as we know, a person can only mind-move a single substance. As my Lord Rastran knows from his own ability. It is unfortunate that we lost one such gifted child to Lord Thorlberd's niece.'

Linsak's face showed nothing, but Rastran felt her insolence. He himself had been on the leading warship when Zastra's forces had attacked the convoy. He had ordered the captain make for the safety of Murthen Island. It had been the right tactical decision; the migaradon should have finished the rebels off, but to some it might look as if he had run away.

'She was lucky. Next time it will be different.'

Five warships lay in Murthen Island's harbour, ready to strike out at his command, and he had more mindweavers under his control than anyone in the whole of Golmeira. He would take personal satisfaction in killing his cousin. Or better still, capturing her and taking her in chains to his father. She had got the better of him all those years ago at Golmer Castle, but that had been kids' stuff. Now he was a man, fully trained. *You have no idea of my powers, Zastra. Your crossbow skills won't save you this time.*

'What about the Sendoran problem?' Linsak asked. 'The last batch were too weak to be much use. Many died before we could even begin to probe their minds. If my Lord would allow them a little more food and perhaps some basic medicines we might have enough healthy Sendorans to work with.'

Rastran waved his hand dismissively.

'They deserve no such thing. If they die, they can be replaced. Sendor is full of such animals. Why waste good food and medicine?'

'Losing the latest shipment has deprived us of new subjects, and my Lord Rastran's temper...' The sentence was choked off, uncompleted.

'Those that resist deserve to die. It is a lesson to the rest. That one that spat at me deserved his fate. Which reminds me, you'd better have him cut down. No doubt he's beginning to smell.'

Linsak twitched her nose as if to imply that it was Rastran who was giving off a bad stench. She was really starting to annoy him. Rastran leant back against the windowsill and folded his arms.

'So what you are telling me is that you have made no progress overcoming the Sendoran resistance to mindweaving.'

Linsak shuffled nervously. 'Their minds are so different, it is difficult to interpret what they are thinking. We have found a way to access the dream centre of their minds. The nightmare planting is going well.'

'What use are the nightmares of savages to me?'

'Manifold, my Lord. We can disturb their sleep, leaving them exhausted. Some we have even pushed into insanity. The threat of this has loosened some tongues, although most stubbornly refuse to co-operate.'

'And the boy? Zadorax.'

'Every night since last Moonscross, we have forced him to live in a nightmare world of our creation. He will break soon, I guarantee it.'

'You'd better be right. I need him to tell me the secrets of the Caves of Karabek. I want to know every entrance.'

'I thought Master at Arms Ixendred was in charge of taking the caves? He has written yet again, requesting delivery of more sintegrack.'

'The only remaining sintegrack is here on Murthen Island. I will not trust it to anyone else. Once the brat has told me the layout of the caves, I will lead the attack myself.'

Linsak raised an eyebrow. *Was she mocking him?* He tried to probe her, but she blocked him easily, her face blank and unconcerned. He wished he could get rid of her, but after a number of previous incidents, his father had insisted that Rastran could only punish his subordinates when they visibly failed.

'Get out of my sight,' he snapped, taking some satisfaction in dismissing her with such deliberate rudeness. He turned his attention back to the unbroken line of the horizon. No sign of a sail to break the monotony. *Come and play, Zastra, if you dare. I'll make sure you regret it.*

Chapter Forty-two

Kylen paced up and down the deck with increasing impatience as Zastra ordered Mata to drop anchor until the tide was high enough for the *Wind of Golmeira* to pass safely through the treacherous channel of the Western Spur. Zastra refused to let the Sendoran's loud sighs and angry looks pressure her into premature action. Only when the waves had risen high enough to lap against the tidal line of algae and seaweed did she give the order to raise anchor. It was the first time they had traversed the channel in this direction and it would do no one any good if they ran aground on one of the sandbanks. The prevailing wind was against them so she ordered the dinghy be lowered to tow them through. Once they had made it safely back to Sea of Golmeira, Zastra set a course for the Pyramid Isle. Justyn and Nerika refused to countenance an attack on Murthen Island until Zastra had proved it was possible to defeat a migaradon. To their knowledge, the closest migaradon was on the Pyramid Isle. Zastra left the ship in Mata's capable hands while she and Orika practised. Zastra added to her growing collection of bruises and cuts as they battled to control the flight of the wooden hatch.

'Perhaps you should try wearing a saucepan on your head?' Jerenik's helpful suggestion came after an unexpected dip of the raft had caused Zastra to bump her head on the foresail yard.

Zastra bit back a sharp retort. It was bad enough that she was aching all over, without Jerenik making fun of her. She probably should discipline him for insubordination, but she didn't want to begin life as captain handing out punishments. She had no desire to be like Dastrin. She was rescued by Mata.

'Saucepans, is it?' snapped her second in command. 'Well, the galley is a mess since we don't have a proper cook. I want it sparkling, saucepans and all. Anyone else with a liking for smart comments can help you.'

The grin was wiped from Jerenik's face and the rest of the crew turned back to their tasks with a new-found eagerness.

Kylen and Dobery had insisted on joining the expedition. Kylen shared Zastra's cabin while Dobery took a bunk in Burgal's old berth together with Ithgol. Jerenik, much to his annoyance, had been sent back to bunk with the rest of the crew. That evening, Zastra invited Mata, Ithgol and Dobery to join her and Kylen for supper. Kylen did not think much of the idea.

'I refuse to eat with a Kyrg. If you'd seen what they're doing to my people, you wouldn't either. They are savages.'

'I have no more reason to like Kyrgs than you,' replied Zastra, 'but Ithgol has proven himself worthy of my trust. Sendorans were called savages once. I would have thought you'd have more sympathy for Ithgol than the others, not less.'

'Pah!'

'Well, I've invited him now,' said Zastra, exasperated. 'I won't uninvite him.'

'You're the captain.' Kylen gave her a sardonic salute.

The supper was a disaster. Kylen sat at one end of the table and glowered. Ithgol was as uncommunicative as ever and even Mata seemed ill at ease and only responded to direct questions. Zastra tried to act as a good host, encouraging Mata with some general questions about sailing and navigation. Dobery joined in now and then, but with Kylen and Ithgol conducting their own private glaring competition the atmosphere turned heavy and an uncomfortable silence descended over the dining table. At least the food was good. Before they had set off, Pitwyn had sent across the finest produce from Port Krysfera. There was also fresh fish, caught direct from the sea only that day. Dobery passed Zastra a jug of sauce.

'Do you think you and Orika will be ready in time?'

'I don't know,' sighed Zastra. 'You've seen us. It's a matter of chance whether I fly or crash onto the deck.'

'Zastra will succeed,' stated Ithgol. Zastra stared at him in surprise. It was the first words he had uttered the entire evening. Kylen pounced on him.

'What do you know? Your opinion is wanted as little as your presence. Why are you even here? To spy for the other Kyrgs no doubt.'

'I am no spy,' Ithgol growled. Kylen shoved aside her plate of food.

'Why should we trust you? Zastra fights for Golmeira, I for Sendor, but what do you fight for?'

Ithgol's eyebrows bunched together. When he spoke, it was as though the words were being squeezed out of him.

'Zastra is my comrade in arms. That is enough. If you were not so puny, I would punish you for your insults.'

'I'm not afraid to fight.' Kylen stood up with such force that her chair tipped backwards. Ithgol rose to meet her challenge.

'Stop this!' cried Zastra. 'We mustn't fight amongst ourselves. We've more important battles. Kylen, have you forgotten that Ithgol helped rescue you from the transports? You should be grateful to him, instead of being so rude. And Ithgol, I won't have threats in my cabin.'

Kylen picked up her chair and sunk back into it sulkily.

'Just don't turn your back on him,' she muttered.

Ithgol remained standing for a moment. Then, with a small nod toward Zastra, he kicked back his chair and marched from the cabin. Dobery and Mata quickly muttered their excuses and departed also. Zastra rounded on Kylen.

'How long are you going keep this up?'

'What?'

'This stupid anger with everyone and everything. Even those risking their lives to help you. Ithgol will prove invaluable when we try to save Zax and the others.'

'I have more on my mind than hurting the feelings of some Kyrginite savage.'

Kylen flung herself into her bunk, turned towards the hull and yanked her blanket over her head.

Zastra and Orika had improved to the point where Zastra was able to fly in a complete loop around the ship, balanced on the hatch cover. Whooping with exhilaration, she swooped down to where Mata and Kylen were standing together at the stern. In response to her unspoken command, the raft halted and hovered a foot above the deck, allowing her to hop off with a flourish.

'Well, that leaves only the small matter of a giant flying beast to face,' Mata said drily. 'We should reach the Pyramid Isle early tomorrow if the wind holds.'

'At last.' Kylen glowed with excitement.

Zastra picked up the square of wood, suddenly feeling queasy. She retired to her cabin, but found it difficult to sleep. It didn't help that every crewmember wanted to knock on her door to wish her luck. She supposed they were trying to be kind but she just wanted to be left alone. In the end, Ithgol took it upon himself to stand guard, which soon stopped the flow of visitors. As she lay on her bunk and stared at the planking above her head, she made out the sounds of the ship. The wash of the water beneath the bow, the pitter-patter of bare feet as the watch trimmed the sail and the hum of voices and clattering of pans below decks as the rest of the crew prepared supper. They were noises she had grown used to and found oddly comforting. The lives of all these people depended on her and the damaged mind of a frightened girl. So much could go wrong. Zastra gave up trying to sleep and went to find Orika. The girl insisted on living in the healer's room. She was awake and when Zastra sat down beside her she rubbed her eyes.

'Are you scared, Zastra?'

'A little. You?'

Orika nodded. 'We won't tell though,' she whispered, with a small giggle.

'No,' agreed Zastra. 'It'll be our secret.'

Orika smiled shyly and lay down on her bunk. Zastra sat with her until the girl was sleeping peacefully. Then she returned to her cabin to try and snatch some sleep herself.

Zastra was awake and on deck as dawn arrived. The triangular outline of the Pyramid Isle broke upwards out of the sea, black against the yawning orange crescent that heralded the sunrise. Mata ordered an increase in sail and laid the ship on a direct heading towards the island. As the sun rose into a cloudless sky all eyes were fixed upon the horizon.

'Nothing,' remarked Jerenik. 'It must be gone.'

'Don't be so sure,' said Dobery.

A black smudge rose from the tip of the pyramid, shivered and headed towards them. There was no doubting what it was.

Chapter Forty-three

'Make ready,' ordered Zastra. The crew set up the catapults, polished their swords and loaded their crossbows. Even though such weapons were next to useless, Zastra thought it only right to be as prepared as possible. A large net covered the quarterdeck, the ropes triple-spliced to increase their strength. The plan was to try and trap the migaradon once Zastra had dealt with the rider. As she ran the rough cords through her hands, checking for any weak points, Zastra began to wonder if the net was big enough. Well, it was too late to do anything about it now.

'Where's Orika?' There was no sign of the girl. Zastra dashed below and found her cowering in her bunk.

'You must come, Orika,' she pleaded. 'This is what we've been working for. I can't do it without your help.' Trembling, Orika allowed herself to be led up onto the deck. Dobery reached out and took Orika's hand.

'You stay with me, my dear.'

Orika clung on to his arm so tightly that the old man winced. He nodded towards Zastra.

'We'll be all right. Be careful, my dear. And good luck.'

Zastra gave Orika's hand a last squeeze. It felt surprisingly hot.

'Wait until the last moment. Surprise is our one advantage. I know you can do it.'

Orika gave a small whimper and buried her head in the front of Dobery's cloak. Zastra placed the wooden hatch cover down on the deck between the fore and mainmasts and squatted upon it. She bent her head and waited, trying to appear calm. Her crossbow was primed and she cradled it in her arms. Everything now depended on Orika. The migaradon was less than half a league away, its flight so ungainly that it looked like a giant rag flapping in the wind. Zastra waited until the shadow of its wings darkened the bow of the ship. A harsh, confident shriek broke the silence. She opened her mind to Orika and gave the command to go.

Nothing happened.

Come on, Orika, willed Zastra. *We have to do this.*

The raft wobbled and then jerked into the air, launching her up between the masts. She struggled to keep her balance, arms flailing as she tried to steady herself. Before she knew it, she was high above the ship. The wind whipped at her shirt and half-trousers, trying to dislodge her. As Zastra steadied herself, the hatch cover began to slow.

Higher, she urged. The wooden raft responded. As Zastra rose up in front of the migaradon, the rider's chin dropped in astonishment.

'Surprise,' said Zastra, grimly. Her bow was already at her shoulder. She fired. The body of the rider slipped sideways and fell towards the ocean below. In response to Zastra's unspoken command, the hatch cover skirted around the head of the migaradon and nudged up against its side. Zastra sprang off the wooden square and into the saddle. She had barely enough time to grasp the chains that served for reins before the beast let out a cry of utter desolation. It wrenched its head around in a frenzy of anger. With one snap of its mouth, the hatch cover was smashed into pieces. It gnashed at Zastra's leg, tearing at its own scales in its eagerness to destroy her. No matter how hard Zastra tugged the chains, the migaradon refused to obey. They sunk lower, circling round and round as the beast strived to attack Zastra. Its huge tail slammed into foremast of the *Wind of Golmeira*, snapping it clean in half. Shrieking in fury, the migaradon beat its wings and began to climb again, higher and higher. All of a sudden it tipped forwards, flinging Zastra out of the saddle and over its head. Still clinging to the chains, she found herself dangling directly beneath the open mouth of the migaradon. The wide jaws snapped at her, but they were both falling, gathering speed at the same rate and it could not catch up with her. Zastra glanced down. The sea, peppered with sharp rocks, rushed towards them. She was help-less. The migaradon couldn't get her, but she would be crushed between it and the sea or else dashed upon the rocks. The *Wind of Golmeira* was too far away to offer assistance.

Zastra, here. Look. Take!

She felt a sharp prod in her ribcage and looked down to see a wooden pole digging into her side. She reached out and grabbed it, letting go of the chains at the same moment. The wooden pole wrenched her upward with such violence that her right hand slipped off and her left shoulder exploded in pain. Somehow, she retained her grip. The migaradon plummeted past her and crashed into the sea, showering her in a huge plume of spray. The wooden pole slipped out of Zastra's sweaty, one-handed grasp. Time seemed to slow as she plunged towards the green-grey sea. She felt a heavy slap against her side and her shoulder burst in agony. Cold water closed around her. She rose once, gasping for breath, but as she tried to swim, pain and water closed over her and she was plunged into blackness.

Chapter Forty-four

Zastra awoke in her cabin. Yashni was prodding her whilst Kylen and Ithgol looked on anxiously. For some reason the Kyrg and the Sendoran were both dripping wet.

'Dislocated shoulder,' said Yashni. 'I'm sorry, but this will hurt a bit.'

'Ow!' Zastra yelled as Yashni wrenched her arm, sending waves of pain shooting out from her left shoulder.

'That's better. It's back where it should be. You've also cracked a couple of ribs, but at least you're alive. Thank the stars.'

Kylen was trying, unsuccessfully, to restrain a laugh.

'That went well,' she remarked. 'You didn't tell us that the plan was to try and get it to eat you. Luckily, it was distracted enough to crash into the only rocks in the entire area.'

'Well, I didn't like to reveal too much ahead of time.' Zastra returned her grin.

'I particularly liked the bit where you fooled it by making it look as if you fell off. The crew were mightily impressed.'

'I did fall off,' Zastra admitted.

'Don't worry. I'm sure some Golmeiran orator will describe

how the noble Zastra defeated the dread migaradon by pulling it from the sky with a single hand.'

'Only there will be two migaradons,' Ithgol grunted. 'Both breathing fire.'

'The Kyrg may well be right.' Kylen clapped her hands and Zastra felt that a change of subject was called for.

'Why are you two dripping all over my cabin floor?'

Kylen jerked a thumb towards Ithgol. 'This big lump jumped into the sea to try and save you.'

Zastra stared at the sheepish Kyrg.

'I thought you couldn't swim?'

'He can't.' Kylen chuckled. 'He sank like a rock. Hylaz had to jump in and save *him*. However, I can swim perfectly well and I got to you just before you drowned. You could say thanks, rather than complain about a little puddle on your precious floor.'

'I'm very grateful. To both of you.'

'You're welcome.'

Ithgol added a barely audible grunt, still looking a mite uncomfortable.

'Where is the migaradon? Did it sink?'

Kylen shook her head.

'No, they've dragged it alongside the hull.'

Zastra heaved herself up. 'Good. If we can work out why its hide is so strong, we may be able to make a weapon able to kill it.'

'Rather than rely on blind luck, you mean?' asked Kylen.

'Luck?' Zastra pretended to be offended. 'There's a lot of skill involved in falling from the sky and staying alive.'

'Skill indeed,' came the familiar voice of Dobery, 'most of which belongs to Orika, I believe.' The old mindweaver led Orika into the cabin. Zastra stepped forward, wincing as her shoulder and ribs complained. She gave Orika a one-armed hug. 'Thank you, Orika. It was quick thinking, sending me that pole. You saved my life.'

Orika grabbed her and squeezed so hard that Zastra had to clamp her teeth together to stop herself crying out.

'You still fell,' Orika sobbed. 'I was so scared you'd be drowned.'

'Fell? You mean when I pulled the migaradon from the sky single-handed?'

She paid no heed to the strangled noises coming from Ithgol and Kylen.

'I thought I told you to be careful,' admonished Dobery, but he too was unable to keep a smile from his face. 'I don't know if you have proved much to Nerika and the others, except that you seem to be blessed with copious quantities of good fortune. Still, luck is a valuable attribute in a leader.'

'How is the ship? Is the mast badly damaged?'

'It's ruined. Luckily there's a spare in the hold. Mata says it will take a few hours to winch into place. Do you want to come and see the creature?'

Zastra followed the others onto the deck. The migaradon lay alongside, half submerged in the water. It was too heavy to be winched on board. Its body had smashed open against the rocks and its innards lay open to view. The sight was not a pleasant one and the smell was even worse.

'It really is fascinating,' said Dobery. 'See how it has three hearts, lined up along a giant artery. I suspect you have to puncture all three hearts to kill it. Unless of course you can crash it at high speed like you did. The bones are surprisingly light and snap easily.'

'And the hide?'

'Scales.' Dobery leaned over the dead body and tapped at a dark brown circle, slightly larger than his hand. The scales overlapped and covered the entire body. 'They are too strong for an ordinary bolt or sword to penetrate.'

He tugged at the tip of one of the scales, wrenching it away from the body.

'Aha!' he cried in delight. 'They are attached by normal flesh and sinew. Does anyone have a knife?'

Jerenik stepped forward, a large knife in his hand. Dobery hacked at the sinew until the scale was released.

'I'm sure Vingrod could use this to discover how to fashion a blade strong enough to penetrate.'

'Who's Vingrod?'

'One of Justyn's followers. A scientist, and a good one too.'

'Well, let's cut off as many scales as we can while the mast is being fixed,' suggested Zastra. She retreated from the unpleasant stench. 'Then we must get back to Uden's Teeth and tell Justyn to prepare his ships. We haven't time to waste. We need to set the watches and...'

She staggered, suddenly feeling dizzy. Mata caught her just before she fell.

'Leave it to me,' she said. 'You need to rest.'

Once the new mast had been jockeyed into place they headed back to Uden's Teeth under a full press of sail. As evening drew in, Mata arranged for a feast so that the whole crew could cele-brate their victory. Jerenik took the opportunity to recount the moment that the beast had crashed into the rocks. He windmilled his arms and collapsed dramatically to the deck in an impression of Zastra's fall through the air. His performance drew gusts of laughter from the crew.

'I save their lives and all they can do is make fun of me,' muttered Zastra.

'Stop complaining,' said Kylen. 'Just be glad you're alive.'

Spirits were high and the near drowning incident appeared to have lessened Kylen's animosity towards Ithgol. She even brought him a second helping of fish steak.

'Let's just hope you can fight better than you can swim.'

He accepted her offer of food with a grunt.

'You don't say much, do you? A "thank you" would be polite.'

'That *was* one of his grateful grunts,' Zastra remarked. Kylen turned to her.

'Why didn't you guide the migaradon into the net, like we'd arranged?'

'It wouldn't respond to anything I did. Believe me, I tried. It must only respond to its rider. You're welcome to have a go when we get to Murthen Island, if you think you can do any better.'

Chapter Forty-five

A wall of disbelieving faces greeted them as they docked at Port Krysfera. The astonishment on Nerika's face made Zastra feel her ordeal had been worth it. Justyn hailed them warmly.

'I'm glad to see you back. Did you... Did it work?'

'Just like we planned.' Zastra managed to keep a straight face, but only just.

'Are you injured?'

Yashni had set Zastra's arm in a sling to help her shoulder heal.

'I'm fine. Don't worry about me. We must start for Murthen Island at once if we are to get there ahead of Thorlberd's reinforcements.'

'But you've only just returned. Surely you should rest.'

'I told you, I'm fine,' insisted Zastra, determined to show no sign of weakness.

'You promised to help us if we killed a migaradon,' Kylen reminded him. 'Will you stand by your word?'

Justyn rubbed his chin.

'I guess I wasn't expecting you to succeed. Very well. Let preparations be made at once.'

'I don't believe this,' Nerika protested. 'I can't believe you're agreeing to risk our people for a few Sendorans.'

'It's about more than Sendorans. Think about it, Nerika. If the next generation of Thorlberd's mindweavers are being trained at Murthen Island, we cannot wait for him to create a force of such power. It would make him truly invincible. If we free them, we may be able to persuade them to join us. We have only three mindweavers at present. We would need many more to have any chance of defeating Thorlberd.'

'And we need to save Zax,' added Kylen.

'Defeat Thorlberd?' Zastra gave Justyn a long look. 'What happened to just trying to survive?'

'We made our choice when we attacked the transport convoy. When I saw what they had done to the Sendorans and to poor Orika, I knew we'd done the right thing. We can be spectators no longer.'

'Then we are agreed?' Zastra looked around the group. One by one, they all nodded, even Nerika.

'We have another problem besides the migaradon,' said Dobery. 'As Justyn says, there's only myself, Pol and Drazan against twenty mindweavers on Murthen Island. We cannot block all of them. How many of your crews can resist mindweaving?'

'Not many,' admitted Zastra. 'Most of my crew were disabled when we attacked the transports.'

Justyn shook his head. 'Same for the *Darkhorse*, and you know I have little power to fight them myself. I shall need you or Pol by my side, Dobery, when the time comes.'

'Sendorans have strong minds,' said Kylen. 'We can resist the mindfoggers. But we are not sailors.'

'Then I suggest you learn,' Zastra remarked. 'We can split the

Sendorans across each ship, ready to take over if the mindweavers interfere with our crews.'

'It might work,' said Justyn. 'If the Sendorans agree to take orders from our captains.'

Kylen frowned. 'Taking orders from a Golmeiran will not come easy to my people.'

'There is no other way,' argued Zastra. 'You must persuade them, Kylen. No one is asking them to swear loyalty to Golmeira, but we must be together in this, or we will fail.'

Kylen inclined her head. 'Agreed.'

Thanks to the organisational skills of Justyn and Pitwyn, all four ships were ready to leave only two days after the *Wind of Golmeira* returned from the Pyramid Isle. Zastra was on the jetty with Justyn, supervising the loading of the last batch of supplies, when a short woman with grey hair rushed towards them. Looking ready to drop with exhaustion, she placed a bulky package in Lord Justyn's arms.

'Vingrod!' Justyn exclaimed. 'Please tell me you've got something?'

'We've been working non-stop since Lady Zastra returned. As we suspected, none of our normal weapons will work. We tried to mould the scales themselves into weapons, but they are so hard that they wrecked the grindstone. By a lucky accident we discovered that the scales melt in a firedust furnace. It's the intense heat, you see, it's—'

'Get to the point,' Justyn interjected. 'We leave any moment.'

'Apologies, my Lord. We used the melted scales to make spear tips and arrowheads. In tests, we found that arrowheads can penetrate the scales as long as the crossbow is fired at close range. We hadn't time to test the spears, so I can't say if they will work. This bundle contains everything we could make in the time.'

Justyn weighed the bundle thoughtfully.

'Gives us half a chance. Good work.'

'Remember that the beast has three hearts,' Vingrod warned. 'One shot will not be enough to kill a migaradon. You will need a good aim.'

They crossed the southern expanses of the Golmeiran Sea, giving the Sand Islands of the Skurgs a wide berth. Zastra left most of the sailing to Mata. Her shoulder was still sore and she had to give it a chance to heal if she was to be fit for the assault on Murthen Island. At every opportunity, the Sendorans were taught the basics of sailing, but progress was slow. Jerenik, promoted to Watchmaster, was among those giving instructions. When he pointed out the difference between two almost identical ropes to a confused Sendoran, cursing her for her incompetence, Zastra couldn't help a private chuckle. She remembered when they had both been novices, every bit as confused as the Sendorans were now. Yet Jerenik displayed little sympathy for his new charges as he chivvied them along. Kylen kept her side of the bargain, stamping down on any disobedience from the Sendorans and insisting they did as their Golmeiran officers told them.

As they approached the Mongrels, Justyn called a conference on board the *Darkhorse*. Zastra took Kylen and Ithgol with her. Various schemes to attack Murthen Island, from the improbable to the ridiculous were thrashed around, but none seemed to leave much hope for success.

'If Orika was here, we'd have a better chance,' Nerika remarked. 'She gave us an advantage over the migaradons. I can't believe Zastra let her stay behind.' It was not the first time she had voiced this opinion.

'She wasn't fit to come,' Zastra responded wearily. 'She would have been a danger to herself and the ship.' In spite of all Zastra's reassurances, Orika had convinced herself that it was her fault Zastra had nearly drowned at the Pyramid Isle and had reverted back to her terrified, timber-shivering state. Zastra had insisted that it wouldn't be right to force Orika to come along. Needless to say, Nerika had not agreed. Zastra changed the subject.

'Polina, tell us again what that Golmeiran captain told you.'

'He said there were twenty mindweavers and the Bractarian Guard, who are Thorlberd's best soldiers. That's in addition to the normal garrison and the migaradon.'

'Let me have another look at that map of the fortress.'

They all pored over the piece of paper, and after more discussions, a plan was agreed.

'Are we sure we want to do this?' Nerika asked. Justyn stood back.

'We have our plan. It might just work. As long as there are no surprises.'

Chapter Forty-six

Rastran was bored. He decided to visit the dungeons where the Sendorans were stored. He took a perfumed handkerchief with him to cover the foul smell. The brat Zadorax was in a special cell of his own, lying half naked on the floor. Rastran nudged the boy with his foot, turning the body over. Furrows of white skin ran down his dirty cheeks indicating the passage of tears.

'Have you been crying again, boy?'

Zax gave him a glassy, uncomprehending look. Rastran kicked him again.

'Wake up. I want to have a look inside your head.'

The boy coughed weakly, his ribcage heaving unevenly against his dirty skin. Rastran delved into his thoughts, sidestepping the remnants of the nightmare of a Sendoran village being razed that had obviously been planted by one of Linsak's mindweavers. The boy's mind was difficult to penetrate but some images leaked out.

Show me the Caves of Karabek. Rastran extracted an image of torchlit caverns and huddled figures. Sendoran faces lined with exhaustion.

'Yes!' exulted Rastran, but even as he tried to pull out the images they faded. The brat was resisting. The further Rastran pushed, the more the caves receded from view. Blankness descended. The boy had passed out. Rastran balled his fist in frustration. An unconscious mind could not be penetrated. He asked for a bucket of cold water and had it thrown over the boy. Zadorax spluttered into life.

Rastran tried another approach. 'We are expecting your sister to try and rescue you.'

The boy scrambled to his feet.

'She'll make you pay for this.'

Rastran flicked his hair from his forehead. 'I hardly think so. My father has sent me twenty more mindweavers, double what we had. Oh, and another migaradon. My cousin and your sister will die trying to rescue your worthless carcass.'

The boy backed away. Rastran pursed his lips.

'What, are you crying again, little boy?'

As Zadorax fought against his emotions, Rastran burrowed into his distressed mind and extracted images of secret signs and hidden entrances before the brat could stop him.

'That's more like it!' Rastran cried in triumph. 'I'll be sure to tell your sister how helpful you were when I catch her.'

Zax burst into tears. A guard rushed down the steps. Rastran snapped round in annoyance.

'How dare you interrupt? I'll have you flogged.'

'Sails,' the guard said hurriedly. 'Flying the flag of Leodra.'

'How many?'

'Four, my Lord.'

Rastran turned back towards Zax.

'Your sister and my cousin are even more stupid than I thought.

They will soon be joining you. Only, since I have obtained the information I needed from you, I won't be as gentle with them.'

He stepped lightly up the stairs, calling for a draught of cintara bark to be prepared, just in case he needed it. If anything went wrong, the special power it gave him would guarantee victory. He was going to enjoy this immensely. *You'll be begging me for mercy, Zastra, before the day is over.*

Chapter Forty-seven

The rebel convoy headed towards the harbor that lay below the gates of the fortress. Unnoticed, a small boat skirted the far side of the island, shrouded in sea mist. Abruptly it changed course and headed for the island. Five figures leapt out and made for a postern door hidden behind an artfully constructed buttress.

'Just where Polina said it would be,' murmured Dobery, in satisfaction. 'The information from the Golmeiran captain has all been accurate so far.'

'He didn't have much choice, faced with a mindweaver,' Kylen remarked. Jerenik stepped past her to work on the lock. The door sprung open. Four guards and a black cloaked woman scrambled to their feet.

'Too much to hope this entrance was unguarded.' Dobery wore a mask of intense concentration. The mindweaver crumpled to the ground without making a sound. Zastra reached for her sword, but Hylaz had disposed of two of the guards before she had even pulled it from its scabbard. Kylen and Jerenik lost no time incapacitating the others. Zastra unhooked a jula lantern from the wall of the guardroom.

'We must get to the tower before they can release the migaradon. Look out for stairs.'

They headed along a narrow passage that curved inside the wall of the fortress. It ended in a spiral staircase, cut from the same yellowish stone as the fort itself. Zastra led them up. There must have been a hundred steps at least, and she was breathing heavily by the time she reached the top and found herself in a large circular room. A square opening in the ceiling was open to the sky, but she was more interested in what lay directly in front of her. A migaradon, asleep, attached to the wall by a chain with links thicker than Zastra's arm. There was no sign of a rider. The others came up behind her. As Jerenik bustled through, he scraped the tip of his sword against the stone of the door frame. The harsh grating was surprisingly loud.

'Shh!' hissed Zastra, but it was too late. The migaradon awoke instantly and snapped its huge head towards the source of the noise. Zastra pressed her back against curved stone wall of the room and began to edge around it. Her crossbow was already in her hand. The migaradon's eyes followed her as it yawned, revealing rows of packed teeth glistening with saliva. Without warning, it struck. Zastra ducked and splinters of stone rained down on her back as the migaradon's teeth clashed against the wall. She rolled to her left and fired into the huge body, aiming just behind the foreleg. The bolt burst through the scales and the migaradon howled in a mixture of pain and surprise. It slashed out wildly, and Zastra was sent diving as a huge, taloned claw scraped along the wall at chest height. Blood pulsed from the wound caused by Zastra's bolt. She pulled the lever to set another bolt in the chamber and unleashed her second shot, then the third, trusting that the anatomy of all migaradons was the same as the one from the

Pyramid Isle. The beast reared up on its hind legs with a high pitched squeal. Zastra froze, defenceless. There were no more bolts in her crossbow and she knew her sword was useless. With a keening wail, the migaradon crashed to the floor, blood pooling around its belly. Zastra exhaled slowly and nudged the inert body with her foot. It didn't move.

'That's one job done. We need to get down to—'

She was cut off by a familiar metallic cry.

'It can't be!' she cried in disbelief.

'Look! There. Another one.' Jerenik pointed at the square of blue sky above them. A huge winged form blotted out the light as it flew past. Across the room, a ladder lay on its side. Zastra skirted the dead migaradon and levered the ladder into position against the rim of the skylight. Jerenik held it firm as Zastra clambered up and out onto the open roof of the tower. The second migaradon was heading straight for Justyn's ships. She knelt down to reload her crossbow, losing precious seconds as she fumbled one of the bolts. She sighted quickly and fired. Her first bolt struck home, but the migaradon was at the edge of her range and the other two bolts, even with their special tips, bounced off the side of the migaradon and fell harmlessly to the ground. The beast did not falter or change course. Zastra cried out in frustration.

Kylen grabbed her arm. 'There's nothing more we can do here. We have to get Zax. Remember, Justyn has those spear heads. They still have a chance.'

'I hope you are right.' Zastra followed the others back down the spiral staircase. At the bottom, two soldiers tried to block their way.

'Wait! Let me see what they know,' cried Dobery, as Kylen and

Hylaz were about to strike. Both guards glanced at Dobery with fear and then collapsed to the ground, clutching their heads.

'This way.' Dobery made for a set of worn wooden steps that led down into the bowels of the fortress. At the bottom, a pair of huge blackwood doors studded with iron barred their way. A smaller door was cut into it, with a metal grille near the top. A face almost as square as the grille peered through it.

'Yes?' The fleshy face was clearly annoyed at being disturbed.

'Er... food for the prisoners,' said Jerenik.

The face snorted.

''ardly. These animals were only fed yesterday. Are you tellin' me Lord Rastran's goin' soft? What's the password?'

Hylaz lifted a large axe. 'How's this for a password?'

Dobery stepped forward. 'I'll handle this,' he said. 'There's no need for violence.' He peered at the grille with an expression of good humoured confusion.

'Let us in, my good fellow. You can see we are friends.'

The face turned away. 'Oy, you lot!' he called. 'Intruders. Stupid ones too, thinkin' Lord Rastran'd trust the prisoners to some weak minded cretin.'

Zastra felt a painful probe dig into her mind and Dobery staggered backwards as if punched. Jerenik slumped to the ground in a stupor.

'Mindweavers,' gasped Zastra, struggling to repel the attack on her mind. 'Strong ones, too.'

'On second thoughts, Hylaz, a little violence may be just what we need,' Dobery said with a grimace. The big Sendoran set about the door with a will. Splinters flew in all directions but the wood was thick and he made slow progress, sparks flying whenever his axe encountered one of the metal studs.

'Hurry,' Kylen urged. Golmeiran soldiers, drawn by the noise, charged down the wooden steps towards them. Hylaz turned towards the oncomers and brandished his axe.

'No.' Kylen gestured him back. 'Keep at the door. Zastra and I can take care of this.'

Zastra marvelled at Kylen's confidence. The entire flight of steps was filled with soldiers. Kylen flew towards the foot of the stairs. Zastra followed, joining Kylen as she mounted the first step. If they could engage the soldiers while they were still bunched together, they had a chance. If they let them reach the bottom of the stairs, where they could spread out and surround them, they would be done for. Zastra's head throbbed. Somewhere a powerful mindweaver was attacking her, but she refused to let that distract her. A body tumbled past her, and then another. Kylen was making progress up the stairs and was in danger of being surrounded unless Zastra caught up. She thrust, parried and ducked, forcing herself up the stairs until she was once more side by side with the Sendoran. It was similar to the close quarters fighting on board the *Wind of Golmeira*, and her previous experience helped her fight her way to the top of the stairs. The last two Golmeirans took one look at Kylen's face and fled.

'My Lady!' Hylaz's shout was followed by a loud splintering sound. A large hole appeared in the middle of the dungeon door. Hylaz put his broad shoulders through it, making the opening even wider. Kylen and Zastra ran down the stairs, jumping over the fallen bodies and followed Hylaz through the gap.

'Zax,' cried Kylen. 'Zax, where are you?'

Zastra grabbed the back of Kylen's shirt, pulling her up short. In front of them, five hooded figures stood in a line, holding hands. Kylen's cry was choked off and Zastra found herself pinned to the spot as if she were wrapped in invisible chains. Dobery was kneeling on the stone floor, doubled over, sweat pouring from his face.

'They are too much for me,' he gasped. 'I'm can't hold them.'

Zastra felt an arm circle around her neck and cut off her breath.

Chapter Forty-eight

Rastran watched through his telescope in disbelief. Someone aboard the leading rebel ship had killed one of his migaradons. *Impossible.* The ships that dared fly the flag of Leodra had ploughed through his own and were closing on the harbour.

'Where is the other migaradon?' he demanded. 'Get it in the air. Now!'

A soldier disappeared, reappearing a few moments later.

'It's dead in the tower, my Lord.'

'Dead? You lying scum. No one can kill a migaradon.' *And yet, one had just been slaughtered in front of him.*

'Um, there's something else, my Lord.'

'What is it?'

'Someone has broken into the dungeons.'

'The dungeons? Must be that Sendoran bitch. Send the Brac-tarian Guard to kill her and then bring me my cintara bark.' The soldier scuttled from the room, bumping into Linsak on his way out.

'Someone will pay for this incompetence,' growled Rastran. 'And if you don't come up with a plan, it's likely to be you.'

Linsak looked as if she might protest, but thought better of it. 'There's no need to panic. We still outnumber them. Remember, we also have the sintegrack.'

Rastran clenched his fist. 'Of course. We'll blast them off their feet if they try to attack the fortress.'

'I've already stationed some men and women on the western promontory,' said Linsak. 'They will have a perfect view of the road up to the main gate.'

Rastran waved her away.

'Command them yourself. I'll have your head if you fail to stop them.'

Chapter Forty-nine

Zastra was being strangled from behind. She tried to reach up to fend off her opponent, but it felt as if a large rock had been tied to each of her wrists. She couldn't move her arms so much as an inch. Whatever the mindweavers were doing, they were too strong. Beside her, she heard Kylen growl in frustration. The arm around her neck tightened, choking her. Her vision began to swim and blur. A large shadow stumbled past her and towards the increasingly hazy outlines of the five mindweavers. One of the outlines seemed to melt away, and then another. The excruciating weight on Zastra's mind lifted a fraction and she was able to repel the probe. Released, her hands flew to her neck and she crouched down and threw her opponent over her head. She had her sword to her assailant's throat before she realised it was Jerenik. He was blinking in dazed confusion.

'Steady there. I'm on your side.'

Kylen placed the tip of her own sword next to Zastra's.

'Then why did you try and kill Zastra?'

'What? Why would I do that? I mean, she can be annoying, but—'

'Jerenik couldn't help it,' Dobery interjected. 'The mindweavers were controlling him. Hylaz saved us.'

In front of them, three cloaked bodies lay in a heap. Hylaz crashed the heads of the remaining two mindweavers together with a loud thump, and added them to the pile. The room was suddenly quiet.

'Five to one. Always were my favourite odds,' he remarked. 'Reckon my skull is too thick for them mindfoggers to get through.'

'I'm grateful for it.' Zastra massaged her throat gingerly. 'I'd be embarrassed to die at Jerenik's hands.'

They found two large cells, one packed with Sendoran prisoners and another filled with frightened youngsters, but there was no sign of Zax. One of the Sendorans directed them towards the rear of the dungeon. They found Zax lying on the floor of a cell that was fronted by vertical iron bars. He was alone.

'Zax! Are you all right?' Kylen rattled the bars furiously. 'I need to get in.'

Zastra called for Jerenik. He leaned over the body of the square-faced gaoler and tugged at his belt.

'Here you go.' He tossed a set of keys to her. Zastra hurried towards Kylen, fumbling with the keys.

'Is he all right?'

'Does he look all right?' Tears were streaming down Kylen's face. 'Look at him.'

Zax lay lifeless on the floor. At last Zastra found the right key. Kylen burst past her and fell upon her brother. He twitched in response.

'Thank the stars,' cried Hylaz. 'He's alive.'

Kylen stroked the hair from her brother's face.

'Zax, my brave boy. I'm here.'

She clung to him, oblivious to the loud clattering that caused the rest of them turn back to the dungeon entrance. The Bractarian Guard poured through the broken door, black-cloaked mindweavers mixed in with them. Jerenik slumped to the floor.

'Not again.' Zastra sighed. She tossed the keys into one of the cells containing the Sendorans and re-drew her sword.

'Shall we, Hylaz?'

'Why not?' the big Sendoran responded. 'There's only about forty of them. No problem if you can fight like a Sendoran.'

Zastra reckoned Hylaz knew as well as she did that they stood no chance against so many, but they stood together and prepared for the onslaught. Before they could move, they were brushed aside by a swarm of released Sendoran prisoners, unarmed but mightily angry. Their fury took them beyond the first of the Bractarians. Weapons were ripped from startled hands and bodies trampled in the crush.

'So that's fighting like a Sendoran,' Zastra said with a shudder.

Only four guards and a single mindweaver made it through the throng. The mindweaver was too shocked and terrified to even try and control their minds. Hylaz and Zastra dealt with them easily enough and Jerenik opened his eyes.

'Um... sorry?'

Zastra hauled him up and dusted him off.

'Don't worry. You didn't try and kill anyone this time.'

'Where's Dobery? And Kylen?'

They were both still with Zax. Dobery laid a hand on Zax's head.

'I can remove the implanted nightmares, but his mind has suffered great trauma. We must get him to calm and safety as soon as possible.'

A massive blast reverberated around the dungeon. The walls quaked and dust showered down from the ceiling. Dobery looked up in alarm.

'What in the stars was that?'

'Sintegrack,' Zastra answered grimly. 'We must help the others. We didn't plan for this.'

'This is not good,' muttered Jerenik. 'Not good at all.'

'I can't leave Zax,' Kylen protested. 'Not now I've found him.'

One of the released Sendoran prisoners stepped forward.

'We will look after Lord Zadorax.'

'You can barely stand,' Kylen protested.

'We can do enough.' The woman gestured for some of her companions to join her. 'We'd die before we let anything happen to the lad. There's enough of us to keep him safe.'

Another explosion rocked the dungeon.

'If we don't capture the sintegrack, Justyn and the others won't stand a chance,' Zastra insisted.

'Come on then,' said Kylen grimly. 'It's time to find the person responsible for this outrage.'

Chapter Fifty

Rastran chewed anxiously on a thumbnail as he stared out of the window. The four rebel ships had dropped anchor and were disgorging men and women. His garrison had scored some hits with their catapults, but failed to stop the rebels from entering the harbour. He would punish the incompetent captain severely when this was over. It was fortunate they still had the sintegrack.

A servant arrived with a cup filled with brown liquid. Rastran gulped it down. It tasted foul as usual, but moments after swallowing he felt its power coursing through his blood. It was a shame he couldn't take it every day, but he knew the dangers of too much cintara. His father insisted it only be used in a crisis. This was most definitely one of those.

The room shook and a thunderous roar rent the air. Rastran's lip curled upwards. Any rebels that weren't destroyed by the sintegrack would soon turn tail. He flexed his shoulders and exhaled. He was ready. It was time to show them all what he was capable of.

Zastra led the others through the corridors of the fortress, following the sound of the explosions. They emerged onto an open parapet. Golmeiran soldiers were lobbing large bags of smoking sintegrack over the walls, aiming at the rebels as they tried to climb the path up to the gate. Zastra made out Ithgol leading the charge, brandishing two scythal blades. One of the bags of sintegrack exploded, wrenching a boulder from the side of the mountain. The huge rock rolled towards the rebels, gathering speed. Those that could dived out of the way as the boulder bounced past them, before crashing into the bay and sending up a huge plume of water. Others were not quick enough. Zastra's stomach clenched as she saw the devastation the boulder had wrought. Another explosion sent more rocks skittering down the hillside. Ithgol and the others were pinned down, an open target for archers that began to rain bolts down at them from the fortress.

Zastra sprinted across the stone flagging. If they didn't seize the sintegrack quickly, their companions would be slaughtered before they could reach the gates. Kylen and the released Sendorans followed her, wielding weapons wrenched from the dead hands of the Bractarian Guard. The defenders were surprised and outflanked. Their slight resistance broke before the unleashed fury of the Sendoran prisoners. They threw down their weapons and surrendered. The sintegrack secured, Zastra leaned over the edge of the parapet and waved Ithgol and the others forward. Ithgol acknowledged her signal and issued a loud command. The rebels ran towards the gates.

'We've captured the sintegrack,' Zastra cried.

Nerika emerged from behind Ithgol, a bloody gash across her forehead. She barely flinched as a bolt flew past her chest.

'How about opening the gates, princess?'

'Over here!'

Kylen had discovered a narrow flight of stairs leading down

from the parapet to the gate. There were only a couple of soldiers in their way and neither were expecting an attack from within the fortress. Zastra knocked one guard senseless and Kylen dealt swiftly with the other. A huge wooden beam held the gates closed. Outside the rebels were pounding against the gates, increasingly desperate to escape the storm of arrows raining down from the ramparts. Kylen and Zastra set their shoulders to the wooden bar and it took all their combined strength to ease it out of its brackets. They were swept backwards as the huge gates swung inwards under the weight of the rebels.

Nerika did appear grateful. 'Took your time, didn't you? What in the stars have you been up to? Why didn't you kill the migaradon?'

'We did. It turns out there were two. How did you...?'

'We've your Kyrg friend to thank for that.'

'Ithgol?' Kylen looked at him doubtfully.

'I told you he'd be useful.' Zastra clapped Ithgol on his back. One of the Sendorans whispered something in Kylen's ear.

'Take me there. I'll kill the flekk myself.'

'Wait!' cried Zastra, but Kylen was already halfway back to the fortress. Zastra tried to follow, but Golmeiran soldiers began to pour down from the ramparts to attack the rebels. She fought her way through and ran after Kylen. Just inside the fortress, she came upon Dobery, backed against a wall by three mindweavers. She picked up a cudgel and bashed one of the mindweavers over the head. As the black form crumpled to the ground, Zastra set about the other two. They were concentrating so hard on their target that they didn't notice her until it was too late.

'Thank you, my dear.' Dobery bent over to catch his breath. His hair was awry and his face was grey with weariness. 'I fear I'm getting too old for this.'

'Did you see Kylen? I think she went after Rastran.'

Dobery closed his eyes for a moment.

'That way.' He pointed towards a set of doors at the end of the corridor. One of them was ajar. From within, a strangled cry was followed by an unpleasant laugh. It had been many years since she'd had the misfortune of being in Rastran's presence, but there was no mistaking that laugh, or the voice that followed.

'Stupid Sendoran. Did you think you could just come in here and kill me? You and my dim-witted cousin. If only she was here to share your fate.'

Zastra kicked open the door.

'Looking for me?'

Rastran was framed by a large window, the light coming from behind him so that his face was half in shadow. Facing him, Kylen was restrained by some invisible force. Even as she tried to understand what was happening, Zastra was lifted off her feet and flung backwards through the air. Her spine crashed against stone, and she found herself pinned to the wall, halfway between floor and ceiling. It felt as if the wall had inhaled deeply and sucked her into it. She struggled desperately, but couldn't move a single part of her body. Even her fingers were pinned flat against the cold stone.

'As you can see, cousin, I've developed mindmoving powers since we last met. Something your mental resistance is useless against.'

'Let them go, boy.' Dobery staggered through the door, holding onto the frame for support.

'You! Still alive are you, you interfering old fool? Do you think you can stop me? You can barely stand.'

'Look around you, boy. You have lost. Murthen Island is ours. What will your father say to that?'

Rastran's lower lip wobbled. Zastra slipped a couple of inches down the wall and she was suddenly able to flex her fingers. Rastran blinked and Dobery was flung back into the corridor, his cry of alarm cut off by a loud thud.

'Dobery!' Zastra cried, but her old friend did not respond.

'Old fool. My father will thank me when I bring Zastra to kneel before him.'

'Dobery was right.' Zastra forced the words through her clenched jaw. 'You were always a disappointment. You were given two migaradons and both are dead and we've captured the sintegrack. Uncle Thorlberd doesn't like failure, does he? And you just keep messing up.'

'Shut up!' roared Rastran. He strode towards her and she felt as if her body was being squeezed into the wall. She couldn't help crying out as the bones in her left shoulder, still not fully healed, ground against each other. Her cousin exulted in her pain.

'Your bones are mine to control,' he gloated, taking another step towards her. 'I know just where to hurt you. He narrowed his eyes and her shoulder burst in agony. She forced herself to speak.

'You're just... a stupid bully. Thorlberd will never trust you again. He always liked me better than you.'

Rastran's smile disappeared and he closed to within two paces of her, his face suffused with hatred.

'Time to die, cousin.' He closed his eyes. A shadow flew in from the periphery of Zastra's vision, followed by a thud. Rastran was down. There was another thump. Rastran's hold on Zastra was released and she slid to the floor. Kylen was holding a wooden chair leg. The remnants of a broken chair were scattered around the prostrate form of her cousin.

'Well done, Zastra.' Dobery inched back through the door. Zastra's heart sang with relief to see that he was alive.

'I'm the one that got him,' Kylen protested.

'Zastra focused Rastran's hatred on her. It was good thinking. Drew his attention away from you. It's the only reason you were free to do what you did.'

'As usual, a Golmeiran gets the credit. Still, at least I'll be the one to kill this coward.' She raised the chair leg high above her head.

'No!' cried Zastra, easing herself forwards clutching her sore shoulder. 'We are not murderers.'

'He deserves to die. You saw Zax. Don't you dare stop me.'

'He shall be punished. But we are not savages.'

'You tried to call me that, once.'

'And I was wrong. Kylen. Wasn't I?'

The Sendoran hesitated. With a scream, she flung the chair leg away, so forcefully it skittered across the top of Rastran's desk and sent a bottle and a goblet flying. Zastra found some rope and tied her cousin up.

A loud cheer went up in the corridor. Justyn poked his head through the door.

'Zastra. You're alive. What a pleasant surprise. We've taken control of the fortress. What should we do with the prisoners this time?'

'The dungeons,' Zastra replied. 'It seems only fair. This one can go as well.' She lifted Rastran to his feet. He was just beginning to stir.

Justyn nodded. 'Dobery, would you mind helping Pol and

Drazan secure the prisoners? We don't want the mindweavers giving us trouble. I'm sure the Sendorans will be glad to help you, but it pays to be careful.'

Dobery acquiesced wearily. Justyn turned back to Zastra.

'Come with me. I've something to show you.' He led her out onto the parapet where they had captured the sintegrack and pointed to the top of the tower. As they watched, the standard of Thorlberd was lowered before being replaced by the flag Ithgol had made; the crest of Leodra alongside the Golmeiran hawk. All of Zastra's old crewmates cheered.

'I'm not generally one for symbols and flags, but I think it's a fine sight.'

Zastra walked away, not wanting Justyn to see her emotions and mistake them for weakness. *This victory is for you, Father.* She went to the edge of the platform to look out across the island that was now hers. As she did so, she passed a body that looked familiar. She knelt down and turned it over, and let out a low moan. It was Jerenik, his eyes glassy and unseeing. He was dead. She hadn't even realised that he had been with them on the parapet. She touched his cheek. It was as cold as ice. A shadow fell across them both. It was Ithgol. He crouched down and lifted the body gently.

'I will take care of him.'

'I didn't think you liked him.'

'He was a comrade in arms.' That was all Ithgol said before he took Jerenik away. Someone called Zastra's name. She looked around. Chelica, one of the crew of the *Wind of Golmeira* was lying on the ground, bleeding from a wound in her thigh. Zastra ran over, calling for help. Sinisa responded, running over and pulling bandages from a backpack. Zastra moved on, looking for others to help. She recognised more faces among the dead. To her dismay she realised that she didn't know all their names. Yet they had fought and died for her. The bodies of the rebels were outnumbered by Kyrgs and soldiers clad in Thorlberd's black uniforms. One of the Golmeiran soldiers lay face up, a slight figure with a face as white as pure marble. Three moles ran in a line upon his left cheek. Zastra felt a jolt of recognition.

'Gonjik?' Without warning, hot tears began to stream down her face and she couldn't hold them back. A hand rested on her shoulder. It was Kylen.

'Why are you crying? He's one of them.'

'I knew him. He's from Fivepeaks.'

'Was he a friend? A sweetheart perhaps?'

'No... No. I didn't even like him.'

'Then why are you so upset?'

'I don't know. He was just a village lad. He didn't choose to be here. It's not right.'

A stone was dislodged behind them. They turned sharply, but it was only Nerika. Zastra waited for the inevitable cutting remark, but Nerika surprised her.

'Now you know what it is to lead others into battle. It should never be easy. You did well today, Zastra, daughter of Leodra. It was a good victory. We should celebrate.'

'Not yet,' said Zastra grimly. 'Not until everyone is cared for. Including the dead.'

Chapter Fifty-one

That evening they gathered in Rastran's room to share stories. Zax and the other released prisoners had been taken to the *Wind of Golmeira* where Yashni was taking care of them. Nerika related how they had broken through Rastran's fleet.

'It was surprisingly easy,' remarked Justyn. 'For some reason, they deployed only three mindweavers to their ships. A tactical error. I'm told that Drazan took out one and Polina took care of the other two. She's very strong. I've never met anyone who was her equal, except perhaps Master Dobery.'

Polina flushed modestly at the compliment. Nerika took up the tale.

'Once the mindweavers were dealt with, Pol and Drazan disabled most of Rastran's sailors, but then the migaradon came for us. It was bleeding, but we could see that you had only succeeded in landing a single shot.'

Justyn laughed. 'You should have heard Nerika cursing you.'

Nerika sniffed.

'I admit it. I thought you'd failed us. It certainly looked that way. Ithgol seized one of Vingrod's spears and bellowed in that

Kyrginite way of his. The migaradon went straight for him and somehow impaled itself on the spear. That still didn't kill it and it would have carried Ithgol off into the air, since the stupid Kyrg refused to let go of the spear. It took three of us to hold him down and wrench the spear out. The migaradon was so mad at Ithgol it went for him again, and that's when he got in the final blow.'

'Good work, Kyrg,' Kylen remarked grudgingly.

'It would not be pleasant to be killed by a migaradon.'

'Is there such a thing as a pleasant way to die?' asked Zastra.

'I could think of some distinctly unpleasant ways to kill Rastran,' Kylen muttered darkly. 'I wish you'd let me blow up the dungeons with him and his scientists inside. They deserve no less.'

'They may deserve it,' Zastra conceded. 'But then we'd be no better than them. Leaving them to face Thorlberd's anger will be punishment enough.'

'Fine. But someday you may regret not killing that cousin of yours.'

'It's time we returned to Uden's Teeth,' said Justyn. 'When Thorlberd hears what has happened, he'll send his whole army and I don't intend to be around when they get here.'

It took less than a day to pack up and leave. Zastra stood on the quarterdeck of the *Wind of Golmeira*, watching Murthen Island recede into the distance. To her right, one of the *Obala*'s catapults groaned. A smoking bale arced towards one of Rastran's ships, which was tethered a few paces from the main jetty of the island. The deck of the ship was piled high with brown sacks. For a moment, even though the contents of the catapult appeared to have hit home, nothing happened. Then, the ship disappeared, and was supplanted by a huge plume of water. The appearance of the plume was followed a heartbeat later by a thunderous roar. A landslide obliterated the jetty and a vast cloud of dust spread upwards into the clear blue sky. Zastra's lips twitched in satisfaction. Kylen had taken great pleasure in telling Rastran and his mindweaver friends that they had buried the sintegrack directly beneath their cell. A lie, but when Rastran felt the explosion, he must have thought for a moment that his end had come. He and his so-called scientists deserved to feel a little of what they had inflicted on others. They had been left plenty of food and water, and Thorlberd's reinforcements would soon be on the way to rescue them. The decision to destroy the sintegrack had not been reached easily. Nerika and Kylen wanted to take it back to Uden's Teeth. Something to use against Thorlberd, but Zastra had insisted it be destroyed and Justyn had agreed with her. The only scientist who knew the recipe had died in the battle for Murthen Island. With every last bag of sintegrack destroyed, there would be no more. A world without such a destructive weapon was much preferable to one with it, to Zastra's mind.

Above the fortress, her father's crest fluttered in the breeze. A message left behind for her uncle. Soft footsteps on the deck made her turn. It was Dobery.

'It was a good victory, Zastra. Worthy of a Warrior of Golmeira. Your father would have been proud.'

Zastra thought of Gonjik and Jerenik and all the others they had lost.

'We paid a heavy price. They never mention that in the Tales of the Warriors.'

'They don't. But we saved more lives than we took, children among them. We have put a stop to something evil and wrong.

More importantly, all of Golmeira will know that you are alive and that Thorlberd is not invincible. Hope is alive again.'

Kylen emerged from the hold.

'How's Zax?' asked Zastra.

'Sleeping at last. Master Dobery, do you think his mind will ever recover?'

Dobery shrugged. 'I wish I could reassure you, my dear. Rest and love may provide a cure. We must wait and hope.'

'What about the other prisoners?'

'Much the same. The children they were training to become mindweavers will need particular attention. We must be patient.'

'You've forgotten you are talking to a Sendoran,' Zastra said with a laugh.

Kylen turned to her.

'Zastra, you have shown that you are a friend of Sendor. You risked your life for Zax and my people. I owe you more than words can express.'

'My uncle is too powerful for any of us to take on alone. But together we have a chance. We have seen over the past few days that Sendorans and Golmeirans, even Kyrgs, can work together.'

'What are you suggesting?'

'An alliance. To free all our people from Thorlberd's tyranny.'

Kylen gave out a half snort.

'A Sendoran and a Golmeiran alliance? Some would say that's impossible.'

'What do you say?'

Kylen reached out and clasped Zastra's hands in hers. Her grip was firm and warm.

'I say we should get started.'

'I think we already have,' replied Zastra. They watched the horizon until the outline of Murthen Island disappeared into the haze, the flag of her father still fluttering in the breeze.

Coming Soon

Return to Golmeira
BOOK THREE: TALES OF GOLMEIRA

Zastra and her allies have struck a telling blow against her uncle, the usurper Thorlberd, but she will not be satisfied until she has brought her brother and sister safety back to the rebel hideout of Uden's Teeth. The search for her younger siblings means a return to the heart of Golmeira, where Thorlberd's power is strongest, and an unexpected reunion with an old adversary.

Acknowledgements

Grateful thanks to Wendy Tomlinson and Sharon Gubby for critical review of the manuscript. Cover by Andy Boothman. Copy edited by Claire Rushbrook.

Also by Marianne Ratcliffe

Realm of Mindweavers
BOOK ONE: TALES OF GOLMEIRA

Teenage Zastra is a big disappointment to her father, Leodra, ruler of Golmeira, because she hasn't got what it takes to become a mindweaver, one of the highly valued few who can manipulate the thoughts of others. Things get much worse for Zastra when she is roused from her bed to find that Leodra has been betrayed and her beloved Golmer Castle overrun with enemy soldiers. She escapes via the castle's ancient underground tunnels, only to be faced with a terrible choice. Hunted across the turbulent landscape of Golmeira, Zastra must rely on her wits and the help of strangers as she tries to outrun the powerful forces set upon her trail.

'*Realm of Mindweavers* is a great read, exciting, well-crafted and full of powerful well-realised characters.' Brian Keaney, author.

Printed in Great Britain
by Amazon.co.uk, Ltd.,
Marston Gate.